Lonely loggers. One genteel lady. A dangerous combination, Tom Randall thought. He was trying to run a business, not a tea party! And if obstinate Meggy Hampton didn't hightail her moonlight and magnolias back south, the sweet sparks she was igniting would make the camp—and his passion— explode like the Fourth of July!

Tom leaned in and inhaled the fragrance of her hair.

"You have any idea what that does to a man?"

"I should think it means they are perfectly starved for civilized conversation."

Tom snorted. "They're starved, all right, but it's not for conversation. They're starved for something soft. Something that's sweet scented and…" His thumbs began to caress her shoulders. "And warm. And alive."

He stepped in closer, bent his head to sniff the scent emanating from her skin. "It can make a man crazy, being alone," he said in a rough whisper. "I can't let a man near you without risking his life."

* * *

The Angel of Devil's Camp
Harlequin Historical #649—March 2003

Praise for LYNNA BANNING's previous books

The Courtship
"The Courtship is a beautifully written tale
with a heartwarming plot."
—Romantic Reviews Today (www.romrevtoday.com)

The Law and Miss Hardisson
"…fresh and charming…
a sweet and funny yet poignant story."
—*Romantic Times*

Plum Creek Bride
"…pathos and humor blend in a plot
that glows with perception and dignity."
—*Affaire de Coeur*

**DON'T MISS THESE OTHER
TITLES AVAILABLE NOW:**

#647 TEMPTING A TEXAN
Carolyn Davidson

#648 THE SILVER LORD
Miranda Jarrett

#650 BRIDE OF THE TOWER
Sharon Schulze

THE ANGEL OF DEVIL'S CAMP

Lynna Banning

HARLEQUIN®

TORONTO • NEW YORK • LONDON
AMSTERDAM • PARIS • SYDNEY • HAMBURG
STOCKHOLM • ATHENS • TOKYO • MILAN • MADRID
PRAGUE • WARSAW • BUDAPEST • AUCKLAND

ISBN 0-373-29249-X

THE ANGEL OF DEVIL'S CAMP

Copyright © 2003 by The Woolston Family Trust

Visit us at www.eHarlequin.com

Printed in U.S.A.

Available from Harlequin Historicals and
LYNNA BANNING

Western Rose #310
Wildwood #374
Lost Acres Bride #437
Plum Creek Bride #474
The Law and Miss Hardisson #537
The Courtship #613
The Angel of Devil's Camp #649

Please address questions and book requests to:
Harlequin Reader Service
U.S.: 3010 Walden Ave., P.O. Box 1325, Buffalo, NY 14269
Canadian: P.O. Box 609, Fort Erie, Ont. L2A 5X3

For my agent, Pattie Steele-Perkins

With special thanks to David and Yvonne Woolston.
And to fellow writers Suzanne Barrett, Tricia Adams,
Brenda Preston, Ida Hills and Norma Pulle.

Chapter One

Seton Falls, South Carolina
March 1872

Mary Margaret pulled the parsonage door shut with a satisfying thunk and for the very last time twisted the key in the lock. She'd married off five sisters in the past three years, the last one just the day before yesterday. *Now it is my turn.*

She marched down the walkway and out the front gate, lugging her satchel. For half a heartbeat, she wavered. The yellow rose rambling along the fence needed pruning, but with all the preparations for Charlotte's wedding, Meggy had had no time for gardening. She forced her gaze away. It no longer mattered.

She smoothed her black traveling dress, slipping her hand into the left pocket. The letter she'd carefully folded crackled under her fingers. *Dear God in heaven, let this be the right thing to do.*

She heaved the tapestry bag into the buggy and climbed up onto the sagging seat. *I will not look back. I will look to the road ahead and be joyful.*

At last! She was free. No more meals to eke out from the squash and dried beans donated by the congregation. No more wedding dresses for Charity or Charlotte, cobbled together out of old tablecloths and scraps of lace. She had remade most of her old ball gowns into dresses for her sisters, and sold the rest for food. A barrel of flour cost 150 federal dollars, a basket of eggs $25. The war had made such a struggle of life!

She closed her eyes and pressed her knuckles against her lips. *The war took everything, even our hearts and our souls.* She and her sisters had survived, but the scars would always remain.

Leaning forward, she patted the satchel at her feet. Inside, on top of her spare petticoat and her nightgown, lay her father's revolver. She would travel three thousand miles, all the way to Oregon, to marry a second cousin of her father's, a man she had never seen. It was the only proposal she had ever received, and she most certainly intended to arrive in one piece!

She gathered up the worn leather reins. "Move on, Bess."

The mare took a single step forward, and Meggy's heart took flight.

"Colonel, darlin', wake up!"

Tom rolled over on the narrow canvas cot and opened one eye. "What is it, O'Malley?"

"The deed needs doin'," his former sergeant said. "And you're the proper one to do it."

Tom groaned. Being in charge didn't let him sleep much. A logging crew wasn't like an army unit. Loggers were a fractious bunch of misfits with a heightened instinct for survival and an even more heightened taste for liquor and high times. Not one of them would last a day under military discipline. Tom had mustered out two years ago, taken Sergeant O'Malley with him and headed west. The undisciplined men he commanded now obeyed him because he *wasn't* a colonel.

"Tom." The Irishman nudged his shoulder. "You won't be forgettin' now, will you?"

With an effort, Tom sat up. His head felt like someone was whacking an ax into his skull, and the aftertaste of whiskey in his mouth made him grit his teeth. He figured his breath alone could get a man drunk.

"Remind me what it is that needs doing, Mick? If it can wait, let it."

"The peeler, the one that got killed yesterday? The coffin's ready and Swede and Turner's dug the grave. You need to speak some words over the man."

Oh, hell, he *had* forgotten. Wanted to forget, in fact. Which was why he'd finished half a bottle of rye last night. In the past month he'd lost one, no, two bullcooks and a skinner. The timber was turning dry as a witch's broom and then one of his peelers, a square peg on a logging crew if he'd ever seen one, let an ax slice into his thigh and bled to death before they could load him into the wagon.

"The men are waitin', Tom."

"I won't forget, Mick. See if you can rustle up some coffee." He tossed off the grimy sheet, lowered his legs to the packed-earth floor and stood up. "Tell them I'll be there."

The interior of the tent spun and Tom sat down abruptly.

"Get me that coffee, will you?"

"Sure thing, Colonel. And you'll be wantin' a clean shirt and your Bible."

His Bible.

He clenched his jaw. His sister had sent it when he'd first joined the army. She had even marked certain passages she liked. He hadn't opened it since that day in Richmond when he'd read over her grave.

Today would be different, he told himself. For one thing, he didn't know the peeler very well. He'd known Susanna all her short life, had raised her by himself after their father died. A familiar dull ache settled behind his breastbone.

"One more thing, Tom. We found something on the body. You better have a look."

"Later." He stuffed the single folded page the sergeant handed him into his shirt pocket without glancing at it. "Coffee," Tom reminded him. "And make it double strength."

* * *

Meggy dropped to the pine-needle-covered ground beneath the biggest tree she had ever seen. She had climbed halfway up the steep ridge, dragging her satchel, which felt as if it was filled with bricks. Her mouth was parched, her stomach hollow, her eyes scratchy. The supply wagon had left Tennant at daybreak, and she had been walking the past hour. Now it was near noon and she could go no farther.

She gazed up into a sky the color of bluebonnets, listening to the *rat-tat-tat* of a woodpecker. All at once the sound was obliterated by raucous men's voices.

Good heavens, Yankee soldiers. She scooted closer to the massive tree trunk.

That can't be right. The war is over. Besides, this is Oregon. She eased around the tree until she could see to the top of the ridge.

Directly above her, a dozen men in colorful shirts and faded blue trousers stood in a circle. Most had unkempt hair hanging beneath their battered hats. Many had untrimmed beards. Three or four leaned on the handles of shovels.

Their voices ceased as a man taller than the rest marched up. He carried himself ramrod straight. She knew without a doubt he was a soldier.

The circle opened for him, and Meggy spied a rough-hewn coffin. She eased forward for a closer look, watched the tall man take a book from his shirt pocket and begin to read.

Tom cleared his throat, scanned the men gathered at the freshly dug grave site and opened his Bible. He ran his forefinger down the page, stopped at the Twenty-third Psalm. Raising his eyes, he opened his mouth.

''The Lord is my...''

Swede Jensen snatched off his red-and-yellow knit cap and bowed his head.

A flutter of something black through the trees caught Tom's eye. It vanished behind a thick fir tree, then reappeared. A hawk? He couldn't be sure. The summer sun was so intense the air shimmered.

Not a hawk. Too low. Something wrapped up like a cocoon—a bear, maybe? The back of his neck prickled.

Whatever it was plodded up the hill toward him at a steady pace. No, not a bear. A bear would pause and sniff the air. Not an Indian, either. Only a white man would walk incautiously forward in a straight line.

He squinted as the figure moved out of the shadows of the fir grove. Not a man. A woman! All in black from boots to veiled hat, with a shawl knotted about her shoulders. Something in the tilt of her head...

For one awful moment he thought it was Susanna. A knife slipped into his heart and he snapped the Bible shut. Handing it to O'Malley, he started down the hill.

She did not look up. Her leather shoes scrabbling on the steep rocky slope, she kept walking, dragging a satchel in one hand and a bulging sack in the other. She didn't slow down until she almost ran into him.

"My stars, where on earth did *you* come from?"

Tom's eyebrows rose. "More to the point, ma'am, where in hell did *you* come from?"

She let go of the satchel, and it plopped onto the ground with a puff of dust. "The supply wagon from Tennant. The driver brought me out on condition that I deliver this." She thrust the sack toward him.

Tom accepted the bag and peered inside.

"It contains six bars of soap, a dozen lemons and two bottles of spirits. He said it would hold you until next week."

"Only two bottles?"

She nodded. "One is for medicinal purposes. And six bars of—"

"Lemons?"

"Mr. Jacobs said they were to combat scurvy."

Tom stared at her. Her eyes were a curious shade of gray-green, almost the color of tree moss.

"Besides delivering Mose Jacobs's scurvy remedy, what are you doing out here?"

Her spine went rigid as a tent pole. "I am calling on Mr. Peabody. Walter Peabody."

"Why?" Tom said carefully.

"It is a personal matter, sir. Between Mr. Peabody and myself. If you would be so kind as to conduct me—"

"Peabody's dead."

Her face went the color of chalk. "I beg your pardon?"

"An accident. His ax slipped and he bled to death."

The stricken look on her face sent a band of cold steel around his chest.

"But…" Her voice wobbled. "He can't be! We were to be married. I came all the way from South Carolina to marry him."

"I'm real sorry, ma'am. We're just burying him this morning."

"I see." She swallowed and lifted her chin. "Yes, I do see."

Tom stood rooted before her, wondering why he couldn't speak.

"May I…view his remains? You see, we never met. I have no idea what he…" She pressed her lips together.

He could not bear to look at her face. Except for her unsmiling mouth and her pallor, she could be any pretty young woman out for a Sunday walk. He'd seen Union soldiers with less composure.

Tom hesitated. His left eyelid began to twitch. Lifting the travel satchel from the ground, he pivoted away from her. "Come with me."

Meggy followed him up the hill, his low, tersely spoken words sending a swarm of butterflies into her stomach. She stepped on the hem of her dress, stumbled over protruding tree roots as she tried to keep up with his long-legged stride. Where the ground leveled out near a stand of fir trees, he stopped short. "Coffin's over there, next to the grave. Best hurry before we nail it shut."

Her heart hurtled into her throat. She had seen bodies before. Old men. Young men. Federal soldiers as well as Confederate. Why was she so frightened now?

She took a step forward. In the coffin before her lay a slight man with pale-gold hair and mustache, a narrow chin and thin lips.

She stood absolutely still. It was a mistake to look at him, but she couldn't help herself. Walter Peabody would have been her husband, had he lived. She had traveled all the way from Seton Falls to be this man's wife. And now...now...

Now she was not only unmarried, she was also in a fix, stranded out here alone among a bunch of exceedingly rough-looking men. Yankee men. And she had not one single penny in her pocket.

"Seen enough?" A low voice spoke at her back.

"Oh. Oh, yes, I expect so. Thank you. I—"

"Okay, Swede, close it up."

"Sure thing, Tom." The big man dropped the lid on the box.

Meggy's legs turned to jelly, and she looked away.

Then a steadying arm pressed under her elbow. "Name's Michael O'Malley, ma'am. I'm thinkin' you'd be Miss Hampton?"

She nodded at the russet-haired man. He wore a wash-worn Union Army shirt, faded stripes still intact, and wide red suspenders. A Yankee. She started to pull away, but she was so unsteady on her feet she could not stand alone. She let him guide her to the edge of the grave, where the bearded Swede was nailing down the coffin lid. Each blow of the man's hammer sent a tremor through her body.

Whatever would she do now? Walter had paid her train fare, but the stagecoach to Tennant had taken all of her meager savings. Here she was, in a godforsaken wilderness with no money and no prospects.

The tall man, Tom, opened the Bible and cleared his throat. "The Lord is my shepherd...."

Meggy's throat tightened. Poor Walter! Cut down in the prime of his life, with no kin to mourn for him except her.

"He leadeth me beside..."

She moved her lips silently over the words of the psalm. Would Walter Peabody rest in peace among Yankees?

"Yea, though I walk through the valley..."

She opened her mouth and joined in. Tom shot her a glance over the top of the plain wood coffin. The look on his face stopped her breath.

Eyes as sharp as a steel saber cut into her. The blue was so intense her mind conjured the morning glories she'd planted against the back fence of the parsonage. Dear Lord, he looked so angry!

"...in the house of the Lord forever. Amen." He slapped the Bible shut. "Funeral's over."

Meggy gasped. "Oh, surely not," she blurted.

"Should we not..." She racked her brain. With him looking at her that way, his mouth hard, his jaw muscle working, every thought she had flew right out of her head.

"...sing?" she supplied at last. "Perhaps a hymn?"

He pinned her to the spot with those eyes, like two blue bolts of lightning. "No damned hymns." His voice spit the words.

Her frame stiffened from her toes to the top of her head. "Why not?"

"Peabody was a good man. A bit soft, but no hypocrite. I won't sully a decent burial by mangling some hymn none of us can remember."

She stared at him so long her eyes began to burn. And then, still holding his gaze, she opened her mouth and began to sing. "Amazing grace, how sweet the sound...."

The Swede chimed in, then another voice. Mr. O'Malley and two more joined in, and finally everyone was singing.

Except for the tall man with the Bible.

Defiantly, Meggy began the second stanza. "I once was lost, but now am found...."

He stood rigid as a rifle barrel until the song ended, then stuffed the Bible in his belt and reached for the shovel stuck in the loosened earth. The Swede and another man with straight black hair that hung past his collar hefted the coffin into the waiting grave.

A shovelful of dirt plopped onto the pine box, and

Meggy's heart constricted. North or South, the sound of earth on a coffin lid was the same. By the time the war ended, she'd attended enough burials to last a lifetime.

She struggled to think clearly as the dirt clods rained down. Walter Peabody had been her last hope. With all the males in Seton Falls under the age of 16, or over 60 or dead, she'd come west out of desperation. She wanted a husband. Children.

But now she was neither grieving sweetheart nor bereaved widow, but still plain Mary Margaret Hampton, oldest of six sisters and a spinster at twenty-five.

Numb with disbelief, she bent her head, clasped her hands under her chin and closed her eyes. *Lord, it's me again. I entreat you to give this man, Walter Wade Peabody, a place in your kingdom where he may rest in peace. It isn't his fault he left this world in an untimely manner. I assure you, his intentions were entirely honorable. Amen.*

When she opened her eyes, the tall man with the Bible was gone.

"Miss Hampton?" A hand touched her elbow. "Colonel'd like to see you. First tent left of the cookhouse, yonder." The red-haired sergeant pointed to an unpainted wood shack, twice as long as it was wide, on the other side of a clearing. Smoke poured out the chimney at one end.

"The cookhouse, yes, I see it." Her mind felt fuzzy, as if her head were stuffed with cotton bolls. She started up the hill behind Mr. O'Malley.

When they reached the tent, her guide rapped twice on the support pole and pushed aside the flap. Through the opening she spied the tall man lounging on a tumbled cot, his feet propped on a makeshift plank desk, which rested on two thick log rounds.

"Here she is, Colonel."

The tall man stood up, his dark hair brushing the canvas ceiling. Mr. O'Malley stepped away from Meggy and lowered his voice. "You read that letter yet, Tom?"

"Not yet. Fetch us some coffee, will you?"

"Colonel, I wish you'd read—"

"Coffee, Mick. Pronto."

The sergeant gestured to the neatly made-up cot on the opposite side of the tent. "Have a seat, ma'am. Won't be a minute." The flap swished shut.

Meggy remained standing. "I'm sure I should not be here, sir. This is a gentleman's private quarters." She stared at a coal-black raven in a cage hung from the tent pole.

Tom chuckled. "Not private. And I'm not a… Anyway, sit down. This won't take long."

With reluctance Meggy perched on the edge of the cot. The warm air inside the tent was thick with the smell of leather and sweat. Man smells. Not unpleasant, just…different. Strong. *Pungent,* her sister Charlotte would have said. Charlotte wrote poetry.

Tom settled on the unmade cot opposite her, repropped his boots on the plank desk and looked her over with a penetrating gaze. "What do you plan to do, now that Peabody's...gone?"

Meggy's mind went blank. "Do?"

"Ma'am, you can't marry a dead man."

The sergeant bustled in with two chipped mugs of something that looked dark and sludgy. He handed one to Meggy and set the other near the colonel's crossed boots. "There's no cream. Fong churned it all into butter."

Meggy removed her gloves and took a sip of the lukewarm brew. It tasted like the coffee she had concocted out of dried grain and sassafras root during the war. She sipped again and choked. Worse. This tasted like chopped-up walnut shells mixed with turpentine.

O'Malley sidled closer to Tom and bent over the desk. "Read that letter yet?"

Tom downed a double gulp of the coffee. "Nope."

"If I was you, Colonel, sir, I might do that right now." He gestured at Tom's shirt pocket.

Meggy rose at once. "Forgive me, sir. I must not keep you from your business."

"Tom, for the love of God, read the damn letter! Beggin' your pardon, ma'am."

Tom glared at his sergeant, then dug in his pocket and withdrew a folded paper. It crackled as he spread it flat. Meggy found herself watching. There was something odd about the way Mr. O'Malley danced near Tom's shoulder, grinning at her.

Tom scanned the words, then drew his black eyebrows into a frown. "That son of a gun," he muttered. "I wonder when he found the time?"

"Might explain why Peabody looked so peaked the last few months. Must've come off the peeling crew and worked half the night on his own, I'm thinkin'."

Meggy looked from one to the other. What were they talking about?

Tom spun the paper under his thumb until the writing faced her. "This concerns you, Miss Hampton."

"Me? Why, how could it possibly?"

"It's Walt Peabody's will."

Meggy lifted the paper with shaking hands.

"...all my earthly possessions to Miss Mary Margaret Hampton, soon to be my wife."

"Possessions? Oh, you mean his law books?"

"No, not his law books. Seems he built a cabin. For when his fiancée joined him."

Meggy stared at him. "You mean...you mean Mr. Peabody provided for me?" The knot in her stomach melted away like so much warm molasses. Oh, the dear, blessed man. He had left her some property! She sank onto the cot.

"Oh, thank the Lord, I have a home."

Tom shot to his feet. "Not so fast, Miss Hampton. You can't stay here. I run a logging camp, not a boardinghouse."

"But the cabin—*my* cabin—is here."

"A logging camp is no place for a woman."

The red-haired sergeant stepped forward. "Oh, now, Tom—"

"Shut up, O'Malley."

Meggy stood up. "No place for a woman? Mr. Peabody seemed to think otherwise."

"Mr. Peabody isn't—wasn't—the boss here. I am."

Meggy felt her spine grow rigid. It was a sensation she'd come to recognize over the last seven years, one that signaled the onset of the stubborn streak she'd inherited from her father. "That does not signify, for it is—was—Mr. Peabody who wrote the will, not you." She gentled her voice. "And you, sir, even if you are the boss here, are surely not above the law?"

At that instant she noticed that Mr. O'Malley stood off to one side, shaking his head at her. The Irishman was trying to warn her about something, but what? What was it she was not supposed to say?

Silence fell, during which she desperately tried to think.

A woodpecker drilled into a tree outside the tent, and Meggy started. The noise rose above the rasp of cicadas, pounding into her head until she thought she would scream.

"The law," Tom said in a low, hard voice, "protects no one. When push comes to shove, it's not the *right* that wins, but the strong. Coming from a Confederate state, I'd think you'd have a hard time forgetting that."

She clamped her teeth together. Was that what the man had against her? That she was from the South?

"The mighty prevail, is that it?"

"That's it. It's a lesson I learned the hard way. I suggest you are about to do the same."

O'Malley pivoted toward his boss. "Oh, now, Tom, couldn't we—"

"Nope."

Meggy drew in a long breath and used the time it took to expel it to gather her courage. She might as well risk it. She had nothing to lose and everything— a home, a sanctuary out here in this remote bit of nowhere—to gain. She needed time to absorb what had happened. Time to make new plans. Besides, she had no money, and until she could decide what to do next, she was stuck here.

"On the contrary, Colonel… I beg your pardon, what is your family name, sir? I do not wish to be improper in addressing you."

"Randall," he growled. "I come from Ohio."

"Colonel Randall," she continued. "I believe it is you who may learn the lesson here. For it is a known fact that when a suit is brought, and the issue judged by an honest jury of one's peers…"

She left the rest unspoken. It was always best to allow the enemy a graceful exit. "Why, your own president, Mr. Grant, made that very point not long ago in a speech before the Congress of the United States."

Tom took a good long look at the young woman standing before him. She wasn't going to give up, he could see that. Her softly modulated voice never rose, but beneath the controlled tone he detected cold steel. And the look in her eye… Yeah, she sure did remind him of Susanna.

In that instant he knew he was beaten. Women like this one, like his sister, didn't give up. If he pushed, she would fight back, and she would continue until she either triumphed or died trying. He closed his hands into fists. He didn't want to be responsible for another one. She had determination written all over her.

And, he noted, she had unusual eyes, set in a perfectly oval face and framed with thick lashes. Her dark hair was parted in the center and gathered in a soft, black-netted roll at her neck. The only other part of her body he could see was her hands, which were graceful and small-boned, with long fingers and short nails. For all her fragile female appearance, those hands looked capable enough.

For some reason his gut clenched just looking at them.

The good Lord can sure play a joke when He sees fit. The last thing he needed was a woman at Devil's Camp. A pretty woman with eyes like a cool, deep river. The last thing he wanted anywhere near him for the remainder of his life was a woman who stirred his emotions.

He grasped her elbow, turned her toward the tent entrance.

"Meeting's over, Miss Hampton. I'm sending you back to Tennant."

Chapter Two

Miss Hampton regarded Tom with calm eyes. "Might I see the home Mr. Peabody constructed for our future?" Her voice was like honey, warm and so sweet it made his heart catch.

O'Malley nudged his elbow. "Can't hurt, Tom," he said in an undertone. "Might be it'd ease the lady's grief some."

Tom sighed. Being outnumbered wasn't what got his goat. What bothered him was his reaction to her. He didn't want to feel sympathy for this woman. Sympathy led to caring, and the minute his heart was involved he knew it would lead to pain, pure and simple. You could love someone, but you couldn't keep them safe. Ever.

"Cabin's that way, Colonel." The Irishman pointed over his shoulder. "Past the bunkhouse. You can barely see it from here. It's nice an' privatelike, and..."

Tom raised his eyebrows and O'Malley fell silent.

Then Tom waved a hand and the sergeant turned and headed toward the cabin.

Miss Hampton trudged beside Tom through the pine trees, their footfalls muffled by the thick forest duff. Her face had an expectant look, but she kept her mouth closed as they followed O'Malley past the cookhouse. At this altitude and in the midday heat, Tom guessed she was too short of breath to talk much.

He studied her full-skirted black dress as it swayed beside him. It had a wide ruffle at the hem and a bit of delicate-looking lace at the neck and sleeves. She looked as out of place as a rose in a potato field. She'd be used to town life, with gaslight and a cookstove with a built-in hot water basin. She wouldn't last five minutes in a logging camp. He almost chuckled. The food alone would kill her.

The cabin was small, but Tom could see it was well built of peeled pine logs, notched and fitted at the corners. He noted that Peabody hadn't had time to fill the chinks with mud. A good breeze would whistle through the cracks and chill her britches good. Not too bad a thought on a day like today, with the temperature near a hundred degrees and the sun not yet straight up. But in the winter...

He bit back a smile. Like he said, five minutes.

She quickened her pace. "Is that it? Why, it's...charming."

Tom had to laugh. The cabin looked sturdy. Rough and practical, not charming. He'd bet his month's quota of timber she'd never lived in a place with just one window, to say nothing of a front door with leather straps for hinges and no way to lock it.

He tramped up to the plank porch and turned toward her. It was a giant step up from ground level; she'd never be able to negotiate it weighed down by that heavy skirt and a bunch of petticoats.

She stepped up to the edge of the porch and halted. "Well, I never…the door is open! I can see right inside, and…" Her voice wavered. "There isn't one stick of furniture!"

O'Malley cleared his throat. "But there's a fine stove, ma'am. And a dry sink. Creek's nearby, so you won't be havin' to haul your water too far."

Tom clenched his fists. "Shut your trap, O'Malley. A lady can't live out here on her own."

Miss Hampton looked up at him. "This lady can."

Without another word, she hoisted her skirts and planted one foot on the porch. Bending her knee, she gave a little jump. Tom glimpsed a lace-trimmed pantalette as she levered her body onto the smooth plank surface.

"No, you can't," he argued. "I'm short on crew now. I can't spare any men to nursemaid a—"

"I must respectfully disagree, Colonel Randall. I shall manage quite nicely on my own, as I have for all the years since my father passed on."

"This is not a civilized town like you're used to, Miss Hampton. This is wild country. You got heat and dust, flies big as blackberries, spiders that'd fill a teacup.''

She turned to face him. ''We have heat and dust and flies and spiders in Seton Falls, too. I am not unused to such things, Colonel.''

A grin split O'Malley's ruddy face. ''You figure to stay then, lass?''

''Yes, I—''

''No, she doesn't,'' Tom interrupted. ''I have troubles enough with two young greenhorns joining a rambunctious crew, ten thousand board feet of timber to cut within the next two weeks and weather so hot you can fry eggs on the tree stumps. A woman at the camp would be the last straw.''

Before he could continue, she swished through the cabin door. Her voice carried from inside. ''Why, it's quite…snug.''

O'Malley punched Tom's shoulder. ''Snug,'' he echoed with a grin. The Irishman clomped onto the porch and disappeared through the open door.

''Just look, Mr. O'Malley,'' Tom heard her exclaim. ''A small bed could fit here, and my trunk could serve as a table.''

Tom gritted his teeth. ''No bed,'' he shouted. ''No trunk. And no women!'' He stomped through the doorway and caught his breath.

Smack-dab in the center of the single room, Mary Margaret Hampton sank down onto the floor, her black dress puffing around her like an overflowed pudding.

"Possession," she said in that maddeningly soft voice, "is nine-tenths of the law." She patted the floor beside her. "I am in possession."

Tom stared at her. Was she loco? Or just stubborn?

"I will need a chamber commode," she remarked in a quiet tone. "I do not fancy going into the woods at night."

"Get up," Tom ordered.

"I do not wish to, Colonel. This is my home now. Walter Peabody left it to me in his will, and any lawyer with half a brain will agree that I am in the right."

He took a step toward her. "I said get up!"

O'Malley's grin widened. "You're not gonna like this, Tom, but she's got a point."

"She's got chicken feathers in her head," he muttered. He moved a step closer.

She looked up at him and tried to smile. "Please, Colonel Randall. Oh, please. Let me stay here, just for a little while. I will be ever so quiet."

It was the trembling of her mouth that did him in. "How long?" he snapped.

She thought for a moment. "Until I can earn enough money to pay my fare back to Seton Falls."

Tom snorted. "Doing what?"

"I will find some way. I am not without accomplishments."

"Three weeks." He almost felt sorry for her.

"Six weeks," she countered.

Instantly he felt less sorry for her. Damn stubborn female. "Four weeks. During which time I expect you to keep to yourself, not bother any of my crew and be careful with your stove ashes. Timber's bone dry this time of year.''

''Yes, I will do all those things. Thank you, Colonel Randall.''

''And don't bathe in the creek without letting me know. I'll have to post a guard.''

When she didn't respond, he shot a glance at her. Her fingers were pressed against her mouth, and at the corners of her closed eyelids he saw the sheen of tears.

Tom groaned. Women were a menace to the human race! They acted so brave, so fearless, and then when they won, they cried. Susanna had done the same, and this one was no different. He hated the way it made him feel—downright helpless. His gut churned just thinking about it.

''Four weeks,'' he barked over an ache in his throat. ''And then you're on your way back to Tennant, you savvy?''

She nodded without opening her eyes. Tom swung out the doorway, heading for his tent and the bottle of rye whiskey he hadn't finished last night. Maybe a drink would help get her out of his mind.

The minute Colonel Randall and the Irishman were gone, Meggy covered her face with her hands. *Oh, dear God, help me. I don't know what to do now, and I feel so awfully alone.*

After a few moments, she raised her head and took a good look at her surroundings. Through the chinks in the walls she could see glimpses of green leaves and an occasional brown tree trunk. A black iron pot-bellied stove sat in one corner, and a smoothed plank counter ran along the adjoining wall. The single window over the dry sink was so dust-smeared it admitted only a dim gray light. *Well, Meggy, you needn't be a complete ninny. A good scrubbing will fix that.*

As for the rest, sheets and soap, a lantern, table-cloths, her Bible and her secreted copy of *Uncle Tom's Cabin*—all the things she had packed in her trunk to start married life with Mr. Peabody—they would not arrive until next week when Mr. Jacobs drove out from Tennant with his next delivery. She could manage until then, could she not?

She eyed the other two walls. A few nails would serve to hang up her clothes. As for a bed, perhaps she might gather some pine boughs and cover them with the extra petticoat in her satchel.

Her satchel! She'd left it in Colonel Randall's tent. Bother! She'd have to walk back down and…

"Comin' through, ma'am!" Footsteps thumped across the porch. Hastily Meggy rose and stood aside as the sergeant barreled through the door, balancing a cot on one thick shoulder. His other hand gripped her travel satchel, and from under his arm trailed a bundle of bedclothes. She thought she recognized the olive-green blanket. Hadn't she sat on it in the colonel's tent?

Speechless, she watched him plunk the cot down

and shove it against the wall. "Colonel won't mind, ma'am. He never uses this one."

He dropped the bedclothes on top. "Had to scrounge a bit for your chamber pot." He swung two battered milk pails into the corner. "One for haulin' water, one for...you know."

Her face burned.

The sergeant tipped his blue cap and gave her a wink. "Supper's at five. Latecomers leave hungry." With a grin he pivoted and sauntered on his way.

Supper! She hadn't eaten since breakfast, and her stomach felt as hollow as an empty barrel. Oh, yes, supper! She'd be there *before* five. Perhaps she would go down to the cookhouse early and help out. In the meantime, she had to think.

What can I possibly do in this wilderness to earn money?

By the time she had made up the bed, hauled a bucket of cool water from the creek fifty yards from her porch, and used a dampened handkerchief to sponge the travel dust off her face and neck, she had made up her mind. If Colonel Tom Randall raised any objections, why she would... Never mind. She'd think of something.

She tidied her hair under the crocheted black netting and gave it a nervous pat. All she would require was a bit of ingenuity, a generous helping of elbow grease and God's forgiveness. Plus a dollop of luck when she went down to supper.

Her heart flip-flopped at the prospect before her.

Perhaps the colonel would be busy giving orders to his crew and wouldn't notice. Maybe the cook…

She dared not think about it too much. To keep her mind occupied she set about unpacking the rest of her things. She laid the tin of candles on the cot, stacked her underclothes on the sink counter, then slid her father's revolver underneath and covered the pile with a tea towel Charlotte had embroidered for her. A line of poetry was stitched around the perimeter. "Cleave ever to the sunnier side of doubt."

Tears stung her eyelids. She must write to Charlotte, must write to all her sisters, and assure them that she was safe and…and not the least bit frightened.

On second thought, she wouldn't lie. "Safe" would have to suffice!

She ran her hand over the mound of clothing covering the revolver, smoothed down her skirt and headed for the door. At the last minute she whipped the tea towel off the pile of garments and stuffed it into her pocket. She would need it.

Tom watched the black-clad form moving down the path from the cabin to the cookhouse and narrowed his eyes. She seemed to float slowly over the earth, and when he realized why, he grinned in spite of himself.

With extreme care she pushed one foot ahead of her, waited a second, then shifted her weight onto it. Only then did she move her other foot forward. Testing for rocks, he guessed. Or snakes. She looked like a miniature black-sailed ship skimming the ground.

You are one helluva fool, Tom Randall. He'd never get her out of his mind if he didn't stop watching her.

He wrenched his attention back to the open accounts book on his desk. Devil's Camp wasn't near breaking even, much less making a profit. Payroll was high. The men made good wages, and they deserved it; he'd hand-picked most of them when he mustered out of the army. Logging was dangerous, and he needed a seasoned crew. But lumber prices were dropping.

He wondered sometimes why he'd taken on this operation. Maybe because the first thing he saw when he'd ridden away from Fort Riley was trees, tall Douglas firs so thick a man couldn't reach around them. After years of killing Johnny Rebs and then Indians, felling timber seemed like a good, clean thing to do. Trees made lumber, and lumber built houses and barns and churches and stores. Civilization. He liked being part of things that would have a future, things that would live on after his own days on earth were over. He guessed he was like his father in that way.

Maybe that was how Walt Peabody felt about that cabin he'd built for Miss Hampton. At the thought of her, he glanced up to see a black skirt vanish into the cookhouse.

He massaged his tight neck muscles and got to his

feet. Great balls of fire, a woman at supper. He'd best go over and keep order.

Meggy craned her neck to peer through the screen door of the cookhouse. No sign of activity. No cook. No crew of hungry men. She lifted the watch pendant at her breast. Exactly five o'clock.

But she heard the clatter of pots and lids, and wonderful, tantalizing smells wafted from inside. She'd just step in and—

A slight figure in a black cotton tunic bustled out a doorway, swept onto the long, narrow porch outside and banged an iron spoon against a metal triangle. The sound jangled in her ears, and when it stopped another sound took its place. Marching feet.

Her blood turned to ice water. *Yankee soldiers.*

"You stand back, missy," the bell ringer warned. His long pigtail swung behind him as he sped noiselessly across the rough floor. "Men come," he called over his shoulder. "You come with Fong."

Meggy took a step in his direction, but in the next instant the screen door slapped open and a herd of jabbering men, all sizes and shapes, poured into the room, climbing over benches and even the long trestle table, to jostle a place for themselves.

Quickly she followed Fong to the sanctuary of the kitchen, then peeked back around the corner and released a sigh of relief. Not one of them looked like a soldier.

The hulking blond Swede she recognized from the

burial this morning. And the Irishman. Two gangly
youths with identical patches of freckles scuffled over
the space next to the Swede until a man with long,
straight black hair separated them with one arm and
took the place for himself.

More men tumbled in, pushing and shoving and
shouting good-natured insults at each other that made
her cheeks warm.

"You help, missy. Bullcook quit yesterday." The
Oriental shoved a huge bowl of mashed potatoes into
her hands, turned her about and gave her a little push.
"Hurry. Colonel Tom not like to wait."

Meggy gulped. A blob of butter the size of her fist
melted in the center of the steaming potatoes. *She was
so hungry!* She inhaled the delicious aroma and felt
another nudge at her back. "Go now. Eat later with
Fong. Not good one missy with dozen misters."

Quiet fell like a sheet of chilling rain when Meggy
stepped into the dining room. No one moved. No one
spoke. Twelve faces stared at her in complete silence.

She forced her feet to carry her forward to the table,
where she set down the bowl of potatoes.

The Irishman rose and swept off his cap. "Boys,
I'm presentin' to you Miss Mary Margaret Hampton.
She's Walt Peabody's next of kin."

She tried to smile. "Gentlemen."

"That they aren't, lass. Some of 'em haven't seen
the likes of a lady up close for six months, so I
wouldn't be fraternizin' too much."

"Aw, come on, O'Malley, be reasonable," a man shouted. A chorus of similar protests followed.

"Gosh, she shore is a purty one. She kin set on my lap and fraternize all she wants!"

"We want to hear her talk! Been a long time since we heard a woman's voice."

"Let's have us a chiv—"

"Hold it!" a voice boomed from the doorway. Tall and lean, Tom Randall strode toward her, his eyes shooting sparks. Meggy's heart began to skip beats.

"Thought I told you not to bother my men," he said just loud enough for her to hear.

She swallowed. "I was not 'bothering,' Colonel. I was serving potatoes."

He turned away from her without a word. "Boys, we've got us a problem. Maybe one of you can solve it."

A murmur of interest hummed through the room. Meggy noticed how he used his body to shield her from view. Fong was right; one missy and a dozen misters *not* good! She edged backward toward the kitchen.

"The problem," Tom continued, "is this. We've got no meat."

Meggy stopped still and heard her stomach grumble. No meat? What smelled so good, then?

"We haven't had any meat for weeks, Colonel. How long is this gonna go on?"

"That's not exactly true, Price. We've eaten a rabbit or two, and a squirrel."

"And some scrawny little pigeons," someone ventured.

She saw what he was doing—drawing the men's attention away from her—but she was so interested in the meat problem, she hovered near the door to listen.

Tom reached into his bulging back pocket, pulled out a bottle of amber liquid and thumped it down on the table. "This is fine whiskey, boys. One full quart."

Every eye studied the bottle.

"Now I'm going to tell you how one of you can claim this joy juice. It's plain we need meat. Fong tells me a deer's been nibbling his tomato plants at night. I'll give this bottle of liquid fire to the first man who shoots us some venison!"

"Hurray for the colonel!"

"I'm one crack shot," yelled the Swede. "We haf meat by tomorrow."

"A whole bottle for just one deer? Wouldja give me a gallon of rum if I kill an elk?"

"Elk meat tastes funny," the man called Price said. "Least it did back in Kansas."

"Hell, that weren't no elk, that were a beef cow. Are all Kansans that stupid?"

Tom held up one hand and a hush fell. "Let's get on with supper so we can be rolling into the timber at first light."

Fong scurried past Meggy with an oval platter of

sliced tomatoes in each hand. He plopped them down to the accompaniment of groans.

"Not more vegetables," Price moaned. "I'm gonna turn into a carrot before this season's half over!"

Tom slid onto the end of the bench and tapped the whiskey bottle with a ring he wore on his little finger. "Just a reminder, boys. We need meat to go with the potatoes."

Meggy had to laugh. The man was a master at guiding people in the direction he wanted. Her father, minister of the Methodist persuasion until his death in the field at Shiloh, had been similarly persuasive. The difference was that Papa fought for men's souls; Tom Randall cared about men's stomachs.

Such a man surely lacked depth.

She tore her thoughts away from him and tried to focus on the mission she had set for herself. She calculated she would need about ten minutes to do what she had to do.

She spied two blue china plates loaded with food and set aside on a small kitchen table. First, she decided, she would eat her supper.

And then she would use the very trick Tom Randall had just showed her to benefit her own cause.

She did hope that God would forgive her.

Chapter Three

Meggy adjusted her position at the small kitchen table so she could see into the dining hall where the men were eating. As she lifted forkfuls of mashed potatoes and boiled carrots to her mouth, she watched Tom Randall out of the corner of her eye.

He sat facing her, speaking to the tall, dark-haired man across the table, the one who had stopped the freckle-faced boys' scuffle. Tom's blue eyes steadily surveyed the dark man's face; Meggy studied Tom.

The colonel was a handsome man, she conceded. The skin of his face and arms was tanned from the sun, his features well proportioned. He wore a red plaid shirt, stuffed into dark-blue trousers. Even his mouth was attractive. For a Yankee, that is. Southern men generally sported mustaches.

The crew laughed and joked as they ate. Tom did neither. He kept his gaze on his men but didn't join in beyond an occasional word. Many of them eyed the whiskey bottle Tom had set out, and a few even caressed the glass container as they finished their meal and meandered onto the porch for a smoke.

Fong bustled between the huge iron-and-nickel cookstove and the sink, pumping water into food-encrusted pots, shaving in bits of brown soap and setting the utensils aside to soak. Then the cook stood poised in the kitchen doorway, watching for the moment he could swoop down to clear the dirty plates the men had left on the table.

When the main room emptied, Fong shot forward, and Meggy laid her fork aside.

Here was her chance.

Very quietly she pushed back her chair, stood up and glided to the pantry. Inside, barrels of flour, sugar, salt and molasses lined one wall. Woven baskets stuffed with carrots, potatoes, apples and squash teetered on crude plank shelves, and bunches of drying herbs tied together with string hung upside down from nails in the ceiling.

She withdrew the tea towel from her pocket, lifted the first barrel lid and scooped up three handfuls of flour. She dumped it in the center of the towel, gathered up the four corners and then moved to the barrel marked Salt. She sprinkled a pinch on top of the flour, then searched for a container of saleratus. There, on the middle shelf!

She maneuvered the top off the square tin canister,

dipped in her thumb and forefinger and added the white powder to the contents of the tea towel.

In the cooler sat a ceramic crock of pale cream-colored butter. Meggy hesitated a long moment. Did she dare? *Papa would spin in his grave if he knew I was stealing butter from a cookhouse pantry.*

She dug her fingers into the crock, scooped out a slippery handful. *I cannot believe I am doing this!*

She slid the glob of butter in on top of the flour and wiped her fingers on the towel. "Now," she breathed. "What else will I need?"

Her gaze fell on a bushel basket of mottled gold apples by the door. Four went into the tea towel; the fifth and sixth she stuffed into her skirt pocket. Sweeping past the sugar barrel, she hesitated for a split second, then halted and plunged in her clean hand. Her fist closed around coarse brown lumps.

Fong's voice rose from the kitchen like a trumpet call. "Missy help wash dishes?"

Her heart stopped. "Yes, I will," she called out. She dumped the sugar into her pocket, then jiggled up and down so the lumps would sift down around the apples and collect at the bottom. Satisfied, she dusted off her hands and straightened her skirt.

Stepping out of the pantry, she slipped the bulging tea towel under her knitted black shawl and turned to the pile of pots and pans in the sink. Fong's black eyes followed her every motion.

Trust me, she begged silently. *I will pay you back.*

He turned away without a word and dropped an armload of plates into the wide sink. "Fong wash, missy dry."

He lifted a whistling teakettle off the stove. Steam arose as he emptied the kettle, then pumped cold water into the enamelware dishpan and pointed to a clumsily hemmed flour sack. Meggy snatched it up and stood ready.

The man was a wonder. Plates, mugs, pots and lids flew through the soapy wash water and into the rinse bucket. She wiped as fast as she could but could not keep up with him. Last to be cleaned were four black iron skillets in various sizes. Fong wiped out the grease with a wadded towel and hung them upside down near the stove.

Meggy eyed the smallest pan. Just perfect. But how would she get it out the door? Perhaps some conversation to distract Fong just long enough?

"How long have you worked for Colonel Randall?"

"Long time, missy. Since before war. Before that, on railroad crew. Boss find me and I cook in army, now here at Devil Camp."

He sent her an inquisitive glance. "Ladies not allowed in camp. Why Colonel Tom let you stay?"

Meggy blinked. "Why, I don't know, really. I guess he couldn't very well turn me away, since Mr. Peabody willed me his cabin."

Fong grunted and splashed the last plate into the

rinse water. "Make no difference. Boss not like pretty women. Remind him of young sister."

His sister! Not a wife or a fiancée? "Colonel Randall is not married, then?" *How rude of me. First I turn thief, then inquisitor.*

"No woman. Not since sister die."

"Die! Oh, dear Lord, how did she die?"

Fong scrubbed hard at a tin saucepan. "Soldiers in Richmond hang her."

Her hands stilled. "Hanged her! How dreadful! Whatever did she do?"

"They say she Yankee spy."

The plate she was drying clattered to the plank floor. Colonel Randall's sister had spied for the Yankees? Meggy couldn't believe her ears. Of course there had been spies; she knew that. But hanging a woman? Why, it was unthinkable!

"So," she murmured, "that is why he is so unfriendly. Perhaps I remind him of the sister he lost." *Oh, no, it was more than that.* The Confederates had hanged the colonel's sister…and *she* was a Confederate!

Fong's face wrinkled into a frown. "You Johnny Reb, missy?"

"Y-yes. From South Carolina."

The Oriental nodded and plopped another pot into the wash water. "Luck is bad," he muttered. "Two things Colonel Tom not like—pretty woman and Johnny Reb. Luck very bad."

Meggy gulped. And here she was, stealing from the colonel's food supplies. If he found out, he would hang *her!*

"You go home now, missy. Fong sit up, guard tomatoes from hungry deer." He brandished a sawed-off broom handle.

As soon as she dried the last pot and suspended it on the rack above the stove, she clutched the tea towel containing the flour mixture and pressed the smallest of the iron skillets into the folds of her skirt. Keeping her back to the cook, she slipped out the screen door and fled down the porch steps.

Behind her she heard the click of the door latch and Fong's tuneless whistling. The latter blended with the throaty croak of frogs and the scrape of crickets. She stumbled up the path in the dark, felt her way to her own front porch and yanked open the door.

The cabin interior was black as the inside of a chimney. She crept to the bed, found the tin of candles and lit a short, fat one that Charlotte had scented with rose petals. Meggy set it on the counter. The little puddle of light calmed her nerves.

One hour. She needed just one hour.

She dampened her under-petticoat in the water bucket and scrubbed the plank counter. Then, with shaking hands, she poured the contents of the tea towel into the skillet and dug her fingers into the center. Within a few moments the flour and butter mixture was crumbly.

Dumping the lump of dough onto the clean counter surface, she patted it into shape and rolled it between her hands to make a smooth, round ball. When she'd set it on the sill of the open window to chill overnight, she emptied her pocket of the apples and spilled the sugar into the lid of a hand cream container. Then she stripped off her dress and petticoat, sponged her hands and face, puffed out the candle and fell into the bed still wearing her shimmy.

Tom tramped off the cookhouse porch and down the well-beaten path to his tent. He'd left the quart of whiskey in Fong's care, knowing his cook would guard it as zealously as the tomato patch he'd planted at the start of the season. He'd bet Fong would sit up in his garden all night, the whiskey bottle tucked beneath his tunic.

He chuckled. The deer that gobbled Fong's tomatoes would be far bolder than a man hankering to sneak a shot of rye!

He snatched up his account book, thumbed the pages, then slapped it down on the desk again. Damn, he wished he had some of that turkey sauce now!

He whittled the tip of his goose quill pen, fiddled with the bottle of brown ink. Finally he rose and took four steps to the front of the tent, four steps back to his makeshift desk, then repeated the circuit.

He felt another sleepless night coming on. In fact, he was so out of sorts he should probably be guarding the tomatoes and let Fong get some shut-eye. Peabody's death had stirred up old memories.

Every single time he got riled up over something he lay awake thinking about Susanna and the ill-informed junior officers with the oh-so-gentlemanly manners who had executed her. Tom had gotten there too late to save her; instead, he'd had to bury her. He'd spent the last seven years trying to forget his failure.

His belly tightened into a hard knot. Just the sound of a soft Southern drawl set his teeth on edge. Lucky thing Peabody hadn't talked much like a Confederate boy; otherwise, he'd never have been able to stomach the man. But Walt Peabody had spent more years in Oregon than he had in the South and talked pretty Western before the war even started.

Walt's widow, or fiancée, or whatever she was, was another matter. Mary Margaret Hampton was a Southern belle from her toes to her crown, and he'd hated her guts the minute she opened her mouth. A woman exactly like her had accused Susanna and, worse, had testified against her in court.

Tom flopped onto his cot, shucked off his boots and trousers, and stretched out full length with his head resting on his folded arms. He spent too many nights like this, staring at the canvas tent ceiling or out into the dark. He was wasting his life.

A light glowed on the rise beyond the cookhouse. He squinted his eyes. The cabin. Must be a lantern or a candle burning inside; the flame shone through the chinks in the split-log walls.

He watched the light wink on and off as some-thing—likely Miss Hampton—moved back and forth in front of the source. What was she doing, pacing up and down like that? That's what *he* usually did at night. It was damned unsettling to lie here and watch someone else do it. He felt like he was watching him-self.

The light flickered out, reappeared. It reminded him of the signals the Cheyenne made with hand-held mir-rors. He stared at it, trying to clear his mind of Miss Mary Margaret Hampton, until his eyelids drifted shut.

Meggy woke with a start. *What was that?*

Something rustled in the brush outside the cabin. She raised her head, listening. A shaft of moonlight fell through the open window above the sink, silhou-etting the ball of dough on the sill and the six lumps that were her stolen apples.

The rustling came again, closer this time. Without a sound, she sat up and swung her feet to the floor. Pulling her father's revolver from under the heap of garments where she'd hidden it, she hefted it in both hands, crept to the window and peered out.

A huge, soft brown eye peered back at her. A sleek brown head ducked, then lifted again. A wide rack of antlers gleamed in the pale light.

A deer! Probably the one that foraged in Fong's tomatoes. The animal took a tentative step forward, stopped, then sniffed the air.

Oh, no! Not my piecrust!

"Shoo!" she cried. Her voice came out no louder than a whisper. "Go away, please!"

The stag took two more steps. Meggy raised the revolver, closed her eyes and squeezed the trigger.

The shot brought Tom out of bed so fast he smacked his head on the tent pole. Great jumping catfish, what in the—

A woman screamed.

He yanked on his pants, jammed his feet into his boots and began to run. In the dark he could barely see the trail. Keeping low to the ground, he headed in the general direction of the noise.

Moonlight, he thought as he stumbled past the cookhouse, was one of God's greatest ideas!

Chapter Four

All the way up the hill, Tom could hear the sound of a woman crying. It cut into his belly like a shot of rotgut whiskey and made him blind with rage. He didn't know why, but he'd never been able to stomach a woman's tears.

When he could see the dark outline of the cabin in the moonlight, he slowed to a walk. If she could cry, she could breathe. That answered one question.

The other question—Why?—he answered when he stumbled over the carcass of a deer.

Someone had killed tomorrow's supper. The shot must have scared the ginger out of her, but the thought of venison steaks made him smile. He stepped around the dead animal and headed for the glimmer of white on the porch ahead of him.

"Miss Hampton? It's Tom Randall."

When he stepped forward, she jerked upright. "Oh! Please come no farther, C-Colonel Randall. I am not p-properly attired.'' She sounded like she had the hiccups.

Tom spun on one heel so his back was to her. ''Who shot the deer?''

''I—I did,'' she confessed between sobs. ''At least I think I did. I had my eyes closed.''

Tom knelt to inspect the animal. ''Mighty good shot, ma'am. Clean and true, right into the head.''

''Oh, the poor, dear thing. I meant only to scare it away, not kill it!''

Poor dear thing? He sneaked a look at her. Arms locked about her white-shrouded legs, she rocked back and forth, her forehead pressed against her knees.

''I feel just awful about shooting it. It had such big, soft eyes.''

Two things warred for Tom's attention—the revolver lying beside her and her hair tumbling loose about her shoulders. He struggled to keep his mind on the gun.

''Where'd you learn to shoot?''

She choked back a sob. ''My father taught me, before he went off to his military post. He said I had a g-good eye.''

''And a steady hand, it would appear. Miss Hampton, you might as well dry your tears and make the best of it. The boys'll be grateful to you for supplying some good meat.''

"I—I will try." She gazed at him with a stricken look. "I just feel so…mean!"

He stuffed down a chuckle. "You ever shoot anything before?"

She nodded. "I shot a Yankee once. In the backyard of the parsonage. He was after our last two chickens, you see, and I…I hit him in the shoulder. I offered to dress the wound, but he swore something dreadful and skedaddled over the back fence."

So she'd lived in a parsonage, had she? A preacher's daughter with good eyesight and guts. Now, why should that surprise him? All Southerners were murdering bastards hiding under a cloak of gentility. He'd learned that in Richmond. His jaw tightened.

"I hear somebody coming, Miss Hampton. You might want to put on a robe."

Meggy scrambled to her feet. The colonel stood before her, both hands jammed in his trouser pockets. Mercy me, he wore no shirt!

She stared at the bare skin of his chest, at the muscles cording his broad shoulders. Never in her whole life had she seen a man without his shirt, not even Papa. She gulped. Even her intended, Mr. Peabody, had been laid out in his coffin fully dressed.

An odd, restless feeling crept over her as she gazed at the colonel's tall frame. Why, he looked strong enough to—

Sergeant O'Malley crashed out of the trees and into

the clearing. "For the love of God, Tom, what's goin' on? I heard a shot, and when I found your tent empty...well, I thought maybe you'd— What's this, now?"

The Irishman stared down at the dead stag. "Well, I'll be smithereened! You killed us a deer, Tom."

"I didn't exactly..."

Meggy slipped inside the front door and listened to Tom's voice floating from the porch. "Think we can dress it out here?"

"Nah. Too dark. Let's lug it down to the cookhouse. I'll go rustle up Fong and some other help. Maybe those two rascally Claymore lads you took on."

She held her breath. Tom had sidestepped telling Mr. O'Malley who had killed the animal. True, she didn't want to confess the deed, but she doubted the colonel would understand why. No Yankee soldier could fathom Southern sensibilities.

She tiptoed to the counter and rummaged in the pile of garments for her night robe, drew it on over her shimmy and underdrawers and tied it about her waist with a jerk.

No Federal officer she'd ever encountered paid the slightest attention to the feelings of civilians. When the Northern army overran Chester County, the soldiers had swaggered and shouted and stolen her mother's ruby ear-bobs. Why, they did not even *look* like gentlemen. Even the men she and her sisters had tended in hospital were hopelessly ill-mannered and unlettered.

Through the open doorway she watched the two men drag the deer away from her porch. Then Mr. O'Malley tramped off down the hill toward the cook-house and the colonel settled himself on the planks, his back toward her.

A long minute dragged by. Meggy became acutely aware of the noises around her, the breeze sighing through the treetops, the low *hoo...hoo* of an owl. The uneven breathing of the man sitting not three feet away from her.

What was he thinking?

The silence hung on until she thought she would scream. All of a sudden his low voice made her jump.

"Might as well go on back to bed, Miss Hampton. We'll haul the carcass down to the cookhouse so you won't have to look at it in the morning."

"Thank you," she managed, in a tight voice. But she stood frozen to the spot. *Why could she not move?*

Because... Meggy's entire body trembled. Was the sight of a half-naked man outside her front door so disturbing?

Certainly not! It was because she was a tiny bit afraid of him.

Because she disliked him.

Because he, well, he was a Yankee.

Because he was a man.

Her heart hammered. Most definitely not! She put

no stock whatsoever in such things. She and Walter Peabody had contracted a union of souls, not bodies. She always wondered at her sisters, who had grown dreamy-eyed and absentminded when they were smitten by some young gentleman. *Oh, Meggy, just the sound of his voice gives me the shivers!*

She had no time for such sentimental nonsense.

Besides that, she most certainly harbored no such feelings about a man she had known just half a day and was a Yankee besides.

She was tired, that was it. And overwrought. Her nerves were frazzled. This entire day—and night— was a dreadful nightmare, and any moment she would wake up.

"Go to bed," he repeated.

"I would," she murmured, "if I could make my feet move."

He rose and half turned in her direction. "Are you all right?"

"No. I—I mean, yes. Of course."

He stepped up onto the porch. "Need help?"

His movement toward her jolted her into action. She inched backward until her legs touched the cot against the far wall.

"Miss Hampton?"

Her derriere sank onto the blanket. With a supreme effort she closed her eyes to blot out the bronzed skin of his bare chest, his sinewy shoulders and arms. *Mary Margaret, you are hallucinating!*

Voices came up the hill. Someone—it must be Colonel Randall—stepped across the porch and pulled her front door shut.

"Tomorrow..."

She heard his words as clearly as if they were spoken at her bedside.

"Tomorrow, Mick, I want a lock put on this door."

Oh, yes, Meggy thought with relief. A lock was exactly what she needed. A lock would surely keep her safe.

By the time Meggy woke, the sun was high overhead in a sky so blue and clear it looked like a cerulean-painted china bowl. She breathed in the warm, pine-scented air and bolted upright. Mercy, she'd overslept!

With hurried motions she washed her face and arms, pulled on her blue sateen skirt, a white waist and a plain cotton apron, and bound up her hair in a neat black net.

Cautiously she cracked open the front door. No sign of men. No sign of the deer, save for a mashed-down patch of dry grass. Skirting the area, she gathered small sticks and an apronful of pinecones, then started a fire in the wood stove. When it caught, she fed it pine chips apparently left over from construction of her cabin and small sections of a tree stump that had been chopped up and left in chunks. Then she rolled up her sleeves and set to work.

Using a smooth glass bottle of Molly More Rose-water as a rolling pin, she pressed the lump of dough into a round flat circle, laid it in the skillet she'd borrowed from the cookhouse, and crimped the edges with her thumb and forefinger. With the pocketknife she always carried in her reticule, she peeled the apples she'd taken from Fong's pantry, sliced them into the pie shell and sprinkled her pocketful of sugar over the top. A dollop of molasses would have been nice, but she could manage without it. It was one thing to carry a tea towel full of flour and butter, but a handful of sticky syrup?

When the oven was hot, she shoved the skillet in, rinsed off her hands and busied herself gathering more wood to replenish the fire while the pie baked.

Oh, it did smell heavenly, even without the cinnamon she usually sprinkled over the apples. The sweet-tart scent made her mouth water. Papa used to say she could make a pie so tender and delicious it was like an angel's breath melting in his mouth.

To her sister Charlotte the good Lord gave the gift of words. To Hope and Charity, keen eyesight and skill with a crochet hook. To Addie, a singing voice that could reduce a congregation to tears.

But to me, Mary Margaret, God gave the ability to cook.

When the pie was golden-brown, she wrapped her apron around her hand, slid the bubbling confection out of the oven and set the skillet on the windowsill to cool.

Unable to stop herself, she twirled about the room until she was giddy. It was a silly thing to do, but at this moment she didn't care one bit. Her daring venture would be a success, she just knew it!

Off in the distance she heard the crash and thump of a falling tree. Somewhere in the woods beyond were twelve hungry loggers. All she needed was a bit of patience and the Lord's own luck.

She eyed the cooling pie and smiled.

Meggy dipped her bare toe in the slow-moving river and shivered. She didn't care what Colonel Randall said, she desperately wanted a bath and a chance to wash her clothes and her hair. Her scalp tingled at the thought of soapsuds. With the men out cutting trees, she couldn't see the sense in advising the colonel of her plans, as he had requested. What could he possibly care about her personal habits?

Despite the bright sun beating down on it, the water was ice cold. She pulled her arms in close to her body. Rivers at home in Chester County were generally tepid by late summer. Out here in the West, everything was colder, bigger, steeper, rougher. And more frightening.

She waded in until the clear water covered her knees, then submerged the bundle of clothes she carried and tossed a bar of rose-scented soap on top of them. Standing naked in the shallows, she scrubbed her black traveling dress, two petticoats, her under-drawers, even her shimmy. Soft, warm air brushed against her skin, and she sighed with satisfaction. Her apple pie was cooling in the window, and now her laundry was done.

She wrung out the sopping garments, waded to shore and draped them over a sun-drenched choke-cherry bush. By the time she'd washed her hair and dunked her hot, sticky body in the cool river water, her clothes would be dry enough to put on.

Bending at the waist, she unpinned her hair and sloshed water over the heavy chestnut waves, then worked up a lather with her fingers. Oh, how blessed it was to feel clean again! She took a deep breath, leaned forward to dive into the blue-green water, and froze.

Voices floated from the woods behind her. Men's voices.

Good heavens, the logging crew! Meggy clapped one hand over her mouth to suppress a squeal. She plunged in neck deep just in time to see Colonel Randall stride into view at the head of a straggly line of slow-footed workers. Two loggers, the Swede and the plump, sweet-faced man called Orrin, carried a two-man crosscut saw across their shoulders.

Dear God, the colonel was heading straight for the chokecherry bush! He would see her garments and know in an instant she had disobeyed his orders.

Worse, she was stuck out here in this freezing water with her hair piled up under a tower of soapsuds.

She sank into the water up to her chin, and her teeth began to chatter.

She watched him approach, saw him hesitate as the chokecherry came into his view. Her bent knees began to ache.

Suddenly the colonel quickened his pace. Meggy groaned. He had spied her dress, her petticoats, her... Oh, how perfectly mortifying!

Barely breaking stride, he gathered up the items, rolling them into a wet ball as he walked, and tucked them under one arm. Without a backward glance he kept moving, staying well ahead of the men lagging behind him.

When their voices died away, Meggy dunked her head under the surface and swam to shore. Her skin sprouted goose bumps as big as June bugs as she waded out of the river. Heaven help her, she had not one single scrap to clothe herself in except for her shoes! How was she to get back to her cabin?

In disbelief, she circled the chokecherry bush. How *could* he have left her in such a fix? He was a mean, no-count lowlife if ever she'd met one. Imagine, taking advantage of a helpless...

Something caught her eye, and she jerked to a halt. There, in the crotch of that young maple tree—what was that dark roll poking out?

Her clothes! Wadded up in a ball and wet as rain-water.

She snatched them up and with shaking hands pulled on the dripping garments, starting with her underdrawers. Her skin shrank at the feel of the damp, clingy muslin.

That dreadful man!

Every step of the way back to the cabin she rehearsed the stinging words she would level at the colonel when she confronted him.

Tom leaned back on the plank porch, supporting his weight on one elbow. He'd sent the crew on ahead with the promise of venison steaks for dinner, and now he waited for Mary Margaret Hampton. He worked his thumbnail into the wood, outlining a curved half-moon that looked like the letter *C*.

C for cantankerous. *C* for crazy. Chuckle-headed. Calico-hungry. All that and more. His crew was an obstreperous bunch of misfits, and it had taken half the season to turn them into a team. He'd almost lost another man today when that idiot bullwhacker Sam Turner got to showing off and one of the young Claymore boys slipped under the mule team.

On top of that, he was saddled with a cotton-headed female. By damn, he was in no mood for any nonsense, especially not from a little slip of a woman whose sense of independence outweighed her brain power.

When she appeared on the trail that led up to the cabin, Tom lifted his head. She marched along the path with jerky steps, holding her wet, drooping skirt up out of the dust. Her eyes glinted an icy green.

"Evening, Miss Hampton."

She stopped short and pressed her lips together. "What are you doing here?"

"Waiting for you. Thought you might be along pretty soon. I see you found your dress and…things."

"Found and donned, no thanks to you. Whatever possessed you to take them in the first place?"

"Had to," he said quietly. "Behind me were eleven men who haven't seen a woman in six months, let alone one standing in the woods buck naked. What do you think they'd do if they stumbled across some damn fool's frilly underwear hangin' on a bush?"

"Avert their eyes and walk on, of course. As any gentleman would."

Tom rose. "My men aren't gentlemen, Miss Hampton. They're rough and they're rowdy and they're all male. I wouldn't go poking at this particular hornet's nest if I were you."

"I was most certainly not poking—"

"You were taking a bath in the river. Against my orders."

She dropped the folds of her skirt clenched in her fingers and propped her fists on her hips. "You saw me!"

"Couldn't miss you. Hair all sudsed up with white

foam, you looked like a frosted cake floating out there in the middle of the river. I gathered up your clothes so the men wouldn't get interested in finding the owner.''

''Frosted cake! Well, I never!''

''That water's crystal clear,'' he said with a grin. ''The rest of you looked like a shriveled up corn doll.''

''The rest of me?''

''Miss Hampton, don't take another bath without telling me. Like I said before, I'll post a guard.''

Speechless, Meggy stared into the man's face for a full minute. A muscle under his eye jerked. ''A guard,'' she echoed.

''A guard.''

All at once she became aware of how cold and wet she was. Her clammy underdrawers stuck to her thighs and calves; her damp shimmy clung to her back and chest like a coating of cold syrup. Her petticoats dripped water down her ankles and into her shoes. And her dress...well, it felt for all the world like a heavy, cold shroud.

''Go inside,'' he ordered. ''You're shivering. Get out of those wet things.''

''I am n-not s-shivering.'' She had to work hard to keep her voice steady.

He rolled his eyes toward the treetops. ''Go!''

Without thinking, Meggy snapped her heels together and saluted. ''Am I dismissed, then, Colonel?''

Without waiting for a reply, she hoisted her skirt up a few inches and planted one foot on the porch. With a little lift she attempted to heave herself upward, but the weight of her wet clothes was more than she'd bargained for. She stumbled against the edge.

Tom watched her struggle for a moment, then moved behind her, placed his hands about her waist and lifted her onto the porch. The feel of her body under his hands, the whiff of roses that came from her hair sent a red-hot arrow straight to his groin.

With an exaggerated sniff, she stomped across the planks to the front door, yanked it open and banged it shut behind her.

"Headstrong and excitable," he muttered as he clomped down off the porch. "She sure gets an arch in her back over the damnedest things."

On the other hand, she might have been raised on prunes and proverbs, but when she closed her mouth, she was all woman.

"That being the case..." He laughed out loud as he strode down the hill toward the safety of his tent.

"The next time she flames up over something, I guess I'll have to set a backfire."

Chapter Five

Meggy listened to the colonel's boots clump across the porch and fade as he tramped down the path. As fast as her chilled fingers could move, she unbuttoned her wet dress, stepped out of her petticoats and peeled off the cold, clingy underdrawers and shimmy. The late-afternoon air was still warm, but her naked skin pebbled just the same. Hurriedly she laid the wet garments out on the counter beneath the windowsill to dry.

And stopped short.

Her pie! Her beautiful apple pie had disappeared. The black iron skillet sat on the sill right where she'd left it, but it was empty.

Clutching a damp petticoat to her body, she tiptoed forward for a closer look. Gone. Not a single crumb remained in the pan. Something, or someone, had stolen her pie.

She snatched up the skillet and gasped. A shiny

round coin lay underneath it. "Merciful heaven, a five-dollar gold piece! But who—"

The colonel, of course. That scoundrel! Why, he'd just lounged there on her porch, waiting for her to return from the river. Plain as buttermilk he'd helped himself to her creation, without even a by-your-leave.

Seething inside, Meggy struggled to think clearly. At least it was decent of him to pay for his prize. She could use the money to pay for the flour and sugar she'd used, and then...

Absently she hung the damp petticoat on a nail by the door and drew on clean, dry undergarments, her brain turning over the spark of an idea.

Yes! And it would serve him right, too. The very idea of eating her pie...

By suppertime she had made up her mind. Slipping the gold piece into her pocket, she snatched up the iron skillet and sped down the path to the cookhouse.

Fong glanced up from the cookstove as she entered the kitchen. "Ah, missy find fry pan. Have good luck now. Fry steaks for supper." He lifted the pan from her hands and banged it down on the stove top.

Meggy blinked. "Don't you want to ask me about the skillet?"

Fong grinned at her. "Nope. More better you not explain." He turned away, dropped a teacup-size ball of suet into each of the four pans. When it sizzled, he slapped down inch-thick slabs of meat and turned to her.

"You need more flour?"

Her heart nearly stopped beating. "Yes," she said in a small voice. "But this time I can pay." She drew out the gold piece and laid it on the warming shelf.

The cook scooped it into his palm. "Too much, missy. You take what you need for two, three days."

"And...and a skillet?" Meggy held her breath. Without the heavy iron utensil she had nothing to bake a pie *in*.

"Oh, yes. Take big pan this time." He banged a two-pronged fork against the handle of the largest skillet. "This one good. I hear about pie," he added in an undertone.

Meggy swallowed. "Who told you?"

Fong's black eyes sparkled. "Cannot say. But—" he beckoned her closer "—he say needs maybe more sugar."

"Oh! The pie thief is criticizing his booty?"

"*I* not steal," Fong protested. He pointed to the side pocket of his black tunic. "Someone pay. In gold. Good business, missy."

Meggy exchanged a long, significant look with the cook. Was she dreaming, or was he encouraging her in her enterprise?

Whistling idly between his teeth, Fong surveyed his skillet-crowded stove top, jabbed one sputtering steak with the fork and expertly flipped it over. "Next time," he said, "use big pan. Make more dollar."

Was it possible Fong was in cahoots with the colonel? She baked a pie, the colonel stole—well, bought it—and Fong got rich when she paid him for the supplies she'd used? It made sense of a sort.

Except that *she* needed the money, or at least part of it. Otherwise, she would never collect enough for train fare back to...

She caught her breath as a sudden, sharp realization hit her. She could not possibly return to Chester County. By now, the parsonage would be occupied by the new minister and his family, and even though her sisters would surely take her in, she did not relish the role of maiden aunt, a spinster like Aunt Hattie, who'd grown old taking care of other people's children instead of her own, and who'd become addled and crotchety in middle age because no man had ever touched her.

Oh, dear God, please don't let that happen to me. I want a life for me. I want someone to love who will love me back.

Therefore, she resolved, she must go forward. She would go where she could have what she wanted. And if that meant selling another pie and saving her money, then that was exactly what she would do. She did not belong anywhere, now. But she would. She *would*.

Meggy pointed to the largest skillet. "That one, please."

Fong nodded and flipped over two more steaks.

She set plates and mugs and utensils on the table,

lugged out the coffeepot, brought two bowls of boiled potatoes and one of savory-smelling brown gravy, and finally carried out the huge platter of venison steaks just as Fong clanged the dinner bell.

A loud, quarreling knot of men tumbled through the cookhouse door.

"Get yer butt outta my place."

"Anybody know who shot the deer?"

"Shut up and pass the meat!"

"Kinda takes the sting out of bustin' that skid, don't it, Swede?"

"Ya, sure it does, by golly."

The men fell on the food like vultures. As the last man, the black-haired Indian, sat down at the table, Meggy spotted the colonel on the porch, his gait slow and loose jointed, his unruly dark hair curling over the collar of his red plaid shirt. Talk ceased the instant he moved into the room.

Meggy turned back toward the kitchen. Something clunked onto the table, and Tom's voice rose behind her. "Boys, we have among us a sharpshooter of the first water."

Meggy stopped in her tracks.

"Well, who is it?" someone shouted.

"Shut up, ya numbskull. It's the colonel that done it."

"You mean he won his own whiskey? 'Tain't fair!"

"Well, hell, what do we care? We got meat, ain't we?"

"Boys," the colonel said. The sound of his voice brought instant quiet.

Meggy's neck grew warm. Would he tell them who had shot the deer?

"Now, boys, when a person's this good a shot, it pays to take note. First off, it's food on the table. And secondly—"

You're not going to tell them, are you? Meggy wanted to scream. *Why?*

He answered her silent query with his next words.

"And secondly, it might pay to stay clear of the trigger-happy hunter who drilled this buck you're eating with a single revolver shot right between the eyes." He paused for effect. "If you take my meaning."

"Ya," said the Swede. "Well, we all wanting to know who it is."

Tom waited so long to speak Meggy felt drops of perspiration between her shoulder blades.

"Boys, Miss Hampton sleeps with her revolver under her pillow. Not only that, but she's a tad near-sighted. Be best if you didn't go anywhere near her cabin lest she mistake you for Sunday supper."

"You mean *she* killed that deer? A *woman?*"

Meggy's ears burned. Clenching her hands at her sides, she spun to face the colonel across the expanse of pine flooring.

Tom settled himself into the empty chair at the head of the table. "Nearsighted, like I said. But damn lucky."

"I say we should give 'er the whiskey. She earned it."

The colonel gave her a long, steady look that sent an odd shiver up her backbone. Her heart pounding, she pivoted and escaped to the kitchen.

She picked at the dinner Fong set before her. After what seemed like an eternity, the men drifted out onto the porch and Meggy rose. She would clear away the dirty plates, help Fong with the washing up and then forget her humiliation at the colonel's hands and concentrate on making another pie. And this time she would double the sugar.

She stepped into the dining room and halted at the sight of Tom Randall still sitting at the long table, his hands wrapped around a mug of coffee.

"I am not nearsighted!" Meggy blurted. "Why on earth would you say such a thing?"

He regarded her with a look she could only describe as half weariness, half amusement. "Miss Hampton, I want my men to stay clear of you. I want them to feel in mortal danger anytime one of them comes within fifty yards of your cabin."

"But—what about my pies?"

"Your pies? What pies?"

"Oh come now, Colonel. You know perfectly well what pies. Apple pies, like the one you stole—I beg your pardon, *bought*—this afternoon. If the men fear to come near my cabin, my profits will dry up.''

Tom ran one hand through his hair. ''What the hell are you talking about?''

Meggy gazed into his baffled blue eyes. ''Why, I'm talking about… You know nothing about my apple pie?''

''Nope. Wish I did, though.'' He pushed the bottle of whiskey toward her. ''The boys want you to have this. You earned it by shooting that deer.''

She stared at him, then at the bottle, then at him again. ''Oh, I couldn't. I don't partake of spirits.''

Instantly she regretted the words. The round, smooth bottle would make a perfect rolling pin. ''On second thought, perhaps just a tiny drop.''

With a chuckle, Tom shoved the bottle closer to her, slid out of his chair and ambled toward the door. There was something downright amusing in the thought of a preacher's daughter wetting her whistle on rye whiskey. He wondered what she'd be like with some firewater in her. Spirited? Maybe even wild? Nah. Probably even more straitlaced and proper than when she was cold sober.

And what was all that palaver about apple pies?

Maybe he should post a guard. Nah, he didn't trust anyone but Fong and O'Malley. Fong would be guarding his tomatoes, and O'Malley… No, not O'Malley. The sergeant was a sweet-talking Irishman with an eye for a pretty ankle.

Best if he just kept an eye on her himself.

He sighed and looked out into the dusky-gold light of early evening. Crickets scraped their mating songs down by the river. Two sparrows chittered back and forth from the drooping branches of a vine maple. *Of all creatures in which there was the breath of life, a pair of each…a male and a female…*

A raw, hungry feeling filled his gut. He'd give his right arm for a glass of that whiskey.

Stepping down off the cookhouse porch, he headed for his tent. Once inside, he lay full-length on the cot, folded one arm behind his head and looked out toward her cabin.

Sooner or later there'd be a light inside.

The minute she entered the cabin, Meggy set to work mixing her pie dough. She could hardly wait to try out the new whiskey-bottle rolling pin. Experimentally she rolled the bottle over the countertop, listening to the amber liquid gurgle inside the glass. Perfect. And so musical!

She began to hum as she patted the dough into a rounded shape. "'We are a band of brothers, and native to the soil….'" "Bonnie Blue Flag" was such a lively, encouraging tune.

As she worked, she congratulated herself on her inventive use of the spirits the colonel had pressed on her. Well, she *was* inventive. She had to be. That was how she had managed to feed and clothe herself and her sisters during the war. Even after the war, when the marauding Yankees came looking for jewelry and their hidden food stores. Never once in all those years had she given up, and she refused to do so now. She would do whatever was required to survive and triumph, even if it meant rolling out her piecrust with a bottle of—she squinted at the label—Red Eye Premium.

She stared at the whiskey. In all her life, she had never tasted spirits. Maybe she would try just one tiny sip.

It burned her throat like fire, but once she managed to swallow it down, a comforting warmth spread into her midsection. Oh, my. Now she understood what gentlemen meant by Dutch courage. It was… strengthening.

She tried another mouthful. Positively confidence-building. And exactly what she needed at the moment.

Tom focused on the glow of light from the cabin, afraid to move a muscle for fear it was only a mirage his tired eyes had created. Nope, not his imagination. The light spilling between the chinks in the log walls winked on and off as she moved about inside.

How come she was so active at night? What the devil was she doing, pacing? Dancing?

His curiosity mounting, he watched until the light suddenly stopped flickering and shone steadily through the trees. He waited a good fifteen minutes,

then frowned. If she'd stopped whatever she was doing and gone to bed, why didn't she douse the candle?

Had she fallen asleep and left it burning? Sweat
started on his forehead. The timber surrounding their
camp was tinder dry, so parched and brittle it would
ignite with the smallest spark.

Tom sat up. So far the season had been nothing but
a ball of snakes. The crew was growing quarrelsome
and unruly, two bullcooks had up and quit, and a man
had been killed. On top of everything, ever since
March it had been dust dry, without a drop of rain.

He planted his boots on the earth floor of his tent
and stood up. He was not going to lose his harvest of
Douglas fir trees to some damn fool of a woman with
a short candle and a shorter memory!

He saw her through the trees, perched on the cabin
porch, her dark-blue skirt puffed around her hips.
She'd rolled up the sleeves of her white blouse, exposing slender arms and delicate looking wrists, and
her white pantaletted legs swung over the edge. She
looked like a white stalk poking up from a big blue
mushroom.

She was singing under her breath. "'We hoist on
high the Bonnie Blue Flag, that bears a shingle—single star....'"

Tom strode through the brush, making as much
noise as possible to avoid startling her. "Miss Hampton?"

She tilted her head sideways. "Yesh, it is, isn't it?"

"Are you all right?"

"I am quite well, thank you." She enunciated each word with care. "I'm gridding...guarding my pie-crust." She pointed her forefinger at the windowsill where a fist-size ball of dough sat square in the center of the open window. "Made a wunnerful pie-crust...better if it chills overnight."

Tom suppressed a grin. "Had a bit of that rye, I'd guess."

Her head dipped up and down several times. "Tastes jus' awful. Like turpentine. But the bottle's nice. I like the bottle. It rolls jus' right."

Tom said nothing. The light inside the cabin sent a soft glow onto the porch. The faint scent of roses hung in the air. What he wanted to do was sit beside her in the moonlight, but something held him back. His better judgment, maybe. Pretty obvious she'd made good use of the whiskey.

"You ever drink spirits before?"

"Of coursh not. I started with little teeny tiny sipses...sips. After a while it tasted better, and it made me all warmly inside." She cocked her head. "You feel all warmly inside?"

"Nope," he lied. Watching her, he felt more than warm. She looked enchantingly female, her legs dangling off the porch, her skin flushed and rosy. He wanted to touch her so bad he ached.

"Why not? Don' you want to?"

"You offering me a drink?"

She giggled. "Thash funny, Colonel. It's *your* whiskey. You jus' lent it to me for the evenin', cuz of that poor little deer."

Tom kept his mouth shut.

"An' then we went an' ate him all up. So I came back and mished up my pie dough… Did you know I make the best piecrush in Chester County? My papa used to say… What was it Papa shed? Oh, yesh, angel feathers. Make crush like angel—"

"Miss Hampton, you're drunk as a sailor."

"Izzat so? What makesh you think that?"

Tom choked down a guffaw and moved to stand in front of her. "Come on, on your feet. Time for bed."

"Can't. Got to wash—watch my pie dough."

"You can watch it from inside."

"Dowanna. Did you know my sisters are all married?"

Tom placed his hands on her upper arms and pulled her upright. "No, I didn't know that. Can you walk?"

"Addie was first. She married that nice Taylor boy from York County. Then Hope an' Charity fell in love with brothers, can you 'magine that? An' Faith found her lieutenant jus' before he went off to the war."

"Take a step forward, Miss Hampton."

"But not me. I'm th' only one who didn't marry. All my sisters did, but I guessh God forgot about me."

"Walk," he ordered.

"Charlotte, now, she had a passel of beaus 'fore the war, but only one of 'em came back. She's been married two whole months now, and I wonder…"

Tom held her shoulders to steady her. "Come on now, try."

"D'you think she's con-conceived yet? Addie had her twins jus' nine months after the weddin', wasn't that nice? An' you know what, Colonel shir—sir?"

"Walk," he repeated. He slipped his arm about her waist, tried to propel her forward. She felt soft and warm beneath the layers of sateen and muslin. He tried not to think about it, tried to keep his mind focused on getting her to move.

"I think twins would be jus' lovely. A boy an' a girl. 'Course, they look the spittin' image of Addie, right down to her dimples." Meggy laid her hand on his bare forearm. "Was your sister a twin?"

Tom jerked. "Who told you about my sister?"

"Fong did, a li'l bit. Wash she really a spy?"

"Susanna was not a spy!" he said, louder than he intended.

Meggy clapped her palms to her ears, then tipped her head back and flung both arms into the air. "Jus' look at those stars! Aren't they wunnerful? Like great big diamonds sprinkled all over the sky."

Tom glanced up, grateful for the change of subject. It had been a long, long time since he'd noticed the stars. Tonight, even with the moon's light, they looked extra bright.

"'Spose every one of those stars is a li'l world jus' like ours? And way off up there someone's lookin' down on ush? Well, I do wonder what they might think, whether we're pea-peash…frien'ly or warlike. P'rhaps we'll never, ever know. After all, it ish a long ways up there."

"It's a ways to your bed, too," Tom observed. "So far you haven't taken a single step."

"On th' other hand, they might have lookin' glash—glasses so they could look down and study us. Big, big glashes, like army off'cer telescopes that would see everything." She peered up at him. "D'you think they might know about Charlotte's baby? I mean, whether she's carryin' yet?"

Tom gave up. Dipping at the knees, he scooped her up and stepped up onto the porch. Her hair, caught in a black net snood, brushed his chin.

"I wunner if it'll be a boy or a girl? A girl, I'd like that. Boysh can be so rowdy. An' then they grow up an' go off and get killed…oh, it's jus' heart-breakin'."

Tom moved through the doorway and into the cabin. The woman in his arms was soft and sweet smelling. He wanted to hold her. Taste her. All at once he knew this was the last place he should be at the moment.

"Now the young man Sharity married, one of the Vincennes brothers, he came back from the war with a wooden leg. Cut clean off at the knee, but you know what, Colonel shir? It didn't bother Sharity one whit, no shirree. 'It's his heart and soul that I love, not his leg,' she said. Made me cry all over my peash cobbler.''

Tom strode to the cot, laid her down and pulled the blanket up to her chin.

She popped up like a jack-in-the-box and began to unbutton her blouse. "Oh, ish bedtime? But I haven't tol' you 'bout Faith. Faith's diff'rent. She married the other Vincennes brother, a doctor, and she—"

Tom stilled her hands and pressed her shoulders down until she was again horizontal. "Miss Hampton, I bet you never talked this much to anybody in your whole life."

She laughed, a musical purring sound that made the blood thrum in his veins. She was so *female.* His body responded accordingly.

Tom groaned. This was absolutely the last thing he needed—a pretty woman, a pretty *Southern* woman—in need of protection.

"Well, thash jus' Faith for you. She's my shis—sister, but a woman should never, ever treat a husband like that. 'Coursh, I never married, but even so, I know never to..."

She sat up again and peeled off her white blouse before he could stop her. "Colonel, have you ever been married?"

He worked to keep his gaze off the smooth, bare skin her camisole exposed.

"Nope. Lie down, Miss Hampton. Try to go to sleep." To keep his hands busy and his eyes elsewhere, he unlaced her black leather shoes, slipped them off her feet and set them under the cot.

She closed her eyes, then popped them open again. "Why ever not?" She sank back on the pillow once more. "You need a woman. Someone who can bake for you…make you pies an'…"

He needed a woman, all right. But not her. Anyone but her. She knew about Susanna, and, worse, she was a Confederate. He felt angry and exposed.

And hungry and alone, a voice inside his head reminded him.

Her eyelids fluttered shut. "All my shisters married," she mumbled. "But not me. D'you think there's something wrong with me?"

Not hardly! With determined strides Tom crossed the floor, blew out the candle stuck on the plank counter, and checked the latch O'Malley had installed on her door that afternoon. No good. It hooked the door all right, but from the inside. Once Tom left the premises, there was no way of keeping anyone out.

Dammit, O'Malley, you could have thought this through!

He stepped out on the porch, closed the door and eyed the hard wooden planks. Giving her that whiskey had been a mistake. It wouldn't be the first time he'd done something that jelly-brained, but by damn, it would be the last!

With a sigh of resignation he tugged off his boots and folded them in half. Then he lay down, shoved the boots under his head and positioned his body across the doorway.

Chapter Six

"Colonel, darlin', wake up." O'Malley bent over Tom, a wide smile on his ruddy face. He touched the toe of his boot to the sleeping man's shoulder. "Colonel?"

Tom cracked one eye open. "What is it, O'Malley?"

"'Tis past four o'clock, Tom. Time for breakfast before the first cut."

"Yeah. I'm coming."

The sergeant surveyed him curiously. "If you don't mind me askin', boyo, what the devil are you doin' up here?"

Tom sat up. "Minding my own business."

O'Malley's russet eyebrows went up. "I see, now. Like that, is it?"

"Like nothing." He unfolded his boots and jammed his foot into one. "Lady drank too much whiskey last night. And the door—" he sent an accusing look toward his sergeant "—can only be latched from the inside."

O'Malley looked blank for a fraction of a second. "Ah, I see the way of it now. She's drunk, can't lock her door, so you... 'Scuse me, Colonel, but why didn't you just latch the damn thing and crawl out the window?"

Tom grunted. Now that O'Malley mentioned it, he had to wonder the same thing. "Pie dough," he muttered. "Her damned piecrust was on the windowsill." He jammed his other foot into the remaining boot.

"That's not like you, Tom, bein' stopped by a little blob of pastry."

"No," he acknowledged. "It's not." He got to his feet and waved his hand at the door. "Get some coffee, will you, Mick? She's going to need a whole potful."

"Right away, Colonel." He peered at Tom. "You look like you could use—"

"Save it!" Tom snapped. "Time to cut timber."

Meggy woke when a shaft of hot sunlight fell across her face. With a blink, she sat up and groaned. Her head felt like the inside of a ringing church bell.

Oh, Lord, she was sick! She sank back down on the cot and stared up at the split-log ceiling, then shut her eyes. She couldn't afford to be sick. She had a pie to bake!

Forcing her lids open, she looked about the cabin.

An unfamiliar enamelware coffeepot sat on her stove. Next to it was a thick white china mug. The stove was cold, of course; no one in his right mind would build a fire on a day this hot.

Very well, she would drink it lukewarm, and bless the kind soul who'd brought it. Maybe Sergeant O'Malley, who had fixed her front latch.

Her gaze flew to the door. Merciful heavens, it wasn't latched! It wasn't even fully closed. Warm air flowed through the opening, and poured through the window as well.

Her piecrust! By now the sun would have all but melted it. She stumbled off the cot and headed for the window.

The lump of dough was gone. "Oh, not again," she moaned. "I cannot shoot a deer whenever I want to bake." She clutched her head as pain pinched her temples and pounded in back of her eyes. Her skull felt as if it had shrunk during the night.

Tears sprang into her eyes. "I can't," she sobbed. "I'll be sick if I even bend over."

Her vision blurry, she sat down on the cot, then looked down at her knees. Mercy, all she had on was her shimmy! Her white shirtwaist, the sleeves still rolled up, lay at the foot of her bed.

Memory returned in a rush. Last night she had sampled some whiskey, and—had she dreamed this?— the colonel had come and she'd told him all about Charlotte and Charity and—

She clapped one hand over her mouth. She'd gotten herself tiddly! She, Mary Margaret Hampton, daughter of a man of the cloth, a Methodist, no less! Oh, whatever would he think of her?

Who, Meggy? Not Papa. Papa is gone. You mean Colonel Randall, do you not?

"Certainly not! Why, I don't give one green fig for what that Yankee ruffian thinks of me," she said out loud.

But to be truthful, she would be easier in her mind if she could remember what had happened next. And how she'd ended up in bed with her clothes off. She closed her eyes in mortification.

When she opened them, her gaze fell on something rolled up in a tea towel and carefully set in a shaded corner of the counter. Next to it were six ripe apples from Fong's pantry. Inside the towel she found her pie dough. Someone, perhaps whoever had brought the coffee, had kindly rescued it from the beating sun. She could still make her pie!

The thought of building a fire in the stove when the heat in the cabin was already suffocating made her feel ill. She retreated once more to the cot. When she lay perfectly still, she didn't feel like throwing up.

To buoy up her spirits, she tried to sing, but what came out was a raspy whisper.

"'Strong are we and brave, like patriots of old; We'll fight...'"

Her head throbbing, she dragged herself off the cot and staggered across the floor to the counter. If she had to bake a pie, she would bake a pie.

"Aw, Tom, have a heart." Swede Jensen tipped his head up and surveyed the towering fir tree Tom indicated.

"You heard me, Swede. I'll lay it right at your feet. All you have to do is slice it up."

"Slice it up," Swede muttered. "By golly, you make buckin' that there tree sound like cuttin' up one of Fong's carrots."

Tom tied his double-edge ax to the rope dangling from his belt. "Hell, I'm doing the hard part. You're the bucker—your job is to cut up that log."

The Swede continued to grumble as Tom checked his spiked boots and prepared to climb the tall fir.

"I'll limb it on the way up, then take the top down. Be ready for it." He cast a swift glance at the rest of the crew, gathered in a loose semicircle around him.

Mick O'Malley sidled close to Tom. "Looks like a widowmaker to me, Tom. You know you don't haffta go up that sucker."

"Sure I do. I won't ask another man to do anything I wouldn't do myself."

"I don't like the look of it near the top. What with the wind comin' up, it could start swayin' like a sassy lady and pop you right off into thin air."

"I'll make the undercut lower than where you're

looking, Mick. And anyway, I won't pop off. I'll tie onto the trunk and hang on like a treed bear." He turned back to the men. "Any other questions?"

"Yeah," Vergil Price growled. "How the hell we gonna get them logs down this mountain? Trail's too steep for a man, let alone a bunch of scab-barked timber."

"We'll cold deck the logs close by so Sam can haul them out on the skid road with his bull team."

"Skid road!" Price spat into the pine brush. "What skid road? Only road we got is clear t'other side of the creek."

Tom grinned at the peeler. "Glad to see some intelligence in that thick head of yours, Verg. Damn smart of you to figure out we'll have to build a skid road *this* side of the creek."

"Oh. 'Course, Tom. I seed that right off."

The men guffawed. "Seed that right off," someone echoed in a falsetto voice. Vergil, a Kansas boy, was often the butt of the crew's heavy-handed humor.

The peeler glowered and moved a step closer to Tom. "It's just that, well, you know...."

Tom gazed at the man who'd taken Walter Peabody's job. What ailed the fellow? For the last month he'd been bucking for a promotion, and now that he'd gotten it, he didn't want to work?

"Afraid the log's gonna roll over on you, Verg?"

Vergil straightened to his full six feet. "N-no. I could peel the skin off a live rattlesnake if I had to."

"Then a straight hunk of Douglas fir that's gonna hold still for you shouldn't be a problem, should it?" When he didn't answer, Tom repeated the question. "Should it? What's eating you, Verg?"

"It's that woman," the peeler said in a pinched voice.

Tom's head came up. "What about her?"

"Oh, Lordy, here it comes," someone intoned.

Here comes what? Tom wondered. What was going on in the camp this time that he didn't know about?

"Well?"

"I seen her, Tom. An' I can't get her outta my mind. I ain't had a woman in four months, and she's hauntin' me like a demon."

"Hold it! Miss Hampton is a respectable woman. You get your mind off her and back to the timber."

"I watched her in the river yesterday. She's got the prettiest little patch of hair between her—"

Tom's fist connected with the man's jaw, and he went down like a poleaxed cow. Tom bent, grabbed a handful of flannel shirt and hauled him to his feet. "Keep your eyes on your logs, Price, or I'll beat you until you look like one of Fong's rotten tomatoes. You understand?"

Vergil gave him a sullen nod and edged away, refusing to meet Tom's eyes. He hated to lean too hard on the man; Vergil took more than his share of the crew's ribbing.

"All right, now, let's cut timber."

The men dispersed. Sam Turner and a short, muscular man called Eight-Bit Orrin charged off into the woods and began clearing brush for the skid road. The two young Claymore brothers and the other men—Swede, Indian Joe, Vergil Price and O'Malley—moved into position near the fir. When the high rigger brought the tree down, they would crawl over it like ants, cutting it into thirty-foot lengths and skinning off the bark.

When every man was in place, Tom looped his manila lifeline around the thick tree trunk and started to climb.

He pushed away the image Vergil Price had called up of Mary Margaret Hampton naked in the river, concentrated on tossing his lifeline up another ten feet and scrambling after it. A one-man crosscut saw dangled from the manila rope clipped into his steel safety loop.

He covered the first fifty feet in a little over ten minutes, severing limbs with a single blow of his ax as his spiked boots walked up the tree. The lopped-off branches whooshed down to the ground, where Price and O'Malley dragged them onto the slash pile.

The wind picked up. Another twenty-five or thirty feet higher and the tree began to sway. More limbs swished past his boots and thunked into the forest duff below him. From up here the crew looked doll-sized.

Tom had come to like high rigging, despite the danger. A hundred fifty feet up among the pungent fir branches a man gained a sense of perspective about things. About what kind of life he needed to fulfill his purpose on earth. About Susanna and justice gone awry.

He loved trees. They were beautiful. Clean. They built homes and schools and churches and barns, and the sweet greeny smell reminded him that nature was good. It was men who brought evil.

He climbed up another hitch. "Pretty philosophical way up here at the top of the world," he murmured. He often talked to himself on a high-rigging job. Sometimes it was the only time he could hear himself think.

Just as he raised his ax, a shout floated up from below. What the—

He glanced down and almost didn't believe what he saw. A second man was starting up the tree.

Tom let the ax drop and cupped his hands. "Leave off," he yelled.

The man kept climbing. All Tom could see was the top of his head, covered by a dingy blue wool stocking cap. Good God, it was Vergil Price.

"Off the tree, Verg," he shouted. "Not safe!"

Vergil kept coming. Had the man gone loco? Two of them on the same tree would...

Cold sweat ran down his neck. The tree began to shake. Tom cinched his lifeline in tight and hugged the bark. Every one of Vergil's footsteps made the trunk shiver.

He had to do something. One man this high off the ground was risky; two men was suicidal.

And two men with axes…

Holy catfish tails, Price must be off his rocker. Maybe he'd snapped. No time to wonder why now; he'd have to think about it later, Tom decided. One thing he knew for sure, the man wasn't coming up to help him limb off fir branches.

He'd have to shake the peeler down and try not to get killed in the process.

The tree was shuddering now. Tom loosened his lifeline and moved up another ten feet. Pulling his tethered ax up hand over hand, he grasped the handle and sliced off a thick bough. With a crack and a swish it hurtled down past the peeler. Tom cut another, then two more, let them twist their way to the ground. He hoped one of the limbs would convince Vergil to back down the trunk. Three more limbs and he began to pray that a branch would sweep the peeler down along with it. Verg was only twenty or thirty feet up; Tom was sixty feet from the top.

He heard O'Malley yelling something that sounded like "soap." No, rope. The Irishman was trying to lasso Price and pull him off the tree.

Twice the lariat grazed the peeler's shoulder, but he hunched his body close to the tree and the rope fell away. Tom groaned. He would have to climb higher, top the crown and hope the kickback would knock Price away.

Lord God, I don't want to kill him. I just want to live through this!

Two more hitches in his line brought him fifty feet below the tip. It'd have to be enough. The closer Price got, the more the tree shook. He hauled up the ax and started his undercut.

The tree wobbled. Tom dropped the ax and pulled up the saw. He put his back into his strokes and heard the trunk start to creak. The tree swayed under him.

Just a few more clean pulls…

A sharp snap told him the fall was imminent. ''Timber!'' he bellowed. His voice echoed back at him from across the canyon. He dropped the saw, flipped the lifeline down a few feet, then scrambled down so his head was below the saw cut in case the top kicked. Another *car-rack* and then a loud groaning sound filled the air. Tom set his spikes as deep as he could, wrapped his arms around the bark and held on.

The thickly branched crown twisted off the top with a ripping noise and plunged downward. The parent tree jerked, then began snapping violently back and forth. Tom clung tight and prayed.

Below him the severed top screamed through the air and crashed near the base.

Another shout. O'Malley. ''Tom,'' came the voice

again. "Come down, boyo. Whiplash shook Vergil off. He's out cold."

"Damn," Tom muttered. He wanted the man wide-awake so he could beat him into chicken mash. Or fire him. Maybe both.

When the tree stopped shuddering, he flipped his line down a notch and started his descent. In ten hitches his feet hit the ground, and by that time he'd stopped shaking.

He unhitched his line, stepped over his ax and saw, and headed straight for Vergil Price.

Chapter Seven

Tom leveled a hard look at the man lying where he had fallen on top of the slash pile. "Why'd you climb that tree after me? Lucky you didn't break your neck."

"I didn't mean no harm, Tom. Honest. Jes' went plumb crazy, I guess. All I could think of was diggin' my ax into your backside. Dunno what come over me, as I'm sure 'nuf scared of heights."

"I ought to kick your butt off this mountain," Tom said through gritted teeth. He jerked his arm away from O'Malley, who appeared beside him, plucking at his sleeve. "What is it, O'Malley?"

"Don't fire him, Tom. We're already short-handed."

Tom turned to the crew members who stood in a loose circle about the slash pile. "You men want to risk your lives with a logger who's got his pecker where his brain should be? I want him off my crew."

"Even," Mick O'Malley said in the same low voice, "if it means not loggin' your quota and losin' the lumber contract?"

O'Malley was right. Every minute the saws weren't whining in the timber he was losing money. "Okay, I won't fire him."

But Price'd sure have to shape up before Tom would risk his men working near him.

"Get up," he ordered the man on the ground.

The peeler rolled off the bed of branches that had cushioned his fall and stood up, his head drooping. He'd lost the blue knit cap, and Tom found himself looking at a bald spot he'd bet Price didn't even know about. Poor dumb son of a gun was getting old at twenty-seven. Loggers did that. The young ones looked like bent old men of forty, and by the time they reached forty, they looked seventy-five.

If they lived that long. Most of them didn't. At thirty-seven, Tom was the oldest man on the crew.

"Pick up your pay, Price, and go down to Tennant and buy yourself some calico. Don't come back until you've got all the female hankering out of your system."

O'Malley's big grin made Tom think about changing his mind. His sergeant had a heart softer than hot mush.

Vergil Price looked up, a scowl on his narrow face. "It's twelve miles to Tennant, Tom. Lemme take the buckboard?"

"Nope. Wagon's for emergencies, and it stays here. Take one of the mules, or walk. It'll be good for what ails you."

Now the men were grinning, too. "Might help the female hungries, but ain't nuthin' gonna cure Kansas-itis," Eight-Bit Orrin drawled. "Why, it's pretty near fatal. We don't get them diseases over in Idaho."

The Swede clapped a meaty hand on Price's shoulder. "Come back sober," he warned. "Ve don' need no drunken fool to spook our fallers. Ve need yust good, strong men with good, strong brains." He gave the shoulder a hefty punch, and Price staggered off down the trail toward camp.

"Shoulda fired him, boss," one of the men volunteered.

Indian Joe snorted. "Shoulda killed him."

Tom shook his head. "Naw. Felt like it, but that wouldn't teach him anything. All right, back to work. Joe, let's take this fir down so Swede and O'Malley will have something to do this afternoon besides flap their jaws. Wouldn't want them to get bored, now, would we, boys?"

The easy laughter among the men made Tom feel better. He hated making a fool of a man, but sometimes doing just that was what kept his crew alive.

"Claymore!" He barked the name on purpose. The brother who got there first he'd train as a skid greaser. The other, slower boy could haul slash.

He watched the older boy, Seth, tear out of the

brush and head toward him at a run. The kid's face was lit up like Christmas. "Yessir?"

"Claymore, you know what a skid greaser does?"

"Yessir. Slicks up the skid road so's the logs'll slip over easy."

"Think you can handle that? You've got to be quick. Pour on your water and get out of the way."

The boy's freckled face glowed. "Oh, yes, sir! Thank you, sir!" He loped toward the slash pile, where his even more gangly brother stood waiting.

God, Tom couldn't even remember being that young. Only vaguely did he recall his first job as a boy, sweeping out Tilson's Mercantile at night. Things were good that summer. That was the summer Pop taught him to set type at the newspaper office, and to play the fiddle. And his sister Susanna had learned to dance.... Yep, that was a good summer, when Susanna was still alive.

A chunk of cold lead settled in his gut. Just the thought of his sister made him half-crazy. He tried to tamp down the memory of her small, determined face, the stubborn tilt of her chin, the fire in her purple-blue eyes. But pushing it away only made it stronger, and more vivid. Dammit to hell, he didn't *want* to remember. It was true what Pop had said. *Anything you love will bring you to your knees.*

Tom should have protected her. Should have been able to save her. Susanna could not have been a spy; he'd bet his life on it. She was incapable of lying, of the duplicity it would take to be an informant. Down deep he believed she had been unjustly accused.

"Tom."

He looked up to see O'Malley standing close to him. "Yeah, Mick?"

"Just wonderin' if you've been askin' yourself why?"

"Why, what?"

"Why you got riled up enough to hit Price in the first place."

"The man's got a loud mouth," Tom snapped.

His sergeant nodded. "Sure, boyo. Sure."

Tom jammed his hands into his pockets to keep from punching the silly smile off Mick's face. Price *did* have a loud mouth.

But that wasn't the whole of it, he admitted. It was what Price had said, about seeing Mary Margaret Hampton naked in the river. He couldn't stand the thought of another man laying eyes on her.

The crew trudged back to camp closer to dusk than Tom liked. Working until the light began to fade was dangerous. Still, it had been a good day's work, he acknowledged as he tramped along in the rear. In spite of the episode with peeler Vergil Price. The road bed had been cleared, and short fir logs cut and laid crosswise to form the skid surface. Tomorrow Sam Turner, the bullwhacker, would hitch up a yoke of oxen and run some logs over it. If it wasn't slick enough, he'd hear about it.

They rounded the last bend before camp, and Tom slowed. The men would pass right by the creek where Price had spied on Miss Hampton yesterday. Every pair of eyes slid to the left, where the smooth water shone like quicksilver in the slanting light.

To Tom's relief, no female form—clothed or un-clothed—was visible. Miss Hampton was following his orders.

Just as he released a sigh of relief, a jubilant shout rang out ahead of him, and the men broke into a run. Something was up. His stomach tensed, and the back of his neck bristled into that fire-and-keep-firing feeling he always got before a battle. He doubled his pace and caught up to the Claymore brothers at the tag end of the line. What the—

The crew was headed straight for that woman's cabin.

Mary Margaret Hampton sat on her front porch and watched the line of weary men approach. They shuf-fled past the row of saucers she had laid out, eyeing with disbelief the slices of succulent apple pie each small plate bore.

Then the man in the lead, Eight-Bit Orrin, broke ranks and doubled back, and the men stumbled over themselves to get a place in line. Swede Jensen dropped a silver dollar beside one of the saucers and scooped up the contents. Other men did the same.

Swede took a huge bite. "Yust like home," he said. "Oh, golly, is yust like my momma make."

"Better," Orrin countered, his mouth full. Seth and Nobby Claymore scuffled over the last slice until Indian Joe grabbed it. He downed it in complete silence but for the gasps of the two brothers.

When Tom rounded the corner of the cabin, the first thing he saw was a ruffled, pink gingham apron fluttering from a rope clothesline rigged between two pine trees. The sight brought him to a dead halt. Frowning, he peered through the vine maples.

Mary Margaret Hampton sat on the edge of her porch, prim as a budded rose, surrounded by empty saucers.

Tom grunted and stepped into the clearing.

"Good afternoon, Colonel."

"No, it isn't," he snapped. "You think it's a good idea to hang your laundry right under the noses of my men?"

"Why, Colonel, that garment on the line is not 'laundry.' It is…well, it is advertising. And it has accomplished exactly what I wanted, just as I had hoped." She jingled her bulging apron pocket.

Tom scowled across the clearing at her. "What, exactly, are you selling?"

"Why, apple pie, of course. One dollar a slice."

Tom stared at her. Then he counted the saucers.

Six dollars' worth. No doubt about it, she'd cleaned up. It was better than a winning poker hand.

"Just where do you plan on keeping your earnings, under your mattress? I wouldn't trust anyone but O'Malley and maybe Indian Joe within twenty yards of your bed."

Meggy rose and propped both hands on her hips. The silver coins in her pockets clinked, but she said nothing.

Tom's gaze held hers. "I almost fired a man today because of you."

Her gray-green eyes widened. "Because of me? Whatever do you mean?"

"Let's just say his thinking was out of line."

"That would be Mr. Price?"

"How'd you know that?" he growled at her.

"He stopped by the cabin earlier. He gave me an earful about what a harsh and unreasonable man you are. I quite took his point."

Tom sneaked a glance at the clothesline. Lord almighty, the garment even had lace ruffles. "I'll wager he damn well looked at your flag over there."

"Colonel, we are not seeing eye to eye on the matter at hand. I have another pie set aside. Would you care for a slice?"

Tom's mouth watered. His mother and later Susanna had made apple pies. He hadn't tasted one since he'd joined the cavalry. A wave of longing swept over him.

"I do not."

Meggy turned away. "In that case, you will excuse me." She bent to gather up the saucers.

"Just a damn minute," Tom snapped.

He hadn't thought through what he wanted to say. All he knew was that he was mad as a hornet stuck in a pot of honey. Having a woman in camp had been a bad idea from the start.

"I don't want my men anywhere near this cabin. From now on, it's off-limits."

Meggy swung around, an empty saucer pressed to her midriff. "But Colonel, this is my place of business!"

"My men don't need your business."

Her eyes flashed. "I hardly think you can speak for your men on this matter, Colonel. As you can see—" she indicated the empty dishes on the porch "—they seem eager for some variety in their daily fare, to say nothing of genteel conversation."

"Can't help that," Tom retorted. "It's a distraction."

"Oh, I am so pleased to hear that," she said calmly. "The first thing my papa taught me about salesmanship was that you have to get the congrega—that is, the customer into the store before you can sell him anything. I am gratified that my method is effective."

Tom stomped up onto the porch. "Now you listen

to me, Miss Hampton. You and your pies are down-right dangerous.''

Her fine, dark eyebrows arched. ''My pies, dangerous? Surely you don't mean to imply they are…tainted in some way? I'll have you know my pies are sought after in three counties.''

''It's not the pies,'' Tom said in a weary tone. ''It's you. I can't meet my timber quota if I keep losing men because they can't keep their minds on what they're doing. I almost lost a good peeler today because he let his imagination get between his brain and his ax.''

''I am afraid I don't take your meaning.''

Tom stepped toward her, his hands clenched. To her credit, she stood her ground, thrusting the saucer she held in her hands toward him in a vain attempt to halt his progress. He lifted it from her fingers, bent and scooped up the remaining dishes and, without looking, tossed them into the pine needles, where they landed with a soft *ploof*. One rolled to rest almost at her feet.

''Listen to me, dammit.'' He grasped her shoulders and brought his face close to hers. ''You're a woman. My men haven't even talked to a woman since April. Let alone smelled one.''

He leaned in and inhaled the fragrance of her hair. ''You have any idea what that does to a man?''

''I should think it means they are perfectly starved for civilized conversation.''

Tom snorted. "They're starved, all right, but it's not for conversation. They're starved for something soft. Something that's sweet scented and..." His thumbs began to caress her shoulders. "...and warm. And alive."

He stepped closer, bent his head to sniff the scent emanating from her skin. "It can make a man crazy, being alone," he said in a rough whisper. "Reminds him that he's hungry, so damn hungry he doesn't care what it costs him, he's got to—"

He broke off abruptly. "So you see, Miss Hampton," he said in a strangled voice, "I can't let a man near you without risking his life."

She stared up at him. "But Colonel, at this very moment, you are near me, and you are suffering no ill effects."

"I wouldn't be too sure of that." A wave of pent-up longing pulsed through his entire body. Without conscious thought he pulled her forward and covered her mouth with his.

Lord, she was so warm. So sweet.

What the devil was he doing?

He released her instantly and stepped back. "My apologies."

Meggy tried to nod, but her head felt as if it had floated off above the trees. "I quite understand, Colonel." Her voice came out no louder than a whisper. "My cabin shall be off-limits, as you dictate."

Was she actually speaking these normal-sounding

*words to this man? The man who had just turned her
knees into two shaking blobs of warm mint jelly?*

A voice inside her head hummed so insistently she
could not think one sensible thought.

The colonel gave her a curt nod. "Very good," he
said crisply.

"However, I should like to remind you that none
of the men has laid a hand on me except for you."

He jerked upright. "Duly noted," he barked. "My
apologies again, Miss Hampton. Dis-missed!"

Of its own accord Meggy's hand flew up and delivered a snappy salute. The colonel blinked, then
stepped off her porch and strode off down the path
without a backward glance.

She watched his tall form disappear into the trees,
wondering if he realized he was marching back up
the trail in the direction from which he had come.

Then she twitched her skirt and stepped quickly
into her cabin. She didn't care a jot about where Colonel Tom Randall went. The farther away from her the
better, especially since she could scarcely take a
straight step after the mad, heavenly feel of his lips
on hers.

Chapter Eight

Meggy paced about the cabin's single room so fast her shoes whispered against the plank flooring. She hadn't been this upset since…since, well, she couldn't exactly remember. That odious, uncivilized man! How dare he dictate orders to her? Impose his will and curtail her movements?

She reversed direction and picked up her pace, her blue work skirt billowing in her wake. Dust motes swirled in a shaft of late-afternoon sunlight as she flew past the open window.

"Off-limits indeed," she huffed. She wasn't part of his logging crew—far from it. She was a geranium accidentally planted in a patch of joe-pye weed. "Let him confine his concern to his lumbering and leave me alone."

Why, he had even laid his hands on her person. Had kissed her! What effrontery. Just like a Yankee, taking what he wanted without even a by-your-leave.

She changed directions again, skimming about the floor on restless feet. What would Papa say? Surely he would have some calming words to guide her through this pit of unChristian fury. At such a time he would say...what? Oh, yes. *Be not consumed by wrath and thoughts of revenge, but turn the other cheek.*

She sniffed. That was all well and good when dealing with one's fellow Confederates. But a Northerner? An overbearing, bossy, know-it-all Yankee? Never.

I am sorry, Papa, but I am not as forgiving as Charity nor as polite as Charlotte. I know I have a temper and a stubborn streak as wide as Aunt Hattie's front porch, but it was this that fed us and clothed us and kept us safe all during the War, and I cannot stop now.

"I don't care if I ever see Colonel Tom Randall again for all my remaining days on this earth!" She gulped a breath. "And I most certainly do not want him to kiss me again!" She spun on one heel to reverse her path once more.

And then a terrible thought struck her and she stopped short. Her very livelihood was at stake.

She *must* bake her pies, and she *must* sell them. She *must* earn money enough for train fare to carry her...someplace. Someplace where she belonged.

Therefore, she reasoned, her cabin—or at least her front porch, which served as her bakery shop—could not possibly remain off-limits. Colonel Randall would simply have to change his mind.

All the next day, Tom worked hard to put Mary Margaret Hampton out of his mind. He didn't find it easy.

Seventy feet off the ground, clinging to the trunk of a Douglas fir shivering in the wind, Tom groaned as Meggy's perfect oval face suddenly materialized among the branches. When he looped his safety line around the trunk, he saw her dark eyebrows arching in the pattern of the bark, and when he closed his eyes to dispel the image, he imagined her lavender-rose scent wafting on the late-afternoon breeze. He sucked in his breath at the memory.

He'd lost his head yesterday. He'd kissed her, after chewing out Vergil Price for just thinking about it. What kind of man did that make him?

Not only a fool, but a hypocrite as well. One thing he'd always detested was a man with no honor, a man who would say one thing and do another. He lopped off three limbs with his ax and moved up another ten feet. Tomorrow they'd move into the high timber. He would have to blaze a new trail back to camp—one that did not run past Meggy's cabin.

Alone in his tent that night he drank more than his usual quota of the ''medicinal'' whiskey he kept locked in the first-aid cabinet. He'd put in a back-busting sixteen-hour day trying to stay alive while his brain turned to mush and his thoughts flew about like liquored-up butterflies, and he was sure enough feeling the strain. The only thing that didn't remind him of her was the whiskey bottle!

At daybreak, he awoke dry-mouthed and headachy. The instant he opened his lids, Meggy's smooth oval face floated into his consciousness, and he snapped them shut again. He hadn't laid eyes on her in twenty-four hours, and she was still driving him crazy.

His pet raven, hung in its wood-slat cage from the center tent pole, rattled the seed container O'Malley had fashioned. To Tom, it sounded like a load of buckshot ricocheting off a tin roof.

"Quiet!" Tom ordered.

He rolled over on the cot, flung one arm across his face and tried to think. He had to pull himself together. If he didn't, he'd have an accident and kill himself. Or worse—he'd kill someone else. He couldn't afford to lose any more of his crew; he was already two weeks behind his production schedule. Another week's losses and they'd all be out of a job.

The bird's wings rustled. "Yer broke," it croaked. "Yer-broke, yer-broke."

"For Pete's sake, don't remind me," Tom muttered.

"Yer-broke."

Tom clutched his head. "And don't shout!"

He never should have taught that creature to talk. "An intelligent bird," O'Malley had said when Tom had found the hatchling huddled in what remained of its nest after a limbing job took the branch that sheltered it. "Oughtta train it, Colonel. Teach it to talk." That was the last time he would listen to any of his sergeant's wild Irish ideas.

"Meggy," the raven grated. "Meggy-Meggy-Meggy."

Tom lurched off the cot and staggered over to the cage. "Shut up, you meddling son of a gun." He yanked the blanket off his bed and shrouded the cage with it. A muted squawk rose from under the thin wool, followed by a scrabbling sound and then silence.

Tom eyed the blanketless cot with longing. His head pounded. It wasn't light yet, but he had to get his butt moving. His eyes, even his teeth ached, but old Nevermore was right. If he didn't hustle up a few thousand more board feet of lumber, he *would* be broke.

Meggy. Meggy. Meggy…

He jerked on his trousers and stomped into his boots. Maybe his head would clear in the crisp morning air.

What he smelled on the morning air brought him to a halt not two steps from his tent. Pie. He sniffed the air to be sure. Apple pie!

Pale blue smoke curled out the stovepipe that jutted from her cabin roof. Hot damn, it was half past five in the morning, and she was at it again. He quick-marched up the hill until he was three yards from her front porch, then inhaled again. Yep. Apple pie. With plenty of cinnamon. His stomach gurgled.

Through the open window he glimpsed an aproned figure moving about in the candlelit interior. It wasn't even dawn yet, and she was up and busy disobeying his orders. He hammered one fist against the plank door. "Miss Hampton? You in there?"

"One moment, please," a musical voice called. A steaming, delicately browned pie slid onto the window ledge, followed instantly by another, this one with a design slashed in the top crust.

The door cracked open. "It is a little early for business, I'm afraid. The pies are still cool— Oh, it's you!"

"Darn right it's me." He jammed the toe of his boot into the space between the door and the frame so she couldn't shut it. "Just what do you think you're doing?"

"Why, Colonel, what a question! At home, ladies are not accountable for their movements before the sun rises."

"You're not *at* home, Miss Hampton. So answer my question."

A rosy flush colored her cheeks. "It must be perfectly obvious what I am doing. I am accomplishing my morning baking before it becomes too hot."

"I thought I told you to cease and desist."

"Oh, no, Colonel. That is not what you said at all."

"You don't remember, is that it? You don't remember why I made you...uh, your cabin off-limits?" He shoved his entire boot into the doorway. "Don't remember my kissing you to prove my point?"

Something flashed in the depths of her green eyes. "On the contrary, I remember it all too well. It was most forward of you, and I...well, I am not certain I have recovered yet."

An irrational surge of pride rolled into Tom's chest. He thought about his own "recovery," seventy feet off the ground chopping off branches with hands that shook. It pleased him that she might be suffering, too.

"Having trouble with your baking, are you?" The query popped out without an instant's forethought. Hearing his words, Tom stifled a groan.

"Oh, no," she said quickly. "I never have trouble baking pies. It's one of the things I do well, that and cutting down old dresses and remaking them. When I set my mind to something, I forget everything else. Nothing distracts me."

The surge of male pride he'd enjoyed a moment earlier evaporated in a heartbeat. *Nothing distracts me.* The kiss that had haunted his every waking thought since yesterday meant nothing whatever to her. The only thing that meant anything to her was apple pie.

The realization stung. "I thought I made it clear I

don't want my men coming here. This cabin is off-limits.''

She raised her chin and looked at him. "I think not, Colonel. You have no right to deprive me of my livelihood. I simply cannot be bound by such orders.''

"That's insubordination,'' he snapped.

"That is pure unadulterated nonsense,'' she retorted. "This isn't a military camp.''

He shouldered his way through the doorway.

She retreated until her spine met the crude wood counter, her eyes blazing. "I am not yours to command.''

"Oh, no? Think about it for a minute. This is a logging camp, not a croquet party. You're the only female for fifty miles, and I'm honor-bound to protect you. You are entirely dependent on me!''

"On the contrary, Colonel. I rather feel I must rely on the good men of your command…er, camp to protect me. *You* are the only man I have thus far encountered whom I need fear.''

"That's not the case and you know it." He wondered why his voice sounded so growly. He probably needed coffee, and quick.

She went on as if she hadn't heard him. "Therefore, until such time as I am convinced otherwise, this cabin is indeed off-limits.'' She paused to draw in a shaky breath. "But only to you.''

"Me? Me!''

"I believe you heard correctly, Colonel. You.''

"If that isn't the craziest, most double-tongued logic! Dammit, Meggy, I am responsible for you!"

"No, you are not," she said with quiet authority. "*I* am responsible for me. And please do not refer to me as Meggy, which is a family pet name. To you, I am Miss Hampton."

"Look, Meg— Miss Hamp—"

"Please do not interrupt. I have been responsible ever since my father was killed, which deed, I hasten to add, was perpetrated by the Yankees. At Shiloh. I assumed responsibility for myself and my younger sisters at that time, and now that they are all married, I have only myself to care for. To be responsible for," she amended. "I undertake this task most seriously."

Tom looked from her flushed face to her hands, clenched together in front of her waist. She was something, all right. For one thing, she didn't speak so stiff and formal when she was drunk. For another, if he was any judge, she was plainly terrified of him.

But here she was, standing toe to toe with him, her chin up and those green eyes of hers darkened to the color of spruce needles.

An odd sensation crept up his backbone, as if every nerve and muscle were standing at attention. "I lost someone I cared about in the War, too," he heard himself say.

"Yes, I know. Your sister."

"You Rebs killed her. It was a Southern woman who bore witness against her and sent her to hang."

Meggy regarded him for a full minute before she spoke. "Was she guilty?" she said softly.

Tom found he could not answer. Surely she was not guilty. *Wasn't she?*

"I am sorry about your sister, Colonel."

He jerked at the sound of her voice. "I regret your father's death, as well," he replied.

"I think, then, that we are even. Neither of our losses has any bearing on the present situation. *Why* I am responsible for myself, and *why* you both distrust Southern women and feel you must protect me do not signify. I am here. You are here. We must make the best of it."

Tom's mouth sagged open. He'd barreled up here to scare some sense into her; how was it she had put *him* on the defensive?

"Excuse me, Colonel. I have three more pies to bake this morning. Would you be so kind as to announce this fact to the men at breakfast?"

Dazed, Tom nodded.

Meggy straightened her spine. "Well, then. Perhaps you won't mind if I get back to work. Since you won't be stopping by later, I will send your piece down to the cookhouse at suppertime with Mr. O'Malley. I trust he will bring your payment of one dollar the next time he visits."

Again Tom nodded. O'Malley. Pie. Payment. Oh, hell, what use was there in trying to reason with her? Talking sense into her was like trying to swallow a feather pillow.

Chapter Nine

"May I offer you more tea, gentlemen?"

Six enamelware mugs borrowed from Fong's store of cookhouse dishes rose in unison from the plank boards of Meggy's front porch. Six rough, weathered hands held the utensils aloft while Meggy poured freshly brewed tea from an enamelware saucepan.

"I do apologize for my lack of proper tea service," she said as she topped off the last empty mug. "My mother's Haviland tea set is packed away in my trunk."

"That don't matter, ma'am." Swede Jensen blew his breath across the top of his brimming mug, then slurped up a noisy mouthful. "My momma, she allus t'ink t'ings taste better when she use her wedding plates. I never tell her it make no difference."

Meggy looked at the burly blond man perched cross-legged on the edge of her porch. He had stuffed the red wool cap he usually wore under one of the suspenders stretched across his thick shoulders. Every time Meggy rose to brew more tea, Swede leaped to his feet, bowed and held the front door open for her. *My word. Calling a man—even a logger—a gentleman certainly did wonders for his manners!*

"You must tell me more about your mother, Mr. Jensen. Is she a good cook?"

Swede's face crinkled into a broad grin. "Oh, golly yes! Back in old country, she bake Christmas cake that was light yust like snowflake."

Sergeant O'Malley guffawed. "Way I heard it, Swede, you just open your mouth and those little cakes float right in and land on your tongue."

"Nah, that ain't right," Orrin countered. To Meggy, the man's chunky form hunched at the edge of the circle looked like a giant fist.

"You hafta catch 'em first. That's how come Swede here got so skinny—chasin' after all them snowflakes."

"Skinny! You better get some work done on yer eyes, Eight-Bit."

Meggy judged the joke had gone quite far enough. "Nevertheless, Mr.O'Malley, I would like to hear more about Mr. Jensen's mother and her cakes." She glanced around at the six faces turned in her direction. "Since we are all far from our families out here in the woods, I trust we are all interested in recalling memories of our homes. And our mothers."

"We ain't got no ma, Miss Meggy." Nobby Claymore leaned his red head against his older brother's shoulder. "She done died of the quinsy last spring."

Meggy's heart constricted. "Oh, my heavens, I am sorry to hear that."

"'S okay, ma'am," the elder brother said. "We was awful sad for a while, but I reckon she went to be with Pa. She's prob'ly happier up there in heaven than she was down here on earth. Leastways they're together."

"You mean they are both gone, Seth? Your mother *and* your father?"

The two boys nodded. "We gotta ol' maid aunt in Green River. She cried like anything when we joined this here crew," Seth stated.

Meggy's heart gave another, stronger squeeze. "Why, of course she did! Two fine strong boys like you, she must miss you most fearfully."

"Wouldn't be too sure of that, ma'am." O'Malley waved his hand over the steaming cup he held. "When I was the lads' age, me mither was only too glad to shoo me out of her kitchen."

"That's cuz you was orn'ry," Orrin declared.

"And dumb," another voice added. "Still can't tell a jack chain from a mule harness, and you been loggin' more'n a year now."

The sergeant's spine went ramrod straight. "Now why would you be thinkin' a daft thing like that?"

"Word spreads. Yore plumb famous fer fallin' off the log boom that time." Orrin tipped his dark curly head toward Meggy and lowered his voice. "Flat as the Dead Sea and he rolls off and busts his leg!"

"Why, Mr. Eight-Bit, surely you are not taking pleasure in another man's misfortune? That is beneath a man of your...stature."

Orrin wilted. "Oh well, of course not, miss. I ain't—aren't—laughin' at the poor dumb bas— Uh...I'm, uh, well, I'm publicly admiring him, so to speak."

O'Malley's shaggy eyebrows lifted and a pleased smile crooked his mouth. "Y'are? Well, I'll be. Thanks, Eight-Bit."

"What's 'stature' mean?" Orrin whispered to the man next to him.

"Dunno 'xactly. Maybe somethin' 'bout how much you weigh. Which must be considerable, cuz you're grinnin' like a overfed bobcat."

"Gentlemen," Meggy interjected. "I appreciate your stopping by to pay a call. However, stimulating as it is to converse with all of you..." She let her gaze settle briefly on each of her visitors. "...the afternoon has flown by on such swift wings it is time for me to go down to the cookhouse and help Fong with your supper. Surely you will excuse me?"

The men rose, and Meggy shook hands with each one. When she came to the Claymore brothers, she had to fight not to hug the poor motherless waifs to her bosom, but she restrained herself for the sake of their pride, knowing the inevitable joshing they would receive from the men at any sign of affection from her.

"Thank you for our tea, Miss Meggy," Nobby whispered. Then he leaned closer and spoke in a conspiratorial undertone. "Your pies tastes lots better'n snowflakes."

The last man in the circle was Indian Joe, who had sat motionless and silent throughout the hour-long repast. When Meggy reached him, he gravely touched his palm to hers and opened his mouth for the first time.

"Skookum chuck."

"Good grub," O'Malley translated as the Indian strode off down the path to the bunkhouse. "And I'm thankin' you for the men," the sergeant continued. "Nothin' better for morale than a bit of tea and blarney."

Meggy solemnly shook his beefy hand.

"The colonel'd pay his respect personally, but he's busy worryin' over his account books again."

Meggy nodded and began to gather up the mugs and the empty saucepan. "It is just as well, Mr. O'Malley. Colonel Randall and I do not see eye to eye."

"That so, ma'am?" A puzzled look crossed the sergeant's ruddy face. "Kinda odd, that is."

She looked up. "What is?"

"Well, sure and he isn't here, ma'am. He's holed

up there in his tent, but he's talkin' away to you as if you was right there lookin' over his shoulder.''

Meggy jerked upright. Talking? To her? ''What is he saying?''

The sergeant sent her a sly look. ''Oh, I couldn't be repeatin' any of it, ma'am. T'aint fit language for a lady's delicate ears. Afternoon, Miss Hampton.''

Meggy stared at the Irishman's retreating form. She could swear she heard him chuckle as he tramped down the path.

And what was that tune he was whistling? She cocked her head, straining to hear.

Why, of all things… ''Bonnie Blue Flag''!

By the time Fong finished frying steaks and stacking four dozen hot biscuits into a towel-draped laundry basket for the men's supper that night, Meggy had received eight polite inquiries about receiving more ''callers'' on the following afternoon. She could scarcely keep her smile to ladylike proportions as she ate her venison and mashed potatoes at the kitchen table with Fong.

Out of her pie profits, she paid the Chinese cook for the supplies she had used. The smooth-skinned Oriental dribbled a spoonful of gravy over a biscuit he split using the thumb and forefinger of one hand.

''You make plenty dollar, missy?''

''Oh, yes, thank you. Plenty, however, is not the same as enough.''

The black eyes snapped with curiosity. "What for 'enough'? You want help boss so he not go belly-up broke?"

"Enough for train— Colonel Randall is in financial difficulty?"

"All time true, missy. Boss pay men too much. Pay Fong too much."

"But why?"

"Long-time friends. Some from army, some not. All same pay, but not cut enough wood-timber yet."

Meggy sat back. So, Colonel Randall had his economic problems, too. A twinge of sympathy squeezed her heart.

Fong popped to his feet the instant she laid aside her fork. "Say too much, maybe." He whisked her empty plate away. "Colonel-boss not like bellyache talk."

She looked up as he darted from the wooden sink, piled high with dirty cooking pots, to the gleaming nickel-plated stove.

Two piercing blue eyes skewered her from across the wide dining room. Meggy held her breath, watching the colonel methodically cut a piece of the meat on his plate and fork it into his mouth without taking his eyes off her. Gracious, he looked mad enough to bite!

She looked away, letting her gaze follow Fong's path as he flitted from stove to sink, wiping down the big iron spiders, sawing a single-layer sheet cake into serving-size squares. She wished the colonel would not look at her that way.

Purposely she focused everywhere but on him, yet still felt his gaze bore into her, as if he were peering right through her skin. She busied herself with her apron ties.

Well, supposing he did have money worries; it was no concern of hers. She thought of the kerchief full of silver dollars—twelve of them at last count—hidden under her mattress. At night it made a comforting lump under her knees, but now, with Colonel Randall staring at her like that, and knowing he was struggling to meet his payroll—well, he himself had warned her about keeping money in her cabin. She supposed he had a cash safe, but she would rather die than ask...

She shot a surreptitious glance across the room and again met his steely gaze. She sniffed in a breath. When confronting the enemy, do not betray fear.

And never retreat!

In the next moment she found herself moving through the kitchen doorway and into the dining hall. Halfway across, she noted the men had all finished their meals and disappeared. Except for the colonel, who sat watching her come toward him, his fork poised midway to his mouth, the room was deserted.

"Good evening, Colonel."

"Evening, Miss Hampton."

"Would you, um, care for more coffee?"

He lowered his fork hand. "Not till I've drunk this cup," he said in a level voice.

"Oh. Of course. I could not see the contents of your cup from…" Her voice trailed away under his penetrating look.

"O'Malley tells me you're holding tea parties for the crew."

"Oh, they're not parties, Colonel. Merely a bit of polite conversation when the men come calling."

"Making any money? Selling your pies, I mean?"

"Why, how kind of you to inquire. Actually, yes, I am doing quite well. Just a few more—"

"How much do you need?" He snapped the question without taking his eyes off her.

"Let me see. The stagecoach to Mountain Junction costs three dollars. Train fare back home will amount to…seventeen dollars and fifty cents. I have already earned twelve."

"I'll give you the rest outright if it'll speed things up any. My men can hardly keep their minds on timbering since you started up your pie business. Now they're so het up about calling on you, they want to quit half an hour earlier every day."

Meggy could think of nothing to say.

"Meg—Miss Hampton, it'd make my job easier if you'd just, well, accept my offer and clear out."

"Why, I wouldn't think of such a thing! I come from a long line of Hamptons and Davises, sir, and not one of them ever accepted charity. I will not be the one to break that proud tradition.''

''Ten dollars, then. Fifteen. Any price you name.''

''The answer is still no. I will earn the money in a fair and honest way. And besides, Colonel, I believe you need those funds to pay your men.''

''What's the difference? I pay them, they buy your pies. Why not just skip the middle man?''

''I wouldn't think of accepting such an offer.'' But her mind registered a single sharp hurt. Colonel Randall was willing to *pay* her to leave camp? *He must want to be rid of me a very great deal.*

She snatched the plate of half-eaten steak from under his poised fork.

''Hey, I'm not finished yet!''

Meggy backed up a step. ''Yes, you are, Colonel. A gentleman never offers to *pay* for the pleasure of a lady's company. Or even for the pleasure of her departure. You should be ashamed. You should be…court-martialed!''

Tom pushed off the bench and stood up. ''Wait just one damn minute!''

She whirled past him. ''Excuse me, I must help Fong wash the dishes.''

Tom snaked his arm into her path, but too late. His fingers caught her apron tie, and as she marched away the floppy bow at her back unraveled. He stared at the bit of ruffled muslin in his hand.

Jumping catfish, she was about the most unpre-

dictable woman he'd ever had the bad luck to en-
counter. She didn't retreat a single inch, even when
she was outnumbered and her back was against the
wall. She was a riled-up hellcat.

She was bothersome beyond his tolerance.

And she was...female. He brought the apron to his
nose. *And sweet smelling.*

His pulse tripped into double time. Just seven more
dollars, he thought. Two apple pies. He could stand
it one more day, maybe even two if he didn't lay eyes
on her and he didn't catch her scent. He'd stay away.
He'd cut timber until it was too dark to see, and then
he'd come back the long way round so he wouldn't
have to pass by her cabin. He'd take his supper late,
anything to avoid being near her.

It would work out just fine. He'd be free of her in
two days, and then he'd sleep nights. He'd...

Shouts rose from beyond the screened porch.

"Look who's comin' up the hill!"

"It's Vergil Price, on a mule, by golly! And look
what he's got with him."

"Whazzat, Swede? Looks like a barrel of...aw, it
can't be. Price isn't that dumb, even if he is from
Kansas."

"Miss Meggy! Miss Meggy, come look! Your be-
longings have come. By golly, boys, her mother's tea
set and ev'ryt'ing."

"Miss Meggy!"

Jehoshaphat, she'd been adopted by his entire crew!

The men tumbled over themselves shoving through the screen door. "Miss Meggy, look what we brung ya!"

Tom closed his eyes. It wouldn't make a bit of difference. Two more days. Just two more pies and two more days. She wouldn't even have time to unpack.

Tom met Vergil Price's hard-eyed gaze.

"I'm back," the peeler growled. He spat a mouthful of dark tobacco juice onto the ground.

"So I see."

"You can't run me off so easy, Tom. I got rights."

"You do as long as you keep your mind on business."

Vergil slid off the mule and jammed his hands in his back trouser pockets. "I got my mind on business, all right."

The men began to murmur. "Come on, boys," O'Malley sang out. "Let's unload Miss Meggy's trunk." He tugged on the mule's reins and herded the crew up to Meggy's cabin.

Tom studied Vergil Price's combative stance. The man's wiry frame seemed to swell up, his chest puffing out with each breath. He looked like a rooster, Tom thought. Exactly like that mean red rooster Pa used to keep in the newspaper office. Said it kept people out of his hair when he was composing his weekly editorials. A strong-opinioned man needed a protector, he'd joked.

"The only business on this mountain is logging, Price. You got anything else up your sleeve, forget it."

"Oh, it's logging I'm thinkin' of," Vergil assured him. "Why, lately timber's the first thing I think of in the mornin', last thing at night." His thin lips twisted into a half smile.

Something about his eyes bothered Tom, but he couldn't put a finger on what it was. He'd seen that look on other faces, angry faces peering in the window of Pa's newspaper office. Readers outraged over Jason Randall's stance on everything from vigilantes to slave-holding states, even the vote for women.

Susanna had grown up just like him—oblivious to the danger of acting on unpopular beliefs.

But you couldn't arrest a man because he looked at you funny. And Tom couldn't afford to short his logging crew another man, not if he wanted to survive the season.

"You watch yourself, Vergil."

"Oh, I intend to, Tom. Gonna watch real good."

I'm gonna watch so good you'll never suspect. You'll never see it coming.

Chapter Ten

Tom sat up on his cot and sniffed the air. An odd smell hung on the breeze. He peered through his open tent flap into the dark and drew in a long, deep lungful of air. Something…pungent. He was into his boots and trousers before his next breath.

Outside, he lifted his head and inhaled again. Maybe one of the men was smoking a cheroot outside the bunkhouse. Then again…

Through the laced branches of the pine and fir between his tent and the bunkhouse, a ghostly light floated. Not near the bunkhouse. Not near Meggy's cabin. A good ways off the trail.

He watched for a moment longer, then started forward. When he got close enough to see, he rocked back on his heels and pocketed his sidearm.

She was dressed in some sort of white nightgown and she was lugging a shovel almost as tall as she was. A candle-lantern dangled from her free hand.

"What the hell are you doing out here in the middle of nowhere?"

She jumped when he spoke. "I am...well, I am...exploring, you might say."

"Exploring, hell. You're tramping around the woods. Alone. At night! I thought I gave orders—"

"Quite true, Colonel, you did. But that would apply to your crew, not to me. I merely stepped out for a little air on this stiflin' evening."

"In your nightgown? Carrying a shovel? And a candle, for Pete's sake. Don't you know how tinder dry these woods are? Why, the slightest spark—"

"My attire is none of your concern."

"Came to bury your pie money, is that it?"

Her face blanched. "H-how did you know?"

Tom shook his head. "Wasn't hard. At four in the afternoon, every logger I've got out on a cutting run gets real careless, and when we head back to camp, seems they all prefer the old path, the one that runs by your cabin. They can't stay away, and you won't stop baking pies. So I figure you sneaked out here to bury your profits."

"I beg your pardon, Colonel, I did not 'sneak.' I walked out here in full view—"

"Of the moon and an owl or two, maybe a coyote. Did you ever think you might be followed by one of those uncouth hell-raisers I've got working for me?"

"Certainly not. Mr. O'Malley and Swede and the Claymore boys, even Indian Joe, why, they all have

perfect manners in my presence. They are all gentlemen, I assure you.''

"Miss Hampton, your head's full of Southern
chicken feathers.''

"Perhaps yours is full of Northern suspicion!''

"A muddled female has no place in a camp with
twelve randy men. I want you inside at night and
accompanied by O'Malley or Fong when you leave
your cabin during the day. All day. Every day. Now,
give me that shovel and let's get this over with.''

"Colonel, you will please remove your hands from
my shovel! I shall bury my earnings myself, in a secret place known only to me. I have had my fill of
maraudin' Yankees and the trouble they cause, thank
you.''

"You haven't had so much as a taste of trouble,
Miss Hampton. You've had mint juleps and Negro
slaves to serve them all during the war.''

"You think so, do you? I had to beg potatoes and
coffee from the congregation in Seton Falls, sell my
ball gowns to keep my five sisters from starving. And
I've hit a Yankee or two on the backside while
climbin' over our fence after our chickens. I hit one
with my broom. Whacked him good, too.''

"A broom, huh? Whacked a Yankee on the backside with a broom.'' Tom fought the grin that threatened.

"A *damn* Yankee, for your information. And when
I leave this camp, which I do pray is not far in the

future, I will retrieve my hidden money and go back to Chester County, where things are civilized!''

''No, you won't. You haven't done one sensible thing since you got here.''

''Why, I most certainly have— Colonel, what are you doing?''

''Protecting your pie money. And your person. Here we go!''

''You put me down this instant!''

Tom chuckled. ''Is that an order, ma'am?''

''It's… It…well, it's as polite a request as I can make while being manhandled like a sack of corn-meal. Just what do you intend?''

''I intend to bury your money under your porch and send you off to bed.'' He puffed out the lantern and grabbed the shovel. ''Then I'm gonna pray hard for a stagecoach to take you back where you belong. Never should have come out here in the first place.''

''Yes,'' she said, her voice muffled against his shirt. ''That is possibly true.''

''That,'' he snapped, ''is the first intelligent thing you've said since you got here.''

He started back toward her cabin, setting his feet Indian fashion so he wouldn't stumble in the dark and spill her onto the ground. She didn't say a word.

After ten steps he wished she would. She felt soft and warm in his arms, and he needed something to take his mind off what his body was feeling.

His steps slowed. Stopped.

"What's the matter?" she whispered. "Is there a wild animal out there?"

He didn't answer. He set her carefully on her feet, then stepped in close. "There's nothing out here, Meggy, but us. You and me."

"Well, I know that. I meant something, you know, dangerous."

"You don't think this is dangerous? You're out here half-dressed and I can't get you out of my mind and you don't think—"

"I am not half-dressed. I am wearing a..." she glanced down as if to remind herself "...one of my sister Charlotte's night rails. She made all new ones, you see, for her trousseau—she was married recently. Such a lovely wedding it was, with flowers everywhere and—"

Tom grinned in the dark. She was chattering like his raven, Nevermore, spinning a tale like Scheherazade to forestall her death at the hands of the sultan. She was leaving in two days, and he wanted to kiss her again so bad he couldn't breathe. He wanted to hold her and keep her safe from wild animals and sultans and even the damn Yankees. Some part of him knew that didn't make much sense, but his brain was so fevered he couldn't think clearly.

He wanted her. That much he knew. He shouldn't, but he did. It was the first spark of need he'd felt since the War and his sister's death.

"Colonel?"

"Don't talk, Meggy. And don't come any closer."

But she did. She stepped toward him as if she knew all about the feelings churning inside him. "Colonel, let me assure you..." She reached one hand toward his chest.

Tom stood like a stone statue, waiting for her touch.

"I assure you I meant no harm in coming out here to Oregon. The truth is I left home with such high hopes, for I was to be married to Mr. Peabody. It was all arranged, and then when I looked at him in his coffin, I realized that I couldn't do it. I couldn't have married him, after all—I didn't know him from Adam. I thought it wouldn't matter, but it did. People fall in love with...with people they have at least been introduced to."

He caught her hand. "Meggy. We've been introduced. You could fall in love with me."

He couldn't believe he'd said that. The last thing he needed was a woman who could fall in love with him. It was his body talking, not his brain. Hunger for her softness, her femaleness...that's all it was. Lust, not love. He wanted nothing to do with love, wanted nothing to do with caring for someone, feeling responsible for someone who mattered to him.

And, God help him, Meggy was beginning to matter.

It was best she didn't know that. Best she felt noth-

ing for him but the exasperation and disdain she'd
expressed ever since she'd set foot in Devil's Camp.

There was nothing, not one thing, not one spark
that flared between them.

Except for now. Tonight.

Except for that kiss.

And here she was, warm and sweet smelling and
soft—oh God, she was soft—in his arms. He drew in
a ragged breath and took another step forward. "Forget I said that."

Meggy said nothing, just tilted her head up and
smiled. If she lived to be as old as Aunt Hattie, she
would never understand her feelings at this moment.
Here she was, alone in the woods with a Yankee colonel of all things, and her heart fluttered inside her
chest like birds' wings. She wasn't the least bit frightened. Or even ashamed about the circumstances, and
that was curious indeed. Somehow in the presence of
this man, Tom Randall, she felt…emboldened.

Western women were this way, she thought. Strong
and able. They went after what they wanted. The trouble was, she didn't want this. Him. He was tall and
strong and attractive in a rough sort of way, but…

Or did she?

She closed her eyes. *She did!* Something about him
stirred her senses, mixed up her insides like scrambled
eggs, until her body felt detached from her brain, and
her skin felt…hot and tingly.

A feeling she couldn't name pulled at her, made

her feel daring and full of courage. She felt like another person, someone she did not know.

An odd, sweet joy flowed through her, along with a delicious ache, a consuming hunger that teased and tugged. What was happening to her?

Was he feeling it, too?

His finger touched her chin, and then his mouth settled over hers. His lips, oh, his lips were wonderful, the way they moved and coaxed. A warm rush of pleasure licked into her belly and he tightened his arms around her, pulling her close. Her breasts swelled against his chest, aching to be touched.

Was this what Charlotte had felt on her wedding night?

Oh, it must be. Such a glorious sensation of blooming inside her, of reaching for something hot and mysterious and alive.

Touch me. Yes, touch me. She stretched upward, felt his fingers skim down her back and below her waist. She wound her arms around his neck and pressed into him.

His breathing changed. He broke away, panted into her hair. "Meggy."

He lifted both arms away from her, but still she clung to him. "Kiss me again," she whispered. "It feels so…"

His tongue probed, opening her lips to his heat and taste. Below her belly a secret place opened as well, throbbed, and when she felt his hand against her she feared she would melt into a puddle of hot butter.

I will never have this again. I will go back to Seton Falls and never see him again, but oh, my, I do not want this to end. Dear Lord, I do not want him to stop. I want him to touch me all over.

How can I be feeling these wild, wanton feelings? I am a lady. A Southern *lady.*

And Southern ladies did not feel such things, did they? Oh, they must, they must! Charlotte had fairly glowed after her wedding night; it must have been just like this. Only this was more, much more. *This is real. This is now. Just being here with him makes me so happy!*

He was speaking to her. The words buzzed softly in her ear, but she could make no sense of them. "Yes," she whispered. Whatever the question, yes.

She felt his frame begin to tremble, or was it hers? She couldn't tell. He lifted her gown, pressed both hands against the bare skin of her buttocks, lifted her hard against him.

He kissed her again, a long, deep kiss that sent her heart into an agony of yearning. Then he picked her up and began to walk.

He carried her into the woods and up a gentle hill to a copse of vine maples where a thick layer of pine needle duff softened the forest floor. He set her upright and began to unbutton his trousers. His hands shook.

This was madness. Madness! *But do not stop. Do not deny me this pleasure.*

She finished for him, and while he shrugged out of his shirt, she lifted her nightgown over her head and laid it on the ground. Then she knelt upon it and waited for him.

Why am I not ashamed of what I am doing? Or frightened? Why do I feel only uncontainable joy and a humming in my body as if I have only this very moment been born?

Chapter Eleven

He stroked her skin, ran his fingers inside her thighs, into the soft hair at her entrance, then inside, deep inside, sending a spasm of pleasure swimming into her loins. She moved with him, laid her hand on his and looked into his eyes. He stopped his movements for an instant, gazed down into her face, then moved the finger buried inside her until she cried out.

His lips followed the same path his fingers had traced, only slower, with more deliberate concentration, and his tongue, strong and clever, flicked in and out, in and out until she laced her fingers in his thick, dark hair and held him still.

He moved his body over her, pressed his male organ gently against her thighs, all the while watching her face. Then he moved up, seeking entry. At the instant she felt his weight and hardness slide into her, his mouth caught hers, his breathing ragged, his lips hungry. She closed her eyes and let herself go with him.

Tom counted, recited rhymes inside his head, anything to prolong her pleasure and keep his mind off the slick, silky feel of her sheath against his skin. He moved with slow purpose, trying not to hurry. He wanted to finish, wanted to feel the sweet release of his seed spurting into her, but more than that he wanted to hear her cries of pleasure. The sound of his name gasped rhythmically on her lips sent a tremor into his gut, but he managed to hold on.

God, she was like flowers, like fire. He'd bedded women before. He'd never made love like this, hadn't thought an experience like this was possible up until now. *What was it about her that made it so different?*

He raised his hands, touched her breasts with his thumbs, then slid his fingers downward. She was wet, moving with him, inviting him.

She reached her release just as he exploded inside her, pumping hard to capture the pleasure and hold it forever. Her sharp cry brought tears to his eyes.

Long after it was over, he held her close, letting his heartbeat slow, unwilling to free her.

The tree shuddered, then rotated to the left. ''Watch it, boys,'' a voice yelled. ''It's a widowmaker!''

Swede and Indian Joe wrestled the six-foot crosscut saw free of the cut and heaved it into the brush. Stumbling backward, they scrambled away from the twisting fir as far as they could manage.

"Timberrr!" With an ear-splitting groan, the base slid off center and snapped free, punching the butt end backward. A rain of twigs and small branches peppered the two men who crouched against a felled log, arms wrapped over their heads. The fir creaked, then hurtled to earth with a *whumph* that shook the ground. A choking cloud of dust rose in the ensuing silence.

Swede raised his head to see Indian Joe on his feet, brushing debris off his dark wool shirt. "You okay, Joe?"

"I'm standing up," came the terse reply. "Where's the boss?"

"Over by the slash pile. Think he saw it?"

"He sees everything. He'll even know why it went sprung like that."

"Swede! Joe!" The other crew members galloped toward the two sawyers from all directions. Vergil Price was the first to reach them. "I thought you was both goners." For some reason he was smiling.

"By golly, when I see it twist, I t'ink so, too."

Tom strode into the melee, his face grim. "Who the devil sighted that fir?"

Indian Joe raised his arm.

"Joe, you're no greenhorn tree cutter."

The Indian shrugged. "Sometimes happen. We

plan fall, then undercut. Saw hung up so we shifted over some. Too much, maybe.''

Tom let his breath out in a rush. ''Well, dammit, don't do it again.'' His body trembled with relief. Trees that kicked back like that had killed more loggers than he cared to count.

''All right, men. Nobody's at fault here, so let's get back to work. Orrin, check on the bullwhacker, see if he's ready for a load. Price, keep your eye on those Claymore boys. I don't want them getting too close to a cut.''

Swede and Indian Joe tramped into the brush after the two-man saw, and the other men walked off to gather their axes.

For maybe five minutes Tom let the silence and the sharp green scent of fresh sawdust clear his head. He knew it wasn't Indian Joe's fault the tree had backsplit. What he did know was that the crew sensed his pent-up desperation about meeting the lumber contract. It wasn't worth it, pushing the men to double their quota. Sooner or later he'd lose another one of them, and no lumber contract was that important.

He walked into a clearing, shaking his head. That, and the night he'd spent with Meggy, made him tense and edgy.

He had to do something about her, about his feelings for her. She wasn't the kind of woman a man could have one night and come back the next for a second helping. But making love to her had changed things. Changed him. He couldn't just go off to Tennant like Vergil Price and buy some cheap calico. After Meggy, it would never be enough.

But he couldn't go to Meggy. Couldn't let himself even think of compromising her further. With a woman like Meggy you either proposed marriage or let her alone.

"You comin', boyo?" O'Malley stood off to one side, watching him. "Bullwhacker's 'bout ready to haul logs. He's waitin' for your signal."

"Sure. Coming, Mick." Tom turned toward the trail the men had cleared that morning, then felt O'Malley's eyes on him.

"Been smithereened, have ya?"

Tom nodded. He'd never been able to hide anything from Sergeant O'Malley for long. Somehow the Irishman always knew when something weighed on him. Sometimes he knew even before Tom himself did.

"Smithereened and then some, I'd guess from the look of you," the sergeant continued. "'Course, t'ain't nuthin' compared to the way *she's* been actin' lately."

Tom's head came up. "Yeah? And how's that?"

O'Malley's grin broadened until a dimple appeared on each of his ruddy cheeks. "Plumb sorcered. I suggested, subtlelike, that the feeling'd pass quicker if she'd dip into some o' that bottle of whiskey she won.

She looked at me like I was one of the green fairy folk.''

Tom merely grunted. He gave his sergeant a long look, turned on his heel and headed down the trail toward the skid road. O'Malley gazed after him, scratching his beard. He pursed his lips to whistle a tune, then closed his mouth with a click.

The only song that came to mind was ''Bonnie Blue Flag.''

Meggy counted the coins weighting her apron pocket. She had enough, eighteen dollars even. Oh, bless those men, Lord. Their appetite for apple pie would send her home.

She poured the silver dollars into the tin sewing box and set it in the humpbacked trunk that now stood in the corner of her cabin. Tomorrow she would borrow Fong's garden shovel again and dig up the rest of her savings where Tom had buried it under her porch that night.

That night. Nothing in Meggy's whole life had surprised her more than that night with Tom.

Almost at once she thought of Charlotte. She ran her palm over the wooden trunk slats, wondering if her sister realized what a fortunate woman she was with a warm, cozy room and a double bed in which to enjoy the bliss of physical loving night after night for the rest of her life.

Her mother's tales, and Aunt Hattie's, had led her

to believe the mating act was hideously awkward and painful, to be borne bravely by a daughter of the Confederacy, particularly a Hampton, and most especially a Davis, her mother's family.

But poor Aunt Hattie had been simply talking through her bonnet. She didn't know one thing about the wondrous feeling of being with a man.

Meggy glanced into the open trunk. It was lined in rose-printed paper and smelled of the lavender sachet Faith had given her last Christmas. Somehow it reminded Meggy of Aunt Hattie, all shut up tight inside. Underneath the accoutrements of a lady—Meggy's gloves and veils and corsets and petticoats—breathed a flesh-and-blood woman. A woman who not just tolerated but liked—no, enjoyed—no, *reveled in* lovemaking. This was something Aunt Hattie would never understand, not in a month of Sundays.

"I have come to a turning in my life," Meggy whispered aloud. "I quite enjoyed being intimate with a man. With Tom, that is." She didn't know, and didn't care, how it might be with someone else. She liked Tom. It was Colonel Randall she yearned for. Even if he was a Yankee.

Last night she'd lain awake aching for him something fierce, and that had most certainly opened her eyes! For the rest of her life she would remember that night.

But she would not, no, she could not, give free rein to such feelings, especially not with a Northerner.

Now that she had been awakened—and Lord knew that's just what it was, was it not, a glorious, glorious awakening?—she must live up to her family name.

She would not endeavor under any circumstances to be with Tom again. Once made her a woman of lapsed virtue. Twice, and she would be a— She could not bring herself to articulate the word.

She folded her freshly laundered nightgown and petticoats and laid them in the trunk. On impulse she lifted out her mother's fine china teapot, ran her fingers over the gold gilt rim of the lid and sighed. One more afternoon. One more round of jokes and the crew good-naturedly teasing each other, and then she would remove herself from the temptation of being near their leader. Heavens, the mere thought of the man made her blush!

"Gentlemen," Meggy said, "please help yourselves to another slice of pie."

O'Malley, prone on Meggy's front porch with his feet propped against the post and a teacup balanced on his stomach, gave a heartfelt groan. "Sure and it'll be the undoing of me."

"Too late," Orrin quipped. "Already can't button yer—"

The sergeant's boots clunked to the floor. "Mind your language, boyo. There's a lady present."

"Beggin' yer pardon, Miss Meggy."

Meggy sent the pudgy man a smile. "No harm has been done, Mr. Eight-Bit. May I offer you more tea?"

Vergil Price watched the gold-rimmed teapot tip forward and dribble dark liquid into the fragile cup Orrin held out. He thrust out his own cup, one with blue flowers painted on it. In all his life he'd never touched a prettier thing. And when she sat before him, pouring his cup full, he almost forgot what he had resolved. He was always careful not to brush her fingers, or look at her too long, for fear he wouldn't be able to carry out his plan.

"Mr. Price." She dipped her head in his direction. "How are the Claymore boys getting along?"

He opened his mouth to answer, but Indian Joe beat him to it. "One smart. Other strong."

"They're pullin' their weight, Miss Meggy." O'Malley sat up, his teacup clattering on its saucer. "The older boy, Seth, he's scamperin' about the skid road like he was born to it."

"Water bucket's too heavy for him," the Indian replied.

"Huh," Vergil Price scoffed. "He'll grow into it. I did."

Swede Jensen slapped his knee. "Nah, you didn't neither."

The men guffawed. Picking on Vergil was the usual afternoon entertainment.

"Buckets musta been smaller back then," someone said.

"Ol' Verg, he thought he'd be smart, so he punched holes in it so's he could lift it."

"Nah," Swede said again. "He's not that dumb, even if he iss from Kansas."

Vergil stiffened. "Ain't nuthin' wrong with Kansas. Least it's flat. Not like out here, where the land's all poked up outta shape."

"Yes," Meggy said quickly. "These mountains certainly are spectacular."

"Why'dja come out here in the first place, Verg?"

Vergil didn't answer.

Meggy watched the man's eyes narrow. "I'm sure we all have interesting reasons for coming West," she offered, keeping her voice light.

"I bet some gal's father run him off at gunpoint."

"Heck no. Who'd wanna marry a man what only comes up to her shoulder?"

Meggy gulped. "Oh, now gentlemen. I don't believe women are that interested in a man's appearance. It's his character that counts, wouldn't you say?"

"Maybe *she* scared him off. Cricked his neck lookin' up at her, and—"

"Maybe he run from law," Indian Joe said in a quiet voice.

Price leaped to his feet. "Why you...you're a lyin' son of a—"

"Comanche," the Indian interjected.

Meggy decided the time had come to change the subject. "Gentlemen, I have something to tell you."

Tom leaned into the breeze curling about the last twelve feet of the Douglas fir he clung to. High above the ground, he felt strangely at peace, even though every muscle and nerve in his body was strung tight as baling wire. From up here, things looked clearer. The men below looked like busy ants, scurrying along the lengths of a dozen thick downed logs, lopping off branches and skinning off the scabrous bark. The smoothed logs of the new skid road hadn't yet weathered but shone muted gold in the strong morning light. He forced his attention back to the fir tree, now beginning to sway as the wind picked up.

This was the third tree he'd topped since dawn, and it felt good. Working his body to exhaustion helped him sleep nights. He glanced down once more, gauging the direction of the fall.

The men below him suddenly coalesced into a circle. What the devil was going on? Tom let his ax swing on its safety line and cupped his hands. "Watch from above!" he yelled.

Swede waved his red cap to acknowledge the order, then clapped it back on his spiky thatch of blond hair and rejoined the circle.

Tom narrowed his eyes. He didn't dare take off any more limbs—no one on the ground was paying attention. He swore under his breath and started down.

The first word he heard when he approached the knot of agitated men was *Meggy*.

Meggy what? He quickened his pace.

"All right, boys," he barked. "What's so important that you're standing around jawing in a sewing circle? Anything needs talking about, other than cutting timber, can be done at supper."

"Supper'll be too late, Tom."

"Too late for what?" His voice sounded more and more like a rusty saw of late. He'd have to get Fong to brew up some of his throat syrup.

"She's leavin'. Miss Meggy's leavin'."

"Got her trunk all packed 'n everyt'ing. Tom, you can't let her go!"

"Leaving? You mean now?"

"Dat's right, boss. She t'ink to catch the stage that comes through Tennant at noon."

"She does, does she?" Tom growled.

"We couldn't none of us talk her out of it. *Do* something, Tom!"

The closer he got to Meggy's cabin, the more confused Tom felt. *Do something, Tom.*

Do what? Just what was he supposed to do after he'd as much as applied his boot to her backside and then accosted her in the woods and made love to her?

Well, it hadn't been exactly like that, but near enough. It was what he'd wanted to do ever since she came walking up the hill that day they buried Walt

Peabody, her intended. He just hadn't recognized it at the time.

Now he recognized it plenty.

He pounded on her front door until his fist throbbed, but there was no response.

"Meggy? It's Tom. Open up."

Nothing.

He peered through the window. The humpbacked trunk Vergil Price had lugged into camp strapped on the back of a mule was gone.

The mule! Price had borrowed the sorry animal from the livery stable in Tennant on condition it would be returned the next time someone went down the mountain for supplies. He'd bet a week's timber...

She couldn't manage it alone; she had to have had help. Now, who was left in camp...?

Fong. Of course. Blast that Chinaman, he'd do anything Meggy asked him. Any of the men would, but Tom was sure Fong's loyalty lay with him. At least it had until Meggy came along.

He headed toward the cookhouse at a run. The instant the oblong wood building came into view, he skidded to a stop. There she was in the doorway, shaking hands with his cook. The loaded mule stood waiting on the shady side of the porch.

"Meggy!" With a jolt Tom realized he hadn't the foggiest idea what to say to her.

Meggy looked up to see the colonel charging up

the path toward her. She clasped Fong's small, muscular hand and finished her sentence. "And thank you for the use of your baking pans, Mr. Fong. I do appreciate—"

"Meggy!"

Fong patted her hand. "Boss look plenty mad. More better I go water tomatoes now." He slipped through the screen door like a floppy-legged shadow, and Meggy's heart jigged its way into her throat.

"Meggy, what…?"

"Hello, Colonel." She kept her voice steady by concentrating on the collar of his plain flannel shirt. If she looked into his eyes she would falter, and she could not afford to lose her resolve.

"What are you doing, Meggy?"

"I am going down to Tennant to meet the stage. I have earned my eighteen dollars, so I am—"

"I guessed. I saw where you'd dug it up."

Meggy swallowed. "It was thoughtful of you to bury it for me that…night, Colonel. I knew just where to dig."

"After what's been between us, surely you can call me by my name?"

"Yes, of course, Colonel, you are quite right. Tom."

"Where are you going—after Tennant, I mean?"

"That is kind of you to inquire. I thought I would go back to Seton Falls."

"You can't. Not now."

"I must. I cannot remain here. You know it as well as I do."

"You can. The men don't... I don't want you to go."

She smiled up at him. "Not four days ago you offered to pay my train fare."

"Things are different now."

"Precisely. What we did was scandalous," she said in a soft voice.

"Are you sorry?"

She hesitated. "No, in truth I am not sorry. It was wonderful. More than wonderful. I will never forget it." She closed her eyes. "Never."

"Meggy, you can't leave now." He lowered his voice. "You might be...you might have conceived."

Her eyelids flew open. "My sister Charity tried ever so hard to conceive. It took months and months before she did, so I don't think a woman can, the first time."

"Chicken feathers! You've got to wait until you're sure. Until your, uh, female cycle comes. I can't let you—"

She laid her hand on his arm. "That is most honorable of you, Tom. But indeed I think—"

Two gunshots rang out, and they both jerked. "What was that?" Meggy gasped.

"Two shots is a signal. An accident...." Tom was loping down the trail before he finished the word.

"Wait, Meggy," he yelled over his shoulder. "Wait."

Fong appeared out of nowhere and tugged the sleeve of her black traveling dress. "They come here, missy. Use bench for operating table."

"Operating table!"

Fong sent her a wide grin. "Colonel-boss very good surgeon. Save arm, leg, whatever. You stay and help."

Chapter Twelve

Tom sprinted up the path and out of sight, his blue wool shirt blending into the trees beyond her cabin. Meggy's heart squeezed, and at the same time a cool voice of reason spoke inside her head. She couldn't possibly stay at Devil's Camp, no matter what. It would be the end of her.

The screen door swished shut as Fong disappeared into the cookhouse. Meggy stared after him. They didn't need her help; the men were a tight-knit bunch who had handled accidents before. They knew what to do, and she did not. The only injury she had ever treated was the sprained shoulder Addie had gotten when she fell through the front porch railing a week before she was married. Taking care of that was only a matter of common sense—if it hurt, Meggy told her not to move it. She'd trussed her sister up in a sling fashioned out of dish towels, and by the day of the wedding she was fine.

But this—a logging injury, possibly like the one that had taken the life of Walter Peabody... She would only be in the way.

Through the door screen she watched Fong pour boiling water out of the teakettle onto one of the plank tables. He tossed a large wooden brush onto the surface and started scrubbing.

She took a step toward the mule. She had already explained her reasons to Tom; all she had to do now was walk down the mountain with her loaded trunk. She lifted the lead rope just as a shout came from the trees and Swede Jensen hurtled past her into the cook-house. Behind him, Tom appeared, walking quickly with something in his arms.

"Fong!" the Swede yelled. "Boss says to...oh, I see you already done it, by golly." The door slammed open.

"All ready, boss!"

Tom strode down the hill toward them, his face white and strained. The form he carried was small. Slight.

Oh no! Meggy's stomach clenched. It was one of the Claymore boys. Seth, the thirteen-year-old, she guessed. The younger brother stumbled along, sobbing and clinging to Tom's trouser leg. When he saw her, Nobby launched himself at her and buried his face in her skirt.

Tom swept past her. "Get some whiskey," he ordered.

Whiskey? Oh, of course. She'd left the remainder of the bottle she'd used as a rolling pin on her kitchen counter. She dropped the mule's tether, handed Nobby over to Swede Jensen and started for her cabin. Behind her she could hear the lumberjack's voice boom. "A brave man don't cry like girl. Even my momma, when she have baby, does not cry."

"But he's hurt bad, Swede." Nobby's voice wobbled. "He's bleeding."

Meggy picked up her skirts and began to run.

When she returned to the cookhouse, a peculiar quiet hung over the room. Tom bent over the still form laid out on the freshly scrubbed table, his ear to the boy's chest. Swede stood off to one side, one beefy arm encircling Nobby, whose tear-streaked face looked white and pinched.

In the silence, Fong plunked an enamelware dishpan down on a bench, then filled it with water from the teakettle. Three other men, Sergeant O'Malley, Indian Joe and Eight-Bit Orrin, lined up on the side of the table opposite Tom.

"What do you need, boyo?" O'Malley spoke in low tones.

"My medical kit." Tom ran his fingers through Seth's blood-matted hair. "And bandages. He's got a nasty gash over his ear."

O'Malley jerked his thumb at Indian Joe, and silent as a cat the man slipped off to fetch what was needed.

"Here's the whiskey." Meggy set the bottle down next to Fong's dishpan.

"Thought you were set to travel on down the mountain," Tom said without looking up.

"I was. I can't, now."

Tom mumbled something, then straightened. "Boy's got a broken arm. He was wetting down the skid road and he fell under the team. Lucky he's not—" He glanced at Nobby and caught himself.

"We'll splint it. I'll have to set it first, though. Mick, give him some whiskey."

Both Eight-Bit Orrin and O'Malley stepped forward. With his pocketknife, Orrin slit open the boy's shirtsleeve, and when O'Malley lifted Seth's head to the whiskey bottle, he folded the fabric back to expose the broken arm.

Seth groaned and Meggy looked away. It was horrible to see anything hurting, worst of all a child. Indian Joe reappeared and thrust a black leather case into Tom's hand.

Tom bent over the boy. "All right now, son. You've got a man-size decision to make. Your scalp's cut pretty deep and I'm going to have to stitch it closed. That's gonna smart. What'll be worse, though, is setting your arm. That'll feel like something sawing into your bone."

"I ain't scared," Seth said in a small voice.

Tom laid his hand on the boy's forehead. "Which do you want first, then, the little hurt or the big one?"

Seth's eyelids fluttered shut. "The big one, I guess. Best get it over with."

Tom nodded. "Drink some more whiskey, Seth," he said in a gentle voice. "It'll help some."

Meggy's knees folded. She managed to alight on the bench next to Fong, then doubled over at the waist to clear her head. *Mary Margaret, you pull yourself together this instant! This is not what he needs now, a silly woman in a swoon.*

"Eight-Bit," Tom snapped. "Find something we can use to splint it."

"Two nice straight pine branches right here, Tom. I'll peel 'em so they're smooth."

"Okay, here goes." Tom ran his fingers over Seth's forearm, feeling for the break. "Got to figure how to move it so it heals straight," he muttered. "All set, son?"

Seth nodded, his eyes shut tight. Tom manipulated the two bone pieces while the boy clenched his teeth together.

"Yell if you want to, Seth. Just don't move."

"Nossir." The boy's breath hissed in, followed by a guttural moan.

Meggy covered her face with her hands. Tom's voice came to her through a dark fog. "Mick?"

"The boy's had enough liquor to float a strong man to the land of the pixies, Tom."

"Give him some more."

Nobby broke away from the Swede and with a little

choking sound buried his face in Meggy's lap. She wrapped her arms around his trembling shoulders and heard a faint click as the bones meshed.

"Splint!"

"Right here, Tom."

A rustling sound and another sucked-in breath. "Okay, that's it. You're a tough lad, son. The worst is over."

"Yessir," Seth murmured.

Meggy thought she could not stay seated one more minute. She raised her head and met Tom's gaze. Tears shone in his eyes, and he spoke without looking away from her. "Fong, you boil the needle?"

The Chinaman grinned. "Still on stove, boss. Boil long time."

Tom gave her a crooked smile, then turned his attention to the boy sprawled on the table. "Seth, stitching up a cut stings like blazes, so you just use all the swear words your mamma wouldn't like and hang on."

Seth nodded. "Miss Meggy still here?"

"I'm here, Seth."

He reached his good arm toward her. "Might want somethin' to hold on to."

She took his bony, dirt-smeared hand in hers and pressed hard.

"Don't mind if'n I use bad language, ma'am," he murmured. "Ain't feeling 'xactly like myself."

Meggy's heart filled to overflowing. She squeezed

Seth's fingers, smoothed her other hand over his brother's soft brown hair. At that moment she didn't trust her voice any more than her knees.

While Tom scrubbed his hands over the sink in the kitchen, O'Malley sponged the blood from the boy's head wound.

"All set, boss," the Irishman called out. "Bleeding's stopped."

Fong handed Tom a needle threaded with a strand of silk so fine Meggy could barely see it. She watched him draw the flaps of skin together and stitch up the torn scalp. His hands were steady as he worked the needle in and out, the long, sensitive fingers skilled and sure. But sweat beaded his forehead, and each time Seth made a sound, Tom flinched.

So big, strong Tom Randall had a vulnerable spot, too. The thought made her heart tumble over and over as if buffeted by a strong wind. He was a fine man. A wonderful man. A… Why, it hardly even mattered that he was a Northerner!

Saints preserve me, am I falling in love with the colonel?

Tom tied the last knot and clipped the ends with a pair of steel surgical scissors. "That's the last one, Seth. How are you doing?"

"Jus' fine, boss. Arm don't hurt much, and my head feels kinda warm an' nice now that that saw-blade's stopped buzzin' into my scalp."

Tom chuckled. "Tomorrow you'll have a man-size

headache, but you earned it like a trouper." He patted the boy's shoulder. Raising his head he surveyed the faces of the crew gathered around the makeshift operating table.

"I need one of you to watch over him tonight, make sure he keeps the splint straight."

To his surprise, Meggy rose. She met his glance over the supine form of the boy on the table. "Carry him up to my cabin, Colonel. I will watch over him. And over Nobby as well. I am quite sure they will not wish to be separated."

Swede shuffled forward. "We was t'inking you was going away, Miss Meggy."

She continued to look straight at Tom when she spoke. "Yes, Swede, I am. But not just now. Not…for a day or two."

Her eyes held Tom's with a peculiar intensity. He tried to read the meaning behind her gaze, but she lowered the dark lashes to hide her expression.

"Gentlemen, would one of you see to my trunk? And Mr. O'Malley, perhaps you could find a pallet for me and one for Nobby as well? Seth will need the cot."

"I surely will, ma'am. Glad to. Sure an' the boy'll think an angel's come to tend him."

"Here's what's left of yer whiskey, Miss Meggy. Ya might be wantin' some. For Seth, I mean."

"Thank you kindly, Mr. Eight-Bit."

Tom's gaze went from her face to the small white

hand grasping the neck of the amber-colored bottle. He was so glad she wasn't leaving he felt like singing. It took all his concentration to wrestle his thoughts back to his young patient.

"We'll need a stretcher to move the boy. Mick, Orrin, see what you can rustle up."

The two men clattered out the door. Fong removed the basin of bloody water. "Make tomatoes grow fat!" the Chinaman quipped as he started for the kitchen.

Meggy turned her face away.

Hell's half acre, Tom thought. He could tell she wasn't an experienced nurse. He was grateful to her for taking Seth on, as well as his young brother; it seemed the boys had touched her heart.

That left him free to wash up, maybe figure his timber losses for the day before suppertime. He'd ask Fong to send a tray for the boys and Meggy. From the look of her, though, he'd bet she wouldn't eat much. Her face was dead white, and her hands kept fluttering between her throat and her midriff.

Some mix of female Meggy Hampton was. A steel rifle barrel for a spine and a heart like a squashy peach. Plus a body that rose to his touch with an openness and passion he'd never known in a woman.

But it was her spirit he admired most.

And respected. He knew he couldn't lay a finger on her for however long she remained at Devil's

Camp. He knew, all right. His male body would ache like the devil, but he'd sleep alone.

He was beginning to wonder which was worse, wanting her and being honorable, or despoiling her and being human. *Hell on earth or hell in hell?*

Right now it didn't make much difference. He was trussed and logjammed either way.

Chapter Thirteen

Using a makeshift stretcher fashioned from two pine poles and a wool blanket, Sergeant O'Malley and Indian Joe carried a woozy Seth Claymore up the hill to Meggy's cabin. When they had lowered the boy onto her narrow cot, the two men disappeared, then returned with pallets and bedding for Nobby and for herself. She supervised Swede and Indian Joe as they unloaded her trunk for the second time in as many days, then busied herself making up the pallets as O'Malley strung a rope across one corner of the single room.

"I'll be hangin' up a sheet here for yer privacy, ma'am, in case you're wonderin'."

Meggy set the teakettle on the stove. "Mr. O'Malley, I have come to accept your good judgment without question."

The sergeant flushed with pleasure. "Well, ma'am, I'm honored, that I am."

Indian Joe clunked an armload of small pine logs into the woodbox. "You have flint?"

"I have a container of sulfur matches, thank you." She rummaged in the side pocket of the now-open trunk which stood in one corner and slipped the round metal container into her pocket.

The black-haired man straightened. "Flint better. Not get wet if fall in river."

"You can be assured I will endeavor *not* to fall in the river, though I thank you for your advice."

"Best you not take a bath, neither, ma'am," the sergeant said from behind a white muslin sheet. "Leastways not without me or the colonel standin' guard. Like he said before, if you recall."

Meggy started. "Oh, I do indeed, Mr. O'Malley. I most certainly will call upon you when the need arises."

She'd call on the sergeant, yes. But not on the colonel. The thought of taking off her clothes with Tom Randall anywhere near would be most unwise. Foolhardy, even. The very idea sent hot prickles up her forearms.

"Then I'll be biddin' you a good evenin', ma'am. Tom said to signal with your candle if you need anything."

"Signal?"

"Just pass something in front of your light—a dish towel, or your hand."

"He can see me up here?"

"From his tent, yes, ma'am. Well, not you, exactly, just the light when you move around inside. Y'see, Walt Peabody didn't have time to fill the chinks between—"

"I see."

"First couple o' nights you was here, Colonel hardly slept fer watchin' you."

"I see," Meggy said again. The chill in her voice brought a frown to the Irishman's smooth forehead. O'Malley scratched his head.

"Watchin' *over* you, that is. We never had a woman in camp before, miss. Can't blame the colonel for feelin' responsible-like."

Meggy gazed into the man's guileless blue eyes and suddenly all the starch in her drained away. Someone was watching out for *her*? After nine years of watching out for everyone else—five sisters and a maiden aunt, and the old people of her father's congregation, even the hungry pickaninnies who came to the kitchen door—she had someone, the colonel, watching over *her*?

All at once she felt as if her heart were pumping hot maple syrup through her veins. In a haze of warmth she bade good-night to the sergeant and Indian Joe, closed the door and turned her attention to her two charges.

Seth's forehead was cool, and he didn't wake up when she smoothed her hand over his skin and pulled a cover over him. Nobby had pulled his bedroll close to the cot on which his brother lay and had curled up into a ball on the floor beside him. His narrow chest rose rhythmically.

Poor little mite. His tear-streaked face needed washing, but Meggy didn't have the heart to disturb him.

Someone tapped against the door. When she opened it, Swede Jensen thrust a tin cookie sheet into her hands.

"Fong sent some food so you don't miss supper. Good stew he made from the last of the venison, by golly. I t'ink plenty for all three of you."

Meggy smiled at him and sent a message of thanks back to Fong. The savory smell from the blue enamelware bowls woke Nobby. Meggy settled the tray on the floor between them and together they spooned up their dinners. Before he reached the bottom of his dish, Nobby's eyelids began to droop.

"Miss Meggy?"

"Yes, Nobby, what is it?"

"D'you think Colonel Tom'd let me grease the skid road 'stead of Seth?"

"Why, I have no idea. What does one do to 'grease the skid road'?"

"You take a bucket and fill it up 'bout half-full of water and sprinkle it on the logs, see? The skinned ones that Swede and the others laid down so the oxes can drag the logs down the mountain. Ya hafta be quick, 'n run fast, or you'll get trampled on, like Seth. But I could do it, I know I could.''

Meggy swallowed. She fervently hoped the boy would *not* be allowed to take on such a dangerous-sounding task. Nobby was so small and spindly. The thought of his thin legs under the hooves of a team of oxen...

She clacked her spoon into the empty bowl. ''I...I will speak to the colonel about it.'' Most assuredly she would! She would demand that Nobby be kept safe from danger. She didn't care how far behind Tom was in meeting his timber quota, he had no right to—

Another knock sounded at the door.

This time, Indian Joe stood at the threshold, holding a floppy bouquet of some sort in one hand. ''Nettles,'' he announced. ''For boy. Make tea, help bone to knit.''

Meggy reached for the greenery, but the Indian lifted the bunch out of her reach. ''Not touch. Nettles burn skin like fire.''

He laid them on Fong's cookie sheet. ''I fill water bucket on porch. Boil half hour.''

In the next moment, he was gone.

Meggy gathered up the two empty bowls and set Seth's portion aside for when he woke up. Then she lit a candle in the fading twilight, stuck it to the wood counter and dipped a kettle of water from the water bucket.

Nobby curled up on his pallet again and within

seconds was sound asleep. He hadn't even removed his boots!

She laid a fire in the fire box and, using one of her precious matches, blew on the spark until it caught. While the tea water heated, she washed the two dishes and the spoons and dried them with a tea towel on which Charlotte had embroidered a verse of poetry.

All precious things discovered late,
To those that seek them issue forth,
For Love in sequel works with Fate,
And draws the veil from hidden worth.

The candle flame guttered as she moved around it, and all at once she thought of Tom, watching the light from his tent. Watching *her*.

The notion that he was aware of her, even though she was far away from his tent, twisted a blade of pleasure in her chest. If she moved in front of the candle he would know that she had done so. If she—

Again came a rap on the door. *What could it possibly be this time?*

A grinning Vergil Price greeted her. "Miss Meggy, I hope I'm not disturbin' yore evenin'."

"Actually, I was making some tea. Nettle tea," she added at the sudden gleam in Vergil's heavy-lidded eyes. The man made her uneasy in a way she could not pinpoint. With the others, even dark, silent Indian Joe, she felt perfectly at ease, but somehow when

Vergil looked at her it was…well, different. "For Seth," she explained. "To help his bone set."

Vergil advanced into the room without invitation. "Care to set a spell on yer porch? Awful hot night."

"Is it? I hadn't noticed. To be truthful, I have been busy unpacking my trunk and caring for the boys."

Vergil peered over her shoulder. "'Pear to be sleepin'. They won't miss you none."

Meggy back away from him, maneuvering to keep the flickering candle between them.

The candle!

She grabbed the damp tea towel and held it in front of the flame for three heartbeats, then lifted it. "Mr. Price, you could do me a great favor if you would." She pretended to inspect the towel, dangling it again in front of the candle for a count of three. A signal, Mr. O'Malley had said. But what kind of signal? Was Tom even paying any attention?

"Whazzat, Miss Meggy?" He smiled at her, exposing yellow teeth.

She snatched up the enamelware bowls. "Here. Return these to Fong. It will save me a trip down to the cookhouse."

"Wouldn'tcha like to set on the porch first?"

"N-no. I must…keep my eye on Seth's medicine."

"Jes' bein' here with you'd be good enough medicine for me. My, you shore do smell good."

"Mr. Price?" She flapped the towel in front of the candle once more. *Tom,* she called out silently.

"Yes'm?"

"Mr. Price, I—I understand you have just returned from Tennant. Would you care to share some of your, um, insights about the town?"

Vergil's arm stretched toward her.

Tom!

Tom lifted his forehead off his folded arms and shook his head to clear it. He'd fallen asleep over his account ledger again. Someone, O'Malley he guessed, had doused his lantern. No doubt the Irishman would tsk-tsk about it all day tomorrow, but it had happened before. Tom sat up studying the book so many nights he was continually short on sleep. Usually, though, if he fell asleep in spite of his efforts, he slept straight through until morning. Tonight something wakened him. Like a voice, calling his name.

Automatically he glanced out the front tent flap. Light glowed from Meggy's cabin. She must be up, tending the Claymore boy.

The light winked off, as if something had blocked it, then winked on again. Nursing took a lot of moving around, he guessed. Off, then on again. Same length of time, about one long breath's worth.

As if she was...

He reached her porch at a dead run and burst through the door. Vergil Price had her cornered next to the stove.

"Price!" Tom yelled. The man whirled around.

"I told you to stay away from her."

"Wasn't doin' no harm, Tom. Jes' came to…fetch her supper dishes. Wasn't—"

Meggy's chalk-white face told him everything. Price had forced his way in, maybe would have forced her….

Tom grabbed the man's shirt in one hand and latched on to his belt with the other. "Get out." He shoved him out the door and off the porch, watched him stumble off down the trail.

Breathing hard, Tom reentered the cabin. "You all right? Did he hurt you?"

"Yes. No." Her voice sounded unsteady.

Nobby sat bolt upright, his eyes as round as two brown pine knots. Seth, too, had been awakened by the noise.

"You boys all right?"

"Yessir."

"Seth, how's the arm feeling?"

"Don't feel nuthin', Colonel. Sorry about not bein' able to protect Miss Meggy."

"Not much you could have done with a busted arm, son."

"Coulda yelled some."

"I coulda bit him, if'n I'd waked up," Nobby offered. "Next time I'll—"

"Won't be a next time, Nobby. Miss Meggy's going to have a twenty-four-hour guard from now on."

Meggy came toward him. "Tom, you can't afford to spare a man for that. You're already shorthanded."

"So?"

"So, the obvious solution is to…well, at the moment I cannot think. Seth, your dinner is still warm. Here's a spoon. Can you eat left-handed?"

Nobby jumped up. "I'll help him, Miss Meggy."

Tom motioned with his head toward the porch. Meggy nodded. She propped Seth's head on a folded-up blanket and put the bowl in Nobby's hands. Then she moved through the doorway ahead of the colonel.

The instant he swung the door shut, she turned into his arms, her whole body trembling.

"I am so sorry," she whispered. "I didn't know how frightened I was until you shouted, and then my knees just turned all soft, like they did the time that Yankee climbed over the fence into our yard, and my goodness, at least then I had enough presence of mind to go find the broom! This time I couldn't make my feet move…."

"You signaled, didn't you? With the candle?"

"Well, I had to think of something. My father's revolver is at the bottom of my trunk, and I don't *have* a broom!"

Tom stared at her, then started to laugh.

She gave a little jerk. "I fail to see what is so funny."

"It isn't funny, exactly. Well, yes it is. I'll make

sure you have a broom tomorrow.'' Then he sobered. ''But keep the revolver handy.''

''Yes.''

''Then again, I think we have a problem a gun won't solve.''

''You want to fire Mr. Price, is that it?''

''In the worst way. Trouble is, he's a good skinner, and I'm short on crew.''

''I cannot let you lose your timber contract because of me. You must keep Mr. Price on.''

She had stopped shaking, and now she stepped away from him and raised her head. ''It is I who am dispensable.''

Hell's bells, he wasn't going to argue with her. Her presence was *not* dispensable, but for a reason she would never dream of. He wanted her near because it made him feel good. Because the thought of never seeing those thoughtful green eyes looking at him with such unfeigned concern stopped his breathing. If she left him, he would ache for her all the rest of his life.

And what about Susanna? Would you betray the honor of your sister by protecting the enemy who bore witness against her?

Meggy stepped away and looked up at him. ''Tom, I have quite regained my composure now, and I believe there is a solution to this dilemma.''

''Yeah? Well, let's hear it.''

* * *

Yeah, pretty lady, let's hear it. Bet you wouldn't be so all-fired composed if'n you knew ol' Vergil was out here listenin'. And I've got me a plan. Somethin' that's gonna make you look at me with diff'rent eyes.

Somethin' that'll make all you bastards remember me.

Chapter Fourteen

Meggy hesitated a long moment, as if weighing something in her mind. A solution. Yes, Tom wanted to hear her solution. The very idea made her tremble, but when she spoke, her voice was calm.

"During the day, your crew—in particular Mr. Price—is under your surveillance."

"During the day, yes. What about at night?"

"At night, your surveillance will shift to me. And the two boys, of course."

"Meggy, I can't watch your cabin from my tent all night."

"Then, Colonel, you might wish to sleep here. With us."

It made sense in a crazy way. What didn't make sense was the way it made him feel, like a cornered wolf with a powerful appetite.

"Let us have a heart-to-heart talk, Colonel."

"Let's have some whiskey first. My head's spinning like a pole-spiked log."

"Very well." She swished into the cabin, leaving the door ajar. He could hear her saying something to the two brothers, heard the stew bowl clack onto the counter. When she reappeared she had the bottle of liquor she'd won when she killed the deer. And two cut crystal tumblers, dug out of her trunk, he guessed. He hadn't seen glasses that fancy since he'd left home.

She poured one small thumb's worth into one glass and half filled the other. "Is this sufficient, Colonel? Or shall I add more?"

"That's just fine." He reached toward the larger glass, but before he could close his fingers around it, she picked it up herself and took a big gulp. Her eyes watered.

"That one's yours," she said in a wheezy voice. She indicated the thumb-high amount. "It tastes quite like wood varnish, but I do admire the courage it gives one."

"Courage?" Right, courage. Tom grabbed the bottle and filled his glass to the rim.

"For what I am proposing. It appears we are in a fix, but the solution is staring us right in the face." She downed another swallow.

"The way I see it, if I slept here at night you'd be ruined."

"Not with the two Claymore boys as…well, as

chaperons." She dropped her gaze to the whiskey in her hand. "And of course we would retire on opposite sides of the room."

Tom chuckled. "Kinda like the Mason-Dixon line, you mean. You on one side, me on the other."

"And the Claymore brothers in between. Precisely." She took another sip from her glass. "My Aunt Hattie—my mother's older sister? Once she was out all night with a gentleman friend of my father's. Well, it was purely scandalous, but the family managed to scotch all the talk that followed because *I* was in the carriage with them. 'Course, I was only five years old at the time, but I could attest to the fact that the carriage wheel had broken and Aunt Hattie and Mr. Peabody were not alone *together* all night. *That* Mr. Peabody," she added as an afterthought, "was the uncle of Mr. Walter Peabody, whom I would have married had he…"

"Survived," Tom stated.

She went on as if she hadn't heard him. "My, we three did have ourselves a time. We kept ourselves warm under the lap robe and played Twenty Questions until it was daylight."

"Out all night in a carriage is different from sleeping under the same roof," Tom observed.

She looked straight into his eyes. "I know you better than I know any man in this camp, Tom. Better than any man I have *ever* known, if truth be told. I admit I am needing protection now, for Mr. Price has grown…aggressive. You can watch him during the day, but there is no man I trust more than you to watch over me at night.''

The oddest surge of pride went through him. Pride and…caution. "Meggy, after what's happened between us, it's hard to be anywhere near you without—''

"I know. I feel it, too. But I know you are an honorable man, Tom. Besides, we are both as hardheaded as two hazelnuts, so neither of is likely to break a pact we make with the other.''

Tom groaned. "Hardheaded,'' he murmured.

Meggy downed another gulp of whiskey and released a long sigh. "I always have been. Mama used to say I was so headstrong I'd never have any beaus, that men liked to be in charge, or at least think they were in charge. I guess she was right, because Hope and Addie and…well, all my sisters, really, had ever so many beaus. At least until the war, but by then Hope was married and Addie and Faith were spoken for, and…''

"What about you, Meggy? Did you not have beaus?'' Somehow he could not imagine the male population of Seton Falls being so blind.

"Me? Why no, I didn't much. After Mama died— I was just twelve that year—there was so much cooking and sewing and church circle entertaining. My father was the minister, you see. It left no time for gentlemen callers. Besides, there wasn't a young man in the entire county I couldn't talk circles around, and that scared most of them off.''

"What about Walt Peabody, the man you came west to marry?''

"Why, I had never even laid eyes on Walter. He was a family connection, you might say, and when Charlotte married in May, I decided it was finally my turn. His father arranged it.''

"You wanted to marry that much? You'd take a man you'd never even met?'' Tom knew by the look on her face that he'd gone too far, but it was too late.

"Oh, I did, yes. I wanted a home and children in the worst way. I didn't want to end up alone and all pinched up, like Aunt Hattie. My gracious, I don't know why I'm tellin' you all this—I do think perhaps alcoholic spirits loosen my tongue!''

Tom laughed outright at that. Her cheeks were flushed a soft rose, her green eyes sparkling with animation. Yes, he could see where she'd talk circles around a man; her spur-of-the-moment digressions looped and doubled back quicker than an Indian covering his trail. Her words were as fascinating to him, and as unexpected, as Susanna's moody silences had been.

He opened his mouth with his sister's name on his lips, then clamped his jaw shut. In the years since her execution, he'd never spoken of her to anyone. Why he was moved to now was beyond him. The whiskey, maybe.

"Okay, Meggy, you talked me into it." He chuckled at her widened eyes, then stood and clumped off the porch.

"I'll just go down and get my bedroll. You lay out the border between the North and the South."

Meggy washed up the dinner bowls, then heated a basin of water and gently sponged Seth's sweat-streaked face. Finally, with Nobby's help, she unlaced his boots and drew them off. When the injured boy balked at letting her remove his shirt, she decided it would not harm him to sleep fully clothed for one night. It hurt to move his injured arm, he confessed, and the last thing Meggy wanted was to cause him further discomfort.

She dosed him with another cup of nettle tea, tucked Nobby under his blanket and turned her attention to choosing a spot for her own pallet. Tom would be back at any moment; she had to decide where the "North-South" line between them would fall.

She eyed the area between her cot, on which Seth now slept, and her humpbacked trunk in the opposite corner. She would claim the area Mr. O'Malley had curtained off next to her trunk. Seth and Nobby's side of the room would be North. That way, Tom could bed down next to Seth's cot, which would put the sleeping Nobby on the floor between them.

She spread a folded sheet over the straw mattress the sergeant had brought for her, then rummaged in her trunk for a crocheted afghan and draped it on top. It was so hot inside the cabin she doubted she would need it; even the breeze through the open window was warm, carrying the scent of pine and wild mint.

She undressed quickly behind the curtain, drew on a clean muslin nightgown and blew out the candle. Waiting until her eyes adjusted to the darkness, she tiptoed past the two slumbering boys and slid into her makeshift bed. For some reason she thought of Charlotte just then, of Mr. Tennyson's poem embroidered around the edge of her tea towel. *All precious things discovered late...*

Meggy sighed. She had missed a great deal of life. Her "precious things" had been buried so long she thought it likely they would never be discovered at all. When she left Chester County, she had wanted marriage and children. What she found was joy in physical closeness with a man, but it was the wrong man. What she had found turned out to be the path to ruin.

Footsteps sounded on the porch, and Meggy held her breath.

"It's me," a low voice said. "Tom." The door swung open and a tall, shadowy figure entered. "Meggy?"

"I'm here, over by the trunk. There is ample room for you next to the cot."

"Boys asleep?"

"I think so."

He bent to grab hold of something, and she heard blankets swishing across the plank floor. Nobby's bedroll, she guessed; Tom was pulling it away from the cot to make room for himself. He laid out his mattress, tucked a blanket under the edges and sat down on it to shuck his boots. Neither boy woke when they thumped onto the floor, and Meggy exhaled in relief. Both lads were sound asleep.

But *she* certainly wasn't. The silence sang in her head. Then every rustle, every breath Tom drew teased her consciousness. When he stopped moving around at last and lay still, other sounds floated to her ears—the sigh of tree branches outside, the *scritch-scratch* of crickets, the far-off yip of a lone coyote.

"Tom?" she said softly. "We need to talk, about Nobby."

"What about him? Is he sick?"

"He wants to do something called 'grease skid-ding' in place of Seth."

"Skid greasing," Tom corrected with a chuckle. "Over my dead body. I hate to disappoint him, but the answer is no. It's too dangerous."

"Oh, I am so glad. Thank you."

A low, growly laugh came from the direction of his bedroll. "*He's* not going to thank me. Nobby's aching to prove his manhood."

"You'll not let him, will you?"

"Not much you can do once the sap starts rising. But I'll watch him, try to keep him out of trouble."

"Sap?"

He ignored the question. Suddenly he sat up, unbuttoning his shirt. "Damn hot in here."

"Yes, it is. We might open the door to catch the breeze."

Without replying, Tom rose and propped the door open with a chunk of firewood. Meggy saw the faint gleam of his bare chest and she shut her eyes tight, then laughed at herself. What a silly goose she was. Out in the forest that night they had lain in intimate circumstances, skin to skin. She certainly hadn't closed her eyes then!

Still, the knowledge that he lay half-naked not two yards away from her gave her the shivers. She concentrated on the night noises, the inhalation of her three visitors, the male scent in the air, of leather and sweat and pine soap. Her mouth grew dry as wood ashes.

Was he as aware of her as she was of him? She listened intently. Both Seth and Nobby whistled faintly when they exhaled, but she could not hear Tom's breathing.

Because…great heavens, because he wasn't asleep! *He is lying there quiet as a cat, listening to me.*

A hot, slow flush traveled from her knees to her shoulders and tingled down both arms. Don't think about it. Think of something else. *Anything* else.

Without being aware of it, she began to hum.

Tom groaned. "I could do without that," he said in a quiet voice.

"Without what?"

"That song you're singing, 'Bonnie Blue Flag.' No need to remind me."

"I sincerely apologize. I had no idea what I was singing, I was just trying to…to keep my mind occupied."

A heavy silence dropped between them, lengthened until Meggy thought she would scream. Then Tom's quiet voice spoke into the darkness.

"My sister's name was Susanna."

Meggy lay without moving, listening to his hoarse, hesitant words.

"She was named after our mother. They weren't anything alike, but…"

She waited a full minute. "Would you like to tell me about her?"

"I've never spoken of her much until now." He stared up at the roof over his head, his breath growing ragged. "I'm not sure I can."

"Go on, Tom. I am listening."

"They arrested her in Richmond. She'd been there before, of course, visiting a great-aunt who married a Virginia planter and inherited his estate when he died. But this time Susanna carried coded messages in her handbag. They said she was a Union spy."

"Surely there was a trial?" Meggy breathed.

"There was. She sent for me, but by the time I got there, it was over."

"You don't believe she was really guilty, do you, Tom?"

"I didn't believe so then. A Richmond woman swore she saw Susanna in the company of a Union general three days before she was arrested. All the messages she carried were addressed to him. But she was sentenced and executed so fast it smelled of conspiracy."

Why, no wonder he distrusts women. Especially Southern women. Meggy could think of nothing short of a miracle that would heal a wound like that. "And now? What do you believe now?"

"Now I don't know. Until recently I thought she was wrongly accused, that they'd made a mistake. But lately I've been remembering things."

"What things?" Meggy prompted.

"Susanna was always getting caught up in some cause or other. She liked intrigue. She wasn't afraid of taking risks, and she rather enjoyed shocking the family, especially Mother."

Meggy thought hard, weighing the risk, before voicing the inescapable thought that came to mind. Tom needed to explore his feelings about his sister's death, but a Southern woman's observations were not something he would want to hear. Nevertheless, she spoke them anyway.

"It sounds as if in some ways, Susanna never grew up."

"She was seven when our mother died. Nine when Pa was killed."

"Your father, was he killed during the war?"

"My father was shot sitting at his desk in the *Zanesville Banner* office," he said shortly. "He printed an editorial on the vigilantes in Kansas, and that night one of them rode in and murdered him. After that, I raised my sister alone. She was twenty-five when they…"

"I am also twenty-five, Tom. And in some ways I have never grown up. At least that is what Papa used to tell me. Then, when he was killed in the War and I found myself head of the family, I felt so woefully unready. Not grown up at all. I went from being a tomboy to an old maid in a few short years."

"You wouldn't have become a spy."

"I might have, yes. I'd have done anything in my power to help the Confederate cause."

She said nothing further, and Tom felt a grudging admiration for her. It didn't make him feel any better about Susanna, about the possibility that she might actually have been a spy, and thus rightly accused and—he clenched his jaw—justly executed. But at least he was beginning to understand how it might have been, from the Rebel side.

He hated to admit it, but he was grateful to Meggy in a way. Southern women, like Northern women, simply did what they believed was right. That woman in Richmond, the one who had testified against Susanna, had approached him at the funeral, had begged his forgiveness with tears in her eyes. In his anger he had brushed her out of his way and stalked on past. He wondered if he would do the same thing now.

He rolled over, shifted his shoulders to get comfortable on his thin pallet, and wished desperately for another swig of Meggy's whiskey. He strained his ears for her soft breathing, but heard nothing.

She wasn't asleep. Was she lying there, as he was, with every nerve on edge?

He held his breath, listening. Seth snored slightly when he inhaled; Nobby's breaths were quick and considerably more quiet. But Meggy?

Unless she was holding her breath, she was awake, trying to be quiet. Maybe she was thinking.

About what? he wondered.

Any one of a thousand things, you damn fool. Maybe Seth's broken arm, or that bastard Vergil Price. Or maybe she was regretting her decision to stay and care for the injured boy. Maybe she was even thinking of him?

Tom's heart stuttered to a stop. She didn't want to be here. She had wanted to get as far away from him as she could. He realized how happy he was that she had stayed. For some reason, every second he spent in her company, every word she spoke in that clear, musical voice, was like a healing balm that soothed his troubled soul.

The Lord sure worked in funny ways. The solace he derived from her presence, the sheer physical joy he experienced in their union had changed him. A Confederate woman had brought him to his knees.

He sat up. Oh, hell, he wasn't going to get any sleep tonight. The cabin was stifling, even with the door propped ajar and what breeze there was coming through the open window. The air was heavy and still, scented with her perfume, or something kind of sweet, like lilacs. His tent would be a lot cooler. The cabin porch would be cooler.

So why don't you get up and move?

Because it wouldn't smell like Meggy in his tent or on the porch. Because she was here, and miserable as he was, he wanted to be where she was.

He didn't want to think about what in God's name he would do when she left.

When the sky began to lighten, Meggy opened her eyes. Tom's bedroll was already done up and stashed in the corner next to her trunk. She stared at it while she began to plan her day. First breakfast for herself and the two boys, then a bit of personal laundry and maybe a bath. After supper she would ask Tom to look at Seth's broken arm. Another day, two at the most, and the boy could return to the bunkhouse with the men. Nobby, too, she supposed.

Now why didn't that make her happy?

She flopped out of bed, donned a fresh shirtwaist and her work skirt behind the screen, then rolled up her pallet. Tiptoeing past the sleeping boys, she stepped outside and down the pine-needle-strewn path to the cookhouse. She would bring their breakfast back on a tray.

The instant she set foot on the porch, she could hear Fong in the kitchen, banging skillets on the stovetop. She started forward, then noticed a shadowed figure off to one side of the dining room.

Tom sat at the far table, hunched over a tin mug of coffee. She moved past him, toward the open kitchen door. "Good morning."

No answer.

She dragged her gaze away from him and stepped into the kitchen. "Good morning, Fong."

"Not good morning, missy." The Chinese cook was dropping bacon slices into a smoke-blackened pan. "Fox chew at boss's belly again. Make bad tempered like dragon." He pantomimed blowing flames out of his mouth.

Meggy sank onto the straight-backed chair next to the small kitchen table. "What seems to be the problem?"

"Not sleep. Not eat."

"But he *did* sl—" She broke off as Fong sent her a curious look.

"Lie down, maybe. Not sleep. Hand shakes like drink too much."

"But he didn't!" At least she didn't think so. She had been awake for hours herself, waiting to hear his breathing settle into a regular pattern so she could relax. The thought that they had both lain in the dark, listening to the other, struck her as funny. She clapped her hand over her mouth to stifle a giggle.

"Not funny, missy. Not good cut timber with dragon-boss."

Meggy nodded and rose in silence to tend the sizzling bacon while Fong mixed up pancake batter. While he ladled spoonfuls onto the iron griddle, she sneaked a glance into the dining room.

Tom hadn't moved a single inch. His dark head was bent, both hands cradling the enamelware mug before him.

"More coffee tame dragon maybe," Fong murmured behind her.

Meggy turned over the last bacon slice, then wrapped a dish towel around the handle of the blue-speckled enamelware coffeepot. Her shoes made a soft tapping sound as she moved toward Tom.

"More coffee?"

He shoved the mug toward her without looking up. "Thanks."

She filled his cup, then set the pot down on the table. "What is wrong, Tom?"

"Nothing. Everything," he amended.

"Tell me. I trust you will be frank, as I have been with you. It's not as if we are…well, strangers, after what has, um, passed between us."

He raised his head and looked at her with eyes so dark they looked purple. "Might be better if we were."

"Yes, perhaps," she murmured.

"All right, here goes. But you're not going to like it one bit."

Chapter Fifteen

"It's like this, Meggy. Seth's broken arm won't keep him off the crew much more than another day. I'll put him on fire watch, so he won't have to move around much, and he'll want to bed down in the bunkhouse again. That leaves you and me...well, that leaves us—"

"Alone in the cabin together," she finished. "I quite see the problem, and I do appreciate your thinking about a possible solution."

"There is no solution," Tom said in a quiet voice. "If you were some other kind of woman, the kind I could hire on as a bullcook and not give a damn if she gets a hand laid on her backside—excuse the language—well, then, it wouldn't matter. But you're not."

"And that changes everything, doesn't it?"

Tom nodded, circling his forefinger around and around the rim of his mug. Meggy stared at his tanned, capable-looking hand. "You don't know how many times in the last twenty-four hours I have caught myself wondering why 'good' women bake bread and scrub floors and 'bad' women have all the fun."

Tom frowned. "You don't want to think those thoughts, Meggy. That's why you can't stay at Devil's Camp."

"You are correct, of course."

"Yeah, I know. When you first arrived and took up residence in that cabin Peabody built, I couldn't wait to get rid of you."

She tipped the coffeepot to refill his cup, then realized he hadn't taken as much as a sip. "Two days ago I was in a fizz and bustle to leave. At this moment, I am finding it more difficult than I expected."

Tom's head came up, and his eyes sought hers. "I'll tell you the truth, Meggy, I don't want to see you go. You've given me something…." He lowered his voice to a murmur. "Not only that night in the woods, but something else. Can't exactly explain it. And I, well, I want you to trust me, but—"

"It is myself I don't trust, Tom. Not you."

"Jumping scorpions," he muttered.

"My stars and chicken feathers, Mama used to say."

Tom tried to smile. "I'll take you down to Tennant, to catch the noon stage," he said in a tired voice.

"You need not, Tom. I know you are needed on the crew, and that you have a lumber quota to meet."

"I want to," he said shortly. "I don't think I can let you go, otherwise."

"Tom." She barely breathed his name. "Will you look at Seth's arm now, before I get the boys' breakfast? I don't believe I will come up just now."

He held her gaze so long her face heated. "Sure. I'll bring the wagon around at half past seven. Dress light, looks to be a scorcher."

She rose and lifted the coffeepot off the table. *A scorcher.* She almost laughed out loud. A scorcher was an old Southern expression Aunt Hattie used to describe a grand and irresistible passion.

The wagon bounced and rattled its way down the twisting mountain road at a bone-jarring pace. Meggy clung to the wooden bench with both hands, trying not to lean against Tom on the sharp turns. The somber goodbyes of the crew and the shy hugs from Nobby and Seth had left her shaken. Instead of her usual jittery excitement at the prospect of travel, a lead ball seemed to weigh down her insides. She could not think of a single sensible word to say.

Tom, too, was silent.

And he remained so, all during the twelve-mile trip to Tennant. At the edge of the tiny town nestled in the flat, narrow valley, Tom slowed the horse to a walk. Still he said nothing, and when they drew up in front of the weathered sign for the Mountain View Hotel, he reined in and just sat there without moving.

A silent Meggy sat beside him. The stagecoach would be along in an hour, and then this whole mixed-up, awful, wonderful episode in her life would be over.

After a long minute, Tom climbed down and hefted her trunk onto the board sidewalk. Then he strode around to her side and held out his hand. The sun beat down like a hammer, the heat pounding against her temples in relentless waves. A scorcher, he'd said. She winced.

Inside she felt cold. Her head didn't ache, exactly, it just seemed to float off her neck as if it were filled with the pine-scented air. She would never forget that sharp, green smell.

Her vision blurred. She stared at her trunk, then at the shimmery red-and-yellow hotel sign. Her legs felt as if they were made out of cotton. She took Tom's outstretched hand.

The instant his fingers closed over hers, an ache ripped through her belly. *Don't think, don't feel. Just do what has to be done.*

She placed one black leather shoe on the wheel rim and let Tom help her down to the walkway.

He gestured to her trunk. "This will be okay here till the stage comes." His voice sounded hoarse.

"I will wait in the hotel. You must start back now, to make it in time for supper."

He nodded, but still he stood facing her, an odd light in his eyes. Meggy's throat closed over a lump the size of her mother's silver tea ball. On impulse she thrust her hand toward him; she could at least shake hands.

Tom took a step toward her and pulled her into his arms. "Goddammit, Meggy. I'm sorry."

A needle lanced straight into her heart. "I am not sorry. It was good and beautiful with you, not at all like Aunt Hattie said. I will never be sorry." She spoke the words into his soft flannel shirt, smelling perspiration and the faint scent of pine soap and musky pipe tobacco.

She looked up into his lean, sun-bronzed face.

"Goodbye, Tom."

"Goodbye, Meggy." Then his jaw tightened and he muttered, "Oh, hell," and his mouth found hers. It was a long, sweet kiss, and in the middle of it he lifted his head and whispered her name. "Meggy. *Meggy.*"

"Hush," she murmured. "Kiss me once more and then go."

When he released her they stood together, not quite touching, their bodies trembling. With a soft groan Tom wheeled away, walked the two steps to the wagon and climbed back up onto the seat. Without looking at her he turned the horse and headed north toward the mountains.

As he passed, he turned toward her and snapped one hand up in a solemn salute.

Her eyes swimming, Meggy straightened her shoulders and brought her stiffened fingers to her hat brim.

Damn Yankees. They're always doing something to make me cry.

Feeling more wretched than she could ever remember, Meggy walked into the Mountain View Hotel and rang the bell at the registration desk. After a moment, the clerk appeared from a doorway, wiping his mouth with a napkin.

"Yes, ma'am? What can I do for you?"

"What time will the stagecoach arrive?" Her voice wobbled, but she didn't care. Her heart, her whole life at the moment was just as wobbly.

"Today, ma'am, not at all. Got held up in Scot River and won't be in till noon tomorrow."

"Noon tomorrow," she echoed. She could barely make sense of the words. "Tomorrow."

"Yes, ma'am. Only one stage between Scot River and Eagle Point, and the driver busted an axle yesterday."

Suddenly she jolted into awareness. "Tomorrow! But…"

"You hungry, ma'am? Got a nice dining room back there." He jerked his head at the door behind him. "Cook just got some fine thick steaks. Don't mind my sayin' so, ma'am, you look a bit peaked.

Would you care to sit down? I can fetch a glass of cool lemonade if you'd like.''

She shook her head. ''N-no, thank you.'' Oh, she was hungry all right. And thirsty, too. But not for meat or drink. It was her body that ached to be filled, her soul that thirsted. *Oh, Aunt Hattie, what have I done? I have fallen in love with the one man I cannot have.*

She wanted to weep, to scream, to beat her hands against the invisible cage that imprisoned her. She closed her eyes as a huge knot tightened inside her chest.

''Would you have a room available?''

''Oh, yes, ma'am. Top of the stairs, first door on the left. Here's the key.'' He dropped the metal object into her shaking hand.

Meggy turned toward the staircase and grasped the banister to steady herself.

''I'll bring your bag up for you. Maybe you got some smelling salts in there.''

She glanced back to the desk. ''My trunk...''

''I'll watch it.'' He peered at her from behind the desk. ''Don't you worry none, ma'am. Everything's gonna be fine.''

Tears stung her eyes. She tried to smile. Everything would not be fine. Nothing would be ''fine'' ever again. Not without the man she'd come to love. Without Tom.

Oh dear God, why did You tempt me to come out West? What was Your purpose?

She couldn't think. And surely she shouldn't question the mysterious workings of the Lord, in any case. *Forgive me, Lord. I did not mean to sound so peevish. Surely You know what You are doing, even if I do not.*

The room was dim and cool. A soft breeze fluttered the spotless curtains at the window overlooking the street below. She couldn't bear to look out, couldn't bear to gaze down that empty road, wishing…

With trembling fingers she unpinned her hat and set it on the polished chest of drawers. She couldn't bear to look in the framed mirror that hung above the chest, either. Methodically she unbuttoned her blouse, stepped out of her skirt and her petticoat. What insanity, to wear petticoats—two of them!—on a day as hot as this one. Even her underdrawers were damp with perspiration.

She unlaced her corset—another insanity—and let it drop to the Turkey carpet. Stepping out of her shoes, she unrolled the white stockings down her knees and ankles. Such a lot of layers and trussing-up the female of the species endured. Tom wore nothing under his trousers. At least he hadn't that night in the forest.…

With a groan she poured water from an ewer into a white china basin and dipped a clean cloth into it. Tom's body was lean and hard and…straightforward.

Male. And beautiful, so beautiful. She had touched him everywhere and marveled. Tom was…Tom.

Her vision blurred. She slipped off her shimmy and sank onto the puffy bed quilt. It was cool, so cool and smooth against her heated skin. If only the blood would stop pounding through her temples. She laid the damp cloth over her eyes and folded her hands on her midriff. *Oh, God. God, please show me the way.*

Her voice rose, thin and uneven, as if it came from somewhere else. "'…and rather than submit to shame, to die we would prefer; so cheer for the Bonnie Blue Flag….'"

Tom lifted the whip, then let his hand fall. The horse had slowed to a lazy walk, and he hadn't noticed the fact until the wagon wheel rolled into a chuckhole and didn't roll out because it was turning so slowly. He dropped his forehead into his hand.

Horses were smarter than people. When a horse felt something was wrong, it didn't go forward unless it was driven. Well, that was the difference, he guessed. A man could be driven just as hard to go against his instincts, but at least a man could think about what he was doing. A man could think about it and feel the bite of regret every step of the way.

Hell, she was only a woman. Yet she had reached into his private self, into his soul. She had soothed his troubled spirit in ways no woman ever had—not his mother, not even his sister. For the first time since Susanna's death Tom could face the possibility—the probability, even—that she had indeed been guilty. She had been a spy. She had done what she thought was right and had given her life to that cause.

Her guilt no longer mattered. You loved people even if they had flaws. His father had been blinded by his own high standards and opinions; his mother had been overproud of the family position. Family honor.

Susanna had the same blind spots, but it didn't matter any longer. She had marched to her own drumbeat and now she was gone. He had taken responsibility for her when Mother died. He had cared for his sister. Guided and protected her. At least he'd done the best he could.

Somehow it was Meggy who had helped him see that, helped him ease the burden his conscience had carried all these years.

Meggy. He groaned aloud, and the horse pricked up its ears.

He wanted to hear her voice. He wanted to inhale her smell.

He wanted to just *be* with her.

He wanted…

The minute he turned the mare around, she began to pick up her pace.

"Meggy?" Tom rapped on the door again. "Meggy, it's Tom."

The door cracked open, then swung wide.

"Tom! What are you doing here?"

"I think we have some unfinished business." He pressed his hand against the oak panel.

Meggy stared at him. She stood before him clad in nothing but a flimsy-looking camisole—hastily donned, if he was any judge. And a rumpled pair of pantalettes with lace around the hem. In her hands she twisted a damp cloth.

"The stage has been delayed. I—I was lying down."

Tom looked past her to the bed. The imprint of where her body had rested was visible on the soft counterpane.

He shut the door behind him. "You were going to spend the night," he observed.

"Y-yes. And catch the stage tomorrow. At noon." Her eyes did not leave his face. Deep within their soft green depths he saw a flicker of something.

Was she glad he'd come back?

Or filled with pain at the prospect of saying goodbye once again? God knows it had been difficult enough the first time. He wasn't sure he could face it again.

"Tom," she said. "Oh, Tom, I'm so glad…." She looked at the rag in her hand. "I had such an awful burning inside my head. Well, inside all of me, really."

He lifted the cloth from her fingers, dropped it to

the floor, then pulled her forward until his mouth brushed her temple.

"Oh, God, Meggy, I couldn't do it. Couldn't leave you without...without—"

"Yes," she murmured. "I quite understand. I ache all over to be with you."

Instantly he felt alive, his nerves thrumming, his skin hot, as if sharp-pointed needles were dancing over him. He bent his head.

"This is purely scandalous, isn't it?" she whispered against his cheek.

"It is," he agreed. He caught her mouth under his. "I can't help it. It's what's between us."

She breathed his name. "Kiss me again. Please, again."

He let himself taste her, then slid his tongue past her teeth, deep inside her warm mouth, and let his senses drown in her sweetness. Her amazing softness. Her strength.

"Meggy," he gasped. "There's never been anyone like you."

"You have had others, of course." She murmured the words against his neck. "I have had only you. And only once."

"And?" He could barely draw breath.

Her voice trembled. "It was wondrous. You know that it was."

"I do know."

"But it wasn't enough."

"I know that, too. I feel something different happening when I'm with you, as if time has stopped and is just waiting for us. Waiting until we're ready for the earth to take another turn."

"How long will it wait?" she asked in a gentle voice.

"As long as it takes. I want you, Meggy. I lie awake at night wanting you."

She gave a soft laugh. "It was you who took that first pie I made, wasn't it? And left the gold piece?"

"No, but I should have. You scared me. I wanted you out of Devil's Camp. I should have bought you off."

"Now I am out of Devil's Camp, Tom. I think it is this that you wanted." She pressed her mouth to his. "What we both wanted."

He rested his hands at her waist, then raised his thumbs to brush them across her breasts. Her small hands found the buttons of his shirt. Starting at the neck, she undid them slowly, working downward toward his belt.

He didn't move, wasn't even sure his heart was beating. She tugged his shirt free, pushed it aside. Her soft breath washed over his bare skin and then he felt her mouth on him, her quick, sure fingers at his belt buckle.

He must be dreaming. The world had stopped and they were suspended together in a quiet, peaceful place where nothing could intrude. He slid his hands under the camisole and touched her, smoothed his fingertips over her soft nipples until they rose and stiffened.

"Tom," she moaned. The sound ignited a flame in his loins.

The buckle loosened. She slipped both hands beneath his trousers.

"Underdrawers," she breathed. "I've been wondering...."

He almost laughed out loud. But her hands, her warm, steady fingers unsnapped the waistband and slid inside. Tom tipped his head back and stared up at the ceiling. She had no idea what she was doing to him.

Just keep breathing. Count something. He fought for control with every ounce of determination he had.

He drew the camisole over her head and bent his head to her breast. His tongue flicked forward, then back, until her hands stilled. She shrugged off the pantalettes and raised one bare knee to his thigh.

He couldn't stand it. Stepping away from her, he jerked off his boots, then his trousers and drawers. When he moved forward he cupped both hands around her buttocks and lifted.

Meggy could not describe what was happening to her. Afterward, she thought it was some sort of enchantment he had cast on her body, for she could no more stop the exquisite sensations or the terrible hunger that ripped through her than she could fly.

Her knee caressed his bare thigh, and then his hands pulled her close, until their bodies were touching. Desire made her light-headed.

He drew one finger along the folds of her most intimate place, and the small cry she gave seemed to encourage him to do more. She raised her leg higher. Opened wider.

His erect member brushed her belly, and he sucked in his breath with a sharp hiss. "Meggy...Meggy, I want to..."

His finger slid inside where it was wet and swollen. It felt so good, *so good*. She felt light and free and utterly shameless.

Oh, Aunt Hattie, how could you live without knowing this happiness just once?

With a low growl, Tom picked her up and carried her to the bed. Then he lay beside her, holding her close, his breathing uneven, his raw, masculine scent overpowering her. She clung to him, let him touch her in ways she'd never dreamed of. His fingers explored, his tongue followed, spreading heat where it met her flesh, in the shell of her ear, behind her knees. Inside her entrance.

"Talk to me, Meggy. Tell me what you want."

"You," she whispered. "Only you."

His mouth found hers, his lips hot and seeking. Nothing had ever felt like this, tasted like this. It was glorious. It felt as if there was another being within her, a woman she had never before recognized as part of herself. After this, nothing would ever be the same.

He mounted her, murmured her name as he entered her and began to move.

"Yes," she moaned against his lips. "Oh, yes, Tom. *Yes.*"

His body convulsed, and with a choked sob he held perfectly still for an instant, then cried out and plunged deeper. She felt it coming—an expectancy, as if she were climbing up and up and all at once she hung suspended at the top. Waves of pleasure took her, blotted out everything but the man who moved inside her. Behind her closed eyes, light shimmered and pulsed. A scream escaped her, and then Tom was holding her, crying out in turn, his own body jerking and trembling.

He moved inside her, and another spasm shook her. And then another.

"No more," she murmured. "I will surely die."

But he did not stop, and she held him tight through the pulsing.

"Oh, Meggy, Meggy. Let me. I don't want it to end." He licked her nipples and she clung to him and wept.

It was close to dawn when they slept at last, sated and shaken by the power of what they had known. The last thing Meggy remembered was Tom's mouth against her temple, his low, unsteady voice.

"No man could ask for more than this."

Chapter Sixteen

The following afternoon, the stage rolled in an hour late. Meggy unclenched her hands and walked outside into the glare, and the grizzled driver leaned down from his perch. "That yer trunk, ma'am?"

She nodded, unable to speak over the ache in her throat.

"Wherebouts ya headin', ma'am?"

"East," she managed to reply.

"Hop in, then. I'll load yer baggage after I wet my whistle. Ain't no other passengers, so make yourself to home."

Meggy hoisted her carpetbag into the coach and stepped in after it. The shades had been drawn over the window openings to keep out the heat, and with a sigh of resignation she settled into the dim interior and closed her swollen eyelids.

She had come out West to marry Walter Peabody, to find for herself what all women long for—a home, a family, a man she could love for the rest of her days. Perhaps she was destined never to have such things. The only man she had ever felt strongly about was not her Southern kinsman, Walter Peabody, but her Northern enemy, Colonel Tom Randall.

And Tom was a man so scarred by his past losses he would never be able to consider a relationship of commitment.

The carriage jiggled as the driver climbed back up onto his seat. "All aboard," he yelled. He snapped the reins over the four-horse team and the coach plunged forward. Meggy opened her eyes, felt her stomach tighten. *Now what?*

She pulled up the shade over the window and leaned forward for one last look at the timbered mountains to the north. Oh, it was beautiful, she had to admit. So lush, so many shades of green even though seared by the relentless sun all summer long. Tall, straight fir trees covered the steep slopes, and sugar pine and vine maples filled in the lower levels.

Her gaze followed the ridge line, where at this very moment the Devil's Camp crew would be cutting timber. The top of the tree-furred mountain blended into the sky, and a golden haze hung over the forest. Sunset this evening would be lovely. Already the sky glowed rosy-orange behind the—

Meggy shot upright on the hard leather seat. It was midday, too early for the sky to color like that. It took a full minute for the truth to register.

"Stop!" she screamed.

At the same instant she heard the driver's guttural shout. "Fire on the mountain!"

"Stop!"

"Cain't stop, ma'am. When the mountains burn, ya cain't do nuthin' but run like hell. Hang on!"

His whip cracked and the coach picked up speed. Dazed with horror, Meggy stared up the mountainside while her heart thumped wildly under her white muslin waist. The narrow road to Devil's Camp snaked up the grade to her left.

She could barely discern its path.

She poked her head out the opening and shouted at the driver. "Will it spread?"

"Shore thing, ma'am. But don't you worry none, we got the fastest horses this side of the Willamette. We'll be to the camp trail and beyond in a quarter of an hour. Fire won't catch us."

But the crew! Nobby and Seth and the others. *Tom.*

Dear God, they would be trapped!

The stage hurtled on. Meggy hung out the window, straining to see through the thickening haze. Her eyes smarted and now she could smell the acrid scent of burning brush. Halfway up the mountain, dirty gray smoke billowed into the air. As she watched, the dark line of smoke and ash moved upward, toward the summit.

Toward Devil's Camp.

The stagecoach headed into the spreading haze.

The sunlight dimmed, and a strange yellow glow lit the sky. Flecks of feathery ash floated in the air, coating the road ahead with gray frost.

All at once the carriage slowed. Meggy leaned out of the window to see why.

Up ahead, where the Tennant road met the wagon trail up to Devil's Camp, stood a huddle of men. Loggers. Meggy recognized Swede Jensen's red wool cap.

The stage drew up in a cloud of dust. "You fellers needin' transport?" the driver yelled.

"Ve haf oxen and two wagons," Swede shouted back. "Ve be fine."

Meggy scrabbled at the door handle, yanked it open and scrambled out. The crew stood in a knot between a team of oxen and three or four horses and some wagons, one of which she recognized. The wagon Tom had used to bring her into Tennant yesterday.

She caught sight of Sergeant O'Malley, standing with one arm around Seth's trussed-up shoulder. A white-faced Nobby clung to Swede's trouser leg. Meggy headed toward them.

"Where's Tom?"

O'Malley stepped forward to intercept her. "Now, don't you be worryin' none, Miss Meggy."

"Then where is he? I see the wagon, but—"

The sergeant laid a restraining hand on her shoulder. "We met him coming up from town. He left us the wagon, took a horse and went back up. Seems we forgot to bring his pet raven."

Meggy's brain reeled. "He went back to camp to rescue a bird? How could you have let him—"

"Oh, now, Miss Meggy. 'Tis not a matter of 'let.' Nobody gives order to Colonel Tom. You oughtta know that by now."

"What I know is that he's a d-damn fool Y-Yankee," Meggy stammered. Oh, she *wished* she wouldn't cry in front of the men!

The stage driver leaned down. "You comin', ma'am? Gotta keep movin' east or else head on back to Tennant. Otherwise t'aint safe."

"I'm…" Meggy closed her mouth and clutched both arms over her chest. She wanted to, oh, how she wanted to climb back onto her seat and leave Oregon and everything in it far, far behind.

But she couldn't. She couldn't make her feet move toward the stagecoach.

"I will be staying," she said at last. "Take my trunk on to your next stop, if you please."

"Now, Miss Meggy," O'Malley began. "A lady like yourself can't just—"

"Fiddlesticks! A lady can do anything any other woman can do. Just you watch me!"

The coach rumbled on its way. In its wake of swirling dust and ash, Meggy stood absolutely still.

Just what was it a woman *would* do?

* * *

"Stand out of my path, Sergeant O'Malley."

"Meggy, girl, you don't know what you're doin'. The horse you can take and welcome, but 'tis daft to head up a mountain that's on fire."

"That is precisely what Tom did, however. Are you saying your colonel is daft?"

"Ah, now, miss, don't you be puttin' words in me mouth."

Meggy leaned forward in the saddle. "Release the bridle, Mr. O'Malley. Do it now, so I will waste no more time."

"I can't, lass. I can't bring myself to let you do this."

Meggy pulled her father's revolver from the travel bag she'd stowed across her lap. With trembling hands, she cocked it and leveled it at O'Malley's red-bearded chin. "You know I can shoot straight," she said in as level a tone as she could manage.

"But you wouldn't, I'm guessin'. Now, would you, Meggy?"

"I would not want to," she admitted. "But I will if I have to. You must let me go after him."

O'Malley tightened his hold on the mare's bridle. "It's too dangerous. People die in timber fires. Even the colonel—why, he might take a wrong trail, find himself trapped and not be able to—"

"All the more reason why I must go. There is something I must tell him." She slipped the revolver inside her travel bag, then reached down and laid her small hand over the sergeant's beefy paw. "Please, Michael. Please."

The sergeant released his breath in a whoosh. "I'm damned if I do, damned if I don't. All right, then, away with you. Never could stand a woman's tears. Never could argue a woman out of a single thing."

Meggy turned the horse onto the Devil's Camp trail and jabbed her heels into its flanks. The mare bolted forward. She pulled her travel valise tight against her chest and held on.

Tom's eyes burned as the smoke thickened around him. Keeping a sharp eye on the wind direction, he headed up the back side of the ridge. No sign of flames yet. He might still have time.

The raven's wooden cage dangled off the horse's rump, tied to the saddle with a length of braided manila rope. "Damn-broke-damn-broke," the raven chirped in a gravelly singsong voice.

"Shut up," Tom growled. He twitched a blanket over the cage. He wasn't broke yet, but he would be if he couldn't reach the side-stacked timber the crew had stashed along the river's edge. There were three piles, each one a triangle-shaped tower of thick Douglas fir and cedar logs, anchored by a single key log wedged at just the right angle and pinned by a single stake driven into the ground. All he had to do was chop through the stake and knock the key log loose, then get out of the way before the whole shebang rolled over him on its way down the steep incline into the river.

Where the trail leveled out, he reined in and pulled his neckerchief up over his mouth and nose. The air smelled acrid, and the smoke was so thick he could barely see. Still, if he stuck close to the river, he'd stumble across one of the side-stacks sooner or later; they were only a mile or two apart.

The timber would float downriver, carried by the current all the way to the valley floor, if he was lucky. Once it was there, the crew could attack the jammed-up logs with peavey hooks. That way, he could still salvage some of the timber from the season's cut— maybe enough to pay the men's wages and move them on to a new camp.

He ran his hand over his stinging eyes. If he was *really* lucky he'd get out of this alive.

He headed the horse cross-country, toward what he knew was the most remote pile of stacked timber. If he worked fast, he could get to the second stack before the logs from the first one reached that far downstream, and so on until he'd released all three stacks. This way, in case the fire caught up to him—or, worse, started chasing him—he could work his way back down the mountain.

"Broke-broke-broke," the raven croaked from under the blanket. "Meggy-meggy-broke."

Blasted bird. The first chance he got he'd toss it,

cage and all, onto a floating log raft and hope a spike-booted lumberjack with a sense of humor would adopt it. Reaching behind him, Tom patted the double-edged ax he'd tied in back of the saddle. His ticket out of debt. That and locating one of those side-stacks before he was burned to a crisp.

The wind gusted, and a shower of gray-white ash rained down on his shoulders and thighs. Thicker than it was half an hour ago, Tom noted. He lowered his head and picked up his pace.

Meggy lifted the flap and peered into the dim interior of Tom's tent. "Tom? Tom, are you here?"

Everything looked as it had before, except that the raven's cage was gone. She backed out of the tent, remounted and cupped her hands around her mouth. "Tom? Tom, where are you?"

She shouted until her throat hurt, but heard nothing except the sighing of pine branches above her head. No chittering of birds. Nothing. The quiet was unnatural. Even the light was strange, hazy and yellow, with flecks of ash drifting over everything.

Where would he go? Surely not farther up the mountain?

She hadn't met him on the trail she'd ridden up, and as far as she knew there was no other way down to the valley. Had he left the logging path and headed into the timber?

Instinctively, she headed for the river, then began

working her way slowly upstream. The air grew thick as pea soup, choking her lungs as she tried to breathe. Pulling the mare up, she groped under her skirt and ripped off a strip of her muslin petticoat. She tied it about her face, leaving only her eyes and the top of her head exposed, and then headed again for the river. She would soak the cloth in the water, and wet her skirts down as well.

Tom's throat was raw. His eyes stung from the smoke-thickened air. He urged his horse upriver through the choking haze until he stumbled on the first of the timber piles he and his crew had stacked along the bank.

He looked up into the orange-tinted sky. He could hear the insistent roar of flames from the other side of the summit, a mile farther up, and the distant crack of trees exploding in the heat. How much time did he have before the blaze reached him?

He drew up his mount and mopped his eyes with his shirtsleeve. He'd been caught in only one forest fire, on an army reconnaissance patrol in the Okanagan wilderness. One experience like that in a lifetime was plenty. From the amount of smoke and the look of the sky, he'd better get moving if he wanted to live through this one.

He edged the horse clear of the timber stack, dismounted and dragged the double-edged ax from behind the saddle. The riverbank was steep here, and slippery. Back in June he'd purposely chosen this spot to pile the lengths of timber; the bank dropped off sharply, and once the key log was released, the logs would tumble free and roll into the water, to be carried downstream.

He hoped. He ran his thumb gingerly over the ax blade. Sharp enough to slice through steel. He moved into position between the stack and the river and planted his feet apart. He'd have to chop through the pole that pinned the key log, then jump clear before the rolling timber caught him.

Checking the location of his horse, he raised the ax to his shoulder. One well-aimed blow should do it.

He kept his eyes on the pinning pole, lifted the ax off his shoulder and stepped into his backstroke. He swung the head high and to the right, then brought it down. The blade bit through the peeled pine branch, and the key log shuddered.

The pole twisted to one side and the stack began to groan. Tom grabbed the ax and sprinted toward his horse just as the key log shifted and broke free.

The entire pile crumbled into a rolling mass of timber, hurtling past him to hit the river with a great splash. Under different circumstances, a team of river-rats with cant hooks and peaveys would be waiting downstream to corral the floating timbers into a log boom. Working alone, Tom figured the best he could do was to get them moving and hope they didn't jam up.

But the more logs he released, the greater the chances of a log jam. Which meant he had to race downriver and release the next stack before the first load reached it. Might have been easier to work up the mountain instead of down, but with a forest fire nipping at his heels, he wanted to save as much timber as he could.

He stowed the ax and pulled himself into the saddle. He could make it to the next side-stack in time, if he was careful.

And if the fire didn't swallow up the ridge too soon.

Meggy tightened her hand on the reins and nosed her mount to the right, as close to the river's edge as she could manage. The heavy air pressed down on her, searing her throat with ashy grit at every breath. The scrap of petticoat muslin she'd dipped in the river just minutes ago was already dry; she'd have to soak it again. Before her, the bank eased into a narrow stretch of sand. Behind her, tree branches sighed. The wind was picking up.

Up ahead...

She wiped her burning eyes with her dampened skirt hem and tried to focus. The sky, rosy-orange a moment ago, now looked yellow and slightly grainy with bits of swirling ash. The forest floor, once the rich brown of pine needles and soft duff, grew more and more indistinct as the dirty gray flecks sifted over everything.

She was correct in deciding to skirt the river. Otherwise, without a clear path and with no way to determine the position of the sun, she would become hopelessly disoriented. Lost on a mountain that was on fire.

Despite the searing heat, a chill went through her. She would *not* get lost. She would keep her head clear, keep her eyes on the river and find Tom. Any moment now, she would see his tall form riding toward her. Any moment now the fear that clogged her throat and made her forearms prickle would melt away. Tom was all right.

He had to be.

She kneed the mare forward, picked her way carefully through huckleberry bushes and patches of nettle, keeping her head down to make breathing easier. She would not think about how far up into the timber she had pushed herself. How much closer she would have to get to the fire she knew was raging just over the ridge before she found Tom and they could flee downstream, out of danger.

Every muscle in her body tensed as she pressed on. Instinct told her to turn back, to go down the mountain now, while she had a chance.

She could not do it. It would be unthinkable to leave the man she loved alone in this hellish place.

She would keep going.

Chapter Seventeen

He would wait. It might be an hour or half a day, but it wouldn't matter. He'd laid his plans carefully, so carefully, and no one would ever know. No one.

It would be so easy. He wasn't stupid. He saw right off how it would be, how he could work it. Another man, someone with no brains, might not know how. Might not know the lay of the land like he did. He hadn't pissed all over this mountain for nothing. He'd seen everything plain and simple, and he'd planned it all out in his head.

Now all he had to do was wait.

Tom guided his horse through the choking smoke, keeping within sight of the slow-moving river as he worked his way downstream. It couldn't be much far- ther—he'd already ridden well over a mile from the first side-stack back up the mountain. Another couple of turns in the trail and he'd—

He reined up and squinted into the haze. Something, or someone, was moving up ahead of him. He caught just a glimpse of whatever it was, there at the edge of that stand of scrub pine. He watched the shadowy shape and frowned.

Moved too deliberately for an animal, he reasoned. His scalp prickled. What would a man be doing up this far on a burning mountain?

Letting his free hand drop to the horse's neck, he smoothed his fingers over the coarse hair and prayed the animal wouldn't nicker.

The figure moved toward him. A horse and a rider. Face covered against the smoke and clad in black…

Good God, it was a woman!

"Meggy!" The name slipped out of his mouth in a hoarse cough. "Meggy, what the hell—"

"Tom?" She stepped the horse forward. "Is that you, Tom? Oh, thank the Lord, I've found you."

"*Found* me? I'm not lost! What the devil are you doing here? I thought you were on the stage from Tennant."

"I was. And then I saw the sky all red and your men gathered at the road head, and I—"

He grabbed the reins out of her hands. "You crazy damn fool woman. Don't you know a forest fire when you see one? Turn that horse around and get out of here, pronto."

She didn't move. "Mr. O'Malley said you had ridden up here. I came to find you." Her voice sounded raspy.

Tom shoved the canteen he'd looped over his saddle horn toward her. "Drink," he ordered.

She unscrewed the cap and tipped the metal container to her mouth.

"Now, get going."

She pressed the canteen into his hand and ran her tongue over her lips. "Not without you."

"Are you loco? God knows how long before that fire comes over the summit. I've got stacks of felled timber to see to before it starts down this side."

Meggy nodded but didn't budge. "I saw some piled up by the river back a ways. We'll do it together."

Tom slapped the reins into her hands. "The hell we will. Head downriver. Now! That's an order. I'll be right behind you."

He thought she smiled as she turned her horse, but he couldn't be sure. Anyway, it didn't matter. They were both heading away from the fire.

Around the next bend he came upon the second timber stack, larger than the first, but closer to the bank. When the key log broke free on this one, he'd have to scramble.

He dismounted and reached for the ax. "Keep moving," he yelled at Meggy.

She moved a few yards beyond the end of the stack

and twisted to face him. "I have something to say to you."

He sent her a look that would fry O'Malley's eyebrows, but she sat unmoving, her shoulders set.

"It will wait until you are finished here," she added.

Tom blew his breath out in a muttered curse and stalked across the riverbank to the stake pinning the stacked logs. Raising his arms, he hacked at the pole.

It took two blows, but finally it gave way. He started to jump clear of the tumbling logs, but his boot slipped in the mud. Instantly he righted himself and dived for safety, but a fir timber twisted backward and slammed into his right shoulder.

His arm went numb, but he managed to keep going, barely making it to safety as the stack crashed past him into the river. His lungs laboring, he leaned on his ax for support. The pain hit him like a bolt of lightning, and he went down on one knee.

Then Meggy was beside him, urging him to stand up, drawing him toward his waiting horse.

"Can't mount," he managed to gasp. "Can't move my right arm." He swayed on his feet, willing himself not to black out.

Without a word she lifted the ax away and retied it behind his saddle. Leading his horse close to a downed pine tree, she fixed him with a steady gaze. "Stand on this log," she ordered. "That's how I learned to mount when I was a child."

Tom shuffled forward a few feet and planted his boot on the fallen log. Meggy's small hands clasped his thighs to steady him. The log slanted slightly, caught at one end in the fork of another tree. Gritting his teeth at every step, he inched up its length until his waist was even with the horse's broad back.

He tried to move without jarring his arm, but with every step it felt like his shoulder was on fire. He managed to get his right leg over the horse's rump and then roll clumsily into the saddle.

"Let's go," he shouted. "Keep to the river."

She stayed ahead of him for the agonizing miles it took to reach the third stack of timber. When he reached it he just stared. Maybe he could try it left-handed.

Meggy turned her mount and fell in behind him. "Give me the ax," she said. She reached behind him to untie it.

"You ever use an ax?"

"Only to chop kindling. We had a hired man to cut wood for us."

"It's dangerous."

She flashed him a look. "I know."

"Then why—?"

"Because it's important. You didn't come up here to rescue your pet raven. You came up here to save these logs."

"Meggy, don't try it. I don't want you to risk it."

"You did," she said simply.

"You're more important than the timber. I've got two stacks already on their way downriver. Should be along any minute."

Meggy glanced at the gurgling water. "Then I'd best hurry." She leaned the ax against a vine maple, caught the back side of her skirt and brought the hem up between her knees, tucking it into her waistband. "I can move faster this way," she explained.

"I don't want you to do this."

"I know," she said again. "But you can't stop me. You can't afford to dismount, for you might never get remounted."

Tom thought for a long minute. "Put your mare over here," he instructed at last. "Don't look at anything but the stake, and when it's cut through, don't wait to see what happens, just get out of the way. Make sure you're clear before you stop running."

Meggy nodded. She picked up the ax, hefted it onto her shoulder and paced out her escape route. She had about fifteen feet from the key pole to the end of the stack.

Tom's voice rose over what suddenly sounded like thunder. "Wind's changing. Leave the ax behind."

Again she nodded. She couldn't take her eyes off the slender pine branch straining against the weight of all those monstrous logs. She could whack a Yankee looter on the backside with a broom, bring down a deer with a single shot.

But what on God's green earth made her think she

could step into a logger's shoes and free tons of lumber?

It was her. He couldn't believe his eyes, but there she was, her skirt trussed up like a Turk's. She had a mask over her nose and mouth that looked like a strip of petticoat.

And the colonel. He'd watched that log nip his shoulder. For a moment he'd thought the timber would do the job for him, but then the colonel had stood up and she'd helped him get back on his horse.

They wouldn't get far, even if she managed to swing that ax hard enough to cut the piled-up timber free. The fire was behind them and moving downhill fast. If the stacked timber didn't get them, the flames would.

It would look like an accident.

Meggy set her feet into motion, deliberately forcing them to carry her into position facing the towering pile of logs. The peeled pine branch the crew had pounded into the riverbank looked too spindly to hold back the timber. She knew that, slender as it was, the pole was the only thing standing between those huge logs and her body.

Perspiration slicked her palms. Again she gauged the distance to the end of the stack. Once released, would the logs roll forward faster than she could run to safety?

She lifted the ax, tested its weight and balance in her hands. It was half again as long and twice as heavy as the one she'd used at home. Still, the principle would be the same, would it not? Keep the sharpened head slanted at the proper angle and strike a solid blow.

Then she must quickly wrench the embedded blade free and strike again. She wondered how many blows it would take.

With an inward groan she lowered the heavy steel implement and let it rest on the ground before her. She could not do it. She was not strong enough. She leaned over the oak ax handle, trying to calm her galloping heart. *What a silly, cowardly goose I am.*

Tom's voice came to her over the rush of blood in her ears. "Don't try it, Meggy. It's not worth the risk."

"No," she said after a moment. "Probably not."

"I can see flames coming over the ridge. Let's get out of here before we're trapped."

"Trapped! Oh, Tom, you don't think—"

"No time to argue, just get mounted. Even with good horses we'll be lucky to outrun a forest fire."

Once more Meggy eyed the timber stack that towered over her head. It would help him. He would need the money when—if—they got off this mountain. Tom would need to establish a new lumber camp; his crew was counting on him.

And, she realized with a start, *she* was counting on

him. My stars, wouldn't Aunt Hattie have words about that! Imagine, throwing in her lot with a Northerner. Why on earth?

She hoisted the ax and again swung it to her shoulder. *Why indeed.*

Because she loved him. Because she cared about what Colonel Tom Randall cared about, even if he was a Yankee. And she guessed that included his future in the lumbering business.

After all, it might be *her* future as well.

She walked to her mare and made a show of checking her carpetbag and adjusting the bridle. "You go on ahead, Tom. It is most unladylike to mount with my skirt trussed up like this. I...I don't want you to watch."

He gave her a lopsided grin. "I've seen everything there is to see. However, I won't watch. I will wait, however."

"Tom..."

"I know what you're thinking, Meggy. Give it up."

She made no response. Instead, she moved gingerly to within striking distance of the pine stake pinning the stacked lumber.

"Meggy, dammit, put that ax down."

"No." She touched the blade to the stake, mentally selected her cut point. "We need this timber."

"Meg—"

"Hush up, Tom. I must concentrate."

She kept her gaze on the short length of pine, raised the blade and stepped into the blow. The sharp steel edge crunched home.

One more. She wrenched the head free and lifted it again.

The damaged stake made a cracking sound, and then with a squeal began to bend under the force of the logs pressing behind it.

"Run!" Tom yelled. "Move!"

Meggy dropped the ax and propelled her legs in the direction of his voice. Behind her a thunk sounded, followed by a grinding noise. The logs were rolling.

She put her head down and dived for her horse.

Tom's good hand was there. She gripped it hard, listened to the timber crash into the river with a slap and a sploosh. Then she scrambled into the saddle.

Glowing embers floated in the air before her. Live embers, she realized. Any one of them could start a blaze in the thick brush surrounding them.

"Stay with me," Tom shouted. He slapped the rump of her mount with his good hand. "Go!"

His horse jolted forward. She did her best to follow him through the smoke-thick air, but she was barely able to see the rear of his horse.

Suddenly he halted. It happened so fast Meggy almost blundered into him, but she pulled hard to the left, reined up beside him and peered into the gloom.

A figure stood in their path, feet planted wide, aiming a revolver at Tom's heart.

Chapter Eighteen

"Afternoon, Tom."

Meggy's belly gave a sickening lurch at the sound of the man's voice.

"Price," Tom acknowledged. "I thought you left camp with the rest of the crew."

"That's what I wanted you to think. Ain't been easy breathin' smoke and cinders, waitin' on ya all this time."

"Guess not," Tom responded in a level tone. "Care to tell me why you did?"

As he spoke, he lowered his left hand to his thigh, as if resting the fingers holding the reins. Out of the corner of her eye, Meggy watched those fingers edge toward the blanket covering the birdcage that hung off the cantle. She jostled her mare to distract Price's attention.

"Nah. Don't believe I do, Tom. Makes no never-mind, now that I've got the upper hand."

Tom nodded. "Miss Hampton's got no part in our quarrel, Verg. And my back's beginning to feel a mite warm with the flames moving toward us like they are. How about letting her ride on ahead?"

She grasped instantly what he was trying to do—get her out of the line of fire. She also saw the blanket start to slide off the slatted cage. One black wing became visible.

"Tom," she said under her breath.

He didn't move, but she knew he was listening.

"You funnin' me, Colonel? After all the work I gone to, why would I let the lady go?"

"Move left," Tom intoned. "Now look, Verg. Miss Hampton's been in the saddle all day. She's so tuckered she can hardly control her horse."

He poked his stirrup into her mare's side. "Whoa there, Nancy."

Meggy sidestepped her horse to the left, watched with satisfaction as Vergil Price's gaze followed her, then flicked back and forth between the two of them. Good. He was distracted.

"On second thought, mebbe you're right, Tom." Price dragged his shirtsleeve over his eyes and coughed. "Dang smoke's gettin' so thick a body can hardly breathe. Mebbe Miss Meggy'd like to come on over here and keep me company?"

"Sure she would, Verg. Keep the smoke from blowing in her face. *Go,*" he whispered to her.

"That is very chivalrous of you, Mr. Price."

Meggy kept talking as the horse moved under her. "What with all the debris in the air, it is most frightfully difficult to take a breath. Perhaps you would have some advice to offer?"

She stepped the mare past Price's thin figure, then turned to face Tom. The merest shadow of a smile played about his mouth.

She chattered on. "It is much better facing this direction, Mr. Price. Though why that should be I cannot imagine, since the flames are now shooting high above the tops of those trees. Why, just look at that!"

At that instant, the raven flapped its wings and croaked. "Wake-up-wake-up. Colonel-wake-up."

Price's gun arm jerked. Tom spurred his horse straight toward him.

The shot went wild. Price swore, re-aimed the revolver just as Tom pulled up less than a yard away.

"Oughta finish you off for that," Price growled. "Might as well do it now as later, seein' as how I'm gonna need your horse to get down this mountain. Me an' Miss Meggy, that is."

"No!" Meggy snapped. "I am not moving a single step."

Price's thin, graying eyebrows rose. "Have to kill you both, I reckon. Never shot no lady before, but there's allus a first time. Never set no timber on fire before, neither."

Meggy caught her breath.

"You sure you got two bullets left?" Tom's cool tone gave her a moment to rally her wits.

"Yup. Loaded it myself not three hours ago. You dismount now, Miss Meggy, and give over your horse."

Meggy grabbed her carpetbag and slid off the mare.

Tom grinned. "Better get at it, then, Verg. Air's so scratchy there's not much pleasure to inhaling." He urged his horse a step closer, forcing Price to angle his gun arm upward.

"My heart's right here, under my pocket flap." He tossed Meggy a quick look as he touched his left forefinger to the flannel.

Price goggled at him. "You invitin' me to shoot you?"

"Why not?" Tom drawled. "You got Miss Hampton's horse, and pretty soon you'll have mine, too. Not much to live for now, is there?" He looked steadily at a point just beyond Meggy's shoulder. "Go on, Verg, while you've got the chance."

Meggy heard the hammer click.

Price closed his mouth. "Now it comes down to it, Tom, I'm kinda sorry." He squinted one eye and sighted down the barrel. Then his eyes went wide as a cold steel shaft nudged the back of his neck. "What the—"

"Please, Mr. Price, do lower your weapon. And quickly, as my hand is not used to such a weighty instrument and I fear my trembling may dislodge the trig—''

Price tossed the revolver onto the ground in front of him. Just as Meggy bent to pick it up, the wiry logger lunged for her mare, clambered awkwardly into the saddle and jabbed his boot heels into the horse's flanks. Stunned, Meggy heard the animal crash through the underbrush.

Tom leaned down and closed his good hand around her elbow. "Fire's heading straight for us. We've got one horse and one chance. Let's—''

The thunderous snap of an exploding jack pine obliterated his final words.

The sky glowed red through the haze of smoke and cinders. Meggy tightened her arms about Tom's waist, trying not to jostle his injured shoulder. His right arm hung useless at his side; his left hand gripped the reins, guiding the skittish horse along a trail that was now barely discernible in the thickening air. She knew for certain they were traveling down-hill, but beyond that she had no idea where they were. She could no longer see the river, nor could she hear the murmur of the water over the noise of the fire.

Red-hot sparks rained down on them. Where they landed in the dry forest duff, spurts of flame shot up into their path, and the nervous horse danced side-ways.

"Whoa, boy. Easy now." Tom's voice rumbled

against her cheek, which was pressed against the back of his smoke-scented flannel shirt. The raven's cage swung against her knee, the bird hopping about in a frenzy, beating its wings against the slats.

On Tom's orders, Meggy had dipped the discarded blanket in the river, then ripped it in two. Tom had covered his head and face with one half and had ordered her to do the same. Even so, only occasionally could she stand to suck in the acrid air. She tried holding her breath until the need to exhale was overpowering.

Her skirt was dotted with tiny holes where sparks had burned through the fabric.

"You all right?" Tom called over his shoulder.

"Y-yes. Hard to breathe."

"Try to keep your head down. It's going to get worse."

"How much farther?"

He didn't answer right away. "Don't know for sure," he said at last. "The fire is catching up to us. We'll have to run for it."

He kicked the horse into a canter. A copse of vine maples and huckleberry crackled into flame ahead of them, and the frightened animal stumbled off to one side. Tom yelled something.

Meggy shut her burning eyes against the heat and tried to bottle up the scream that clawed at her throat.

"Hold on." Tom shouted the words as he kicked the balky horse into a gallop. Her chin glanced off his backbone with the unexpected jouncing. *Dear Lord, his arm.*

She knew it must be broken. Every motion must cause unbearable pain. She bit down hard on her tongue to keep her stomach from heaving.

A tree snapped to her left. She opened her eyes to see a shower of sparks erupt from a blazing bush, singeing the low branches near the trail. Gold-edged embers swirled so close she could see the wind fan the glowing tips into a new burst of flame. Her throat closed.

The fire was overtaking them. They weren't going to make it.

Tom turned his head. "Meggy!"

She thought her heart would fly out of her chest. "Yes, Tom?" She had to shout over the whoosh and crackle of the flames.

"We're going to have to gamble."

"I know," she shouted back. Her voice sounded as if it came from somewhere outside herself. *A lady never raises her voice.*

The thought was so incongruous in the situation that a little raspy laugh floated out of her mouth.

A lady never rucks up her skirt, either.

A lady never lies in a man's arms, wishing daylight would never come. A lady never—

"Hang on! We're going into the river."

The horse sailed over a lichen-covered log and headed down a steep incline, its hooves scrabbling for purchase on the muddy bank. The birdcage flopped and banged against her knee while the raven inside squawked unintelligible syllables.

Then icy water rose over her shoes and soaked the torn hem of her dress. The next thing she knew the horse was swimming.

"See any logs coming downriver?" Tom yelled.

Meggy strained her eyes upstream, searching for a sign of floating timber. "None yet."

"Good. Don't want them on top of us." He rolled to his left, slid out of the saddle and into the river. Meggy grabbed the birdcage, holding it up to keep it dry as the wheezing horse slowed its strokes. Tom reached for her burden, held it aloft with his good arm while she let herself slip off the horse's rear end.

For a few moments, her gathered skirt and one remaining petticoat buoyed her up, then the sodden material collapsed around her. The next thing she knew, water was lapping under her jaw.

"Are we going to drown?"

"Might not. More than likely get scorched to death. The way the wind's driving that fire, in a few more minutes it'll jump the river."

"We are going to die, then."

For some unfathomable reason she felt perfectly calm. The words she uttered sounded so matter-of-fact, so absurd considering the fix they were in, Meggy wondered if she was losing her mind. People did sometimes, when faced with the unthinkable. *Per-*

haps it is the Lord's way of helping us to meet our end.

"Hold on to this," Tom ordered. He thrust the cage into her arms and reached for the horse's bridle.

"Whoa. Easy, boy." He fumbled underwater, then dragged the saddle free. Relieved of the weight, the horse plunged toward the opposite shore.

"Thatta boy. Swim hard and then run like hell." His gaze followed the animal until it clambered up onto the sandy bank a dozen yards away.

His arm came around her waist. Meggy looked into his dirt-streaked, weary face and knew the truth. The fire would sweep over their heads, would sear the air in their lungs, and they would die in each other's arms.

The Lord is my shepherd....

It would be all right. They would be together.

Chapter Nineteen

Meggy laid her forehead against Tom's chin. The rough stubble was scratchy against her skin, but it didn't matter. Tom held her with his good arm while she paddled with her cupped hands to keep them afloat. The birdcage bobbed near Tom's shoulder.

His eyes studied the riverbank. "When the fire burns down close to the water, that's when it'll jump. When it does, take a deep breath and go under. Don't come up for air until you have to."

"Tom, there's something I want to tell you."

"Yeah?" He shot a glance at the flames, now licking the line of chokecherry bushes at the river's edge. "Be sure to get enough air, Meggy. Empty out your lungs before you inhale."

"Tom," she said again. "Tom, I—"

His gaze returned to her upturned face. "Just one more thing." He tried to smile, but his lips twisted oddly. "I love you more than anyone I've ever loved. I would give my life if I could save you from this."

"Tom. Oh, Tom, I would not want to live without you."

A tree exploded on the bank, throwing flaming chunks of wood into the air—chunks that arced back into the water with a hiss.

"Get ready, Meg. Here it comes."

"I—"

"Take a big breath."

"—love you." She gulped in air.

"Now!"

The water closed over her head.

Sergeant Michael O'Malley smoothed his freckled hand over the neck and shoulders of the chestnut gelding, ignoring the Swede for as long as he could. By all the saints in Ireland, if he knew what the colonel would want him to do, didn't the dumb son-of-a-Viking think he'd be *doing* it? Apparently not, from the barrage of queries peppering his ears.

Where the devil could Tom be? And doin' what, in the name of Saint Brigid?

Even more worrisome, where was Miss Meggy? Tom could take care of himself, but a wee slip of a lass who lifted her teacup with her little finger crooked—what would she know about survivin' a forest fire?

The horse tossed its head and sidled away. "Sorry, boyo. Wasn't watchin' what I was doin'."

From the other side of the animal came Swede's voice again. "So, what you t'ink we should do?"

"Wait it out," O'Malley growled. "That's what the colonel'd say if it was one of us crazy enough to go back up there."

"The men, they t'ink maybe one of us should—"

"No," the sergeant barked. "Tom'd have my hide if I risked another one of the crew. We stick together, and that's that. It's what he'd want."

Another voice spoke. "We gonna be able to finish the season, what with the camp all burned up?"

"If the colonel's alive, we'll finish, all right. May not get our wages till next Christmas, but he's not one to go belly up on a contract without a fight. You know that as well as I do, Eight-Bit."

"Now I see why they call it Devil's Camp," the stocky logger replied. "Not much he kin do if he's burned to a crisp up on that mountain."

"Don't say such a thing, 'tis bad luck, it is. Besides, we don't want the young lads upset, now do we?" O'Malley jerked his head toward the Claymore brothers, sitting in the back end of one of the wagons. Seth held his splinted arm close to his body, while Nobby's tousled head rested in his lap.

The sergeant's gaze moved from the two boys to Swede's troubled blue eyes, and then scanned the mountainside for the hundredth time in the last hour.

Nothing. Just the Devil's Camp trail disappearing into a gray-brown haze of smoke. A mile to the east, the river widened where it joined the south fork of the Tennant River. He studied that, as well.

The slow-moving water shone like polished metal as the sun descended toward the hilltops. He half expected to see the colonel riding toward him on top of the water, like the Lord Jesus Christ, only mounted on a horse.

Indian Joe stepped in close. "You look funny, Mick. What you see?"

"Nuthin', Joe. Just the river and the…" His head jerked up. "There. Up there on the mountain, what's that movin'?"

"Look like a man on horseback." The Indian squinted against the sunlight. "Not woman, but woman's horse."

The men gathered into a knot, watching the mare descend. When the trail leveled out, the rider reined in.

"By golly," Swede sang out. "It's Vergil Price!"

O'Malley felt the back of his neck prickle. "I thought he came down with the rest of us."

Indian Joe frowned. "He not ride in my wagon."

"Not in mine, neither," Eight-Bit added.

"What's he been doin' up there?" O'Malley wondered aloud.

"Here he comes," Eight-Bit said. "Let's just ask him."

* * *

She was dying. All around her the light was dimming, fading to gray and now to black. So easy. So cool and peaceful. She would see Mama again. And Papa. Soon. Very soon.

Her head broke the surface, her mouth opening wide to gulp in air. She could breathe! How gloriously sweet the air was, sweet and life-giving, even if it did make her throat burn.

"Tom!" Her voice came out in a croak. "Tom!"

The raven's cage bobbed a few feet from her shoulder, the current gently pulling it downstream until the rope she had looped about her wrist grew taut. Beside her, the water boiled suddenly, and Tom's lean, angular face appeared. He sucked in air and tried to speak, coughed, and tried again.

"All right?" he rasped. "Are you all right?"

"Y-yes, I am. Unless I am dead. I did feel I was drowning."

His mouth widened into a grin. "Not dead. We're both very much alive." He glanced toward the shore, then his gaze skimmed across the river to the opposite side where flames were already gobbling up brush and trees.

"We're lucky. Fire skipped right over our heads." He looked into her eyes, then flicked his glance beyond her. The grin faded.

"Log boom. Oh Jupiter, the logs!"

Meggy twisted to look. The timber they had released into the river now spread across the entire width. A floating forest was bearing down on them.

"Swim!" Tom yelled. "Get to the side, out of the way."

O'Malley grasped the bridle of Vergil Price's mount with both hands. "And where might Miss Meggy be, now that you're ridin' her mare?"

The lanky rider regarded the men clustered about him with outward calm, but O'Malley saw the bony fingers holding the reins close into a fist. Was that the way of it, then? Was Price hiding something? Mick tightened his grip.

"Well?"

"Oh, me an' Miss Meggy met up along the river, and seein' as Mr. Tom—"

"The colonel was with her?"

"Yeah, me an' the colonel was choppin' a log stack free. You remember, Swede? The timber the crew side-stacked that time in June when—"

"Ya, I remember. T'ree log stacks we pile, so high I can't see over."

"That's right. It was 'bout the time Eight-Bit lost his finger."

O'Malley watched him. "So Miss Meggy offers her horse to you?"

"That's right, she did. Said she'd ride with the colonel."

"Did she, now?"

Tom was no fool. If a man needed a mount, wouldn't he ride double, not take the horse? Something didn't add up.

"You boys goin' on into Tennant?" Price queried.

There was silence for a moment until O'Malley spat onto the ground. "None of us are movin' an inch until we lay eyes on Tom and Miss Meggy."

"Think I'll mosey on ahead, then. A man builds up a mighty big hunger scrambling around in the mountains."

O'Malley yanked on the bit. "I think you'll do no such thing. We're all of us hungry, and thirsty, too. But we're not leavin' until we know."

"Know what?" Price said in a bland voice.

"Know whether Tom 'n Meggy's alive or not. Been some minutes since you got here, Price. How come they're not right behind you?"

Price studied the toe of his boot. "Well, they's riding double, fer one thing. And fer another, Tom's got a busted arm. That might slow him down some."

A dark shape moved at the edge of the sergeant's field of vision. A horse stepped down the trail toward them. Tom's gelding.

Without a rider—or a saddle.

O'Malley sent a surreptitious look at Indian Joe, who inclined his head a fraction of an inch.

"Get down off your horse, Price."

"Aw, now, Mick. No need to—" The rest of his words were lost as he tumbled sideways off the horse.

Indian Joe's calm black eyes peered over the empty saddle.

"Stirrup loose. Too bad."

O'Malley spat again. "All right, Price. Settle your-self in that wagon over there with the others."

"Then what?" Swede and Eight-Bit said together.

"We'll wait," O'Malley said quietly. "And pray like Catholics, all of ye."

Chapter Twenty

Weighed down by her water-soaked skirt and petticoat, Meggy struggled to swim out of the path of the oncoming logs. Her legs couldn't seem to move. Beside her, Tom stroked with his good arm and used his shoulder to bump the caged raven ahead of him.

"Faster," he gasped.

She shook the water out of her face. "I can't." With a frantic breaststroke, she managed to move another two feet forward, but the current pulled her a foot sideways for every inch she gained.

"Another ten feet," Tom urged. "Try." With a powerful kick, he surged ahead of her.

She tried, oh how desperately she tried to follow him. The mass of logs kept coming at them; they were so close now she could see the patterns in the rough bark.

Stroke. Kick hard.

Her body felt heavy, her motions clumsy. But if

she didn't get out of the way, the timber would cover her, push her beneath the surface.

As the timber floated toward her, she raised her arm to protect her face. At the last minute Tom slipped his hand under her armpit and pulled her out of the way. The rafted logs, clustered in twos and threes, were abreast of them.

"Let some go by," Tom yelled. "We'll pick a couple of slow ones and hope they don't jam up."

Meggy blinked at him. "What are we going to do?"

Tom's grin flashed again. "Ride 'em."

"Merciful heaven, now is no time for such taradiddle!"

"I'm telling you straight, Meg. Climb onto the log and hold tight."

Her heart leaped straight into her throat. "You mean…?"

He jerked his head in a nod. "Exactly. Wait for a big one, broad enough to hold you. Grab on and pull yourself up. I'll be right behind you."

Meggy eyed the floating timber. Drowning might have been easier. How in the world could she haul herself and her soggy skirt onto a little bump of fir riding along on the water? *Lord, I never dreamed falling in love with a man would be so dangerous!*

Tom's blue eyes scanned the mass of logs. "Here comes a good thick cedar. Get ready."

The cedar had a smaller length of fir traveling

alongside it. Tom tipped the raven's cage onto its side and lobbed it toward the two logs. The cage rolled into the slot between them, and he reached his good hand toward Meggy.

She felt his strong fingers close over her forearm, felt him position her sideways until they were both swimming parallel to the timber. At his signal, she flung both arms over the log at her side, then felt his shoulder under her rib cage, lifting until she was half in, half out of the water. She tumbled forward until her cheek banged into the birdcage.

The log began to rotate slowly. Instinctively she dug her fingertips into the crenellated bark. "Tom!"

Tom lunged for the log, straddled it, then stretched out full length and hooked one boot over the adjacent timber in an effort to stop the spinning.

The cedar dipped sharply with the addition of Tom's weight. The river washed over her shoulders, and she lifted her head, choking on a mouthful of water. Side by side, the two logs formed a makeshift raft, even though they weren't lashed together. Each log moved independently. Her position was precarious at best.

Frozen with terror, she clung to the wood, shifting her weight from side to side to counteract the rolling motion. Any moment she expected the timber to turn over and drag her underneath.

"Lie still," he called. He pressed his forehead against Meggy's heels. With his good arm, he reached out to the gyrating log next to them. He'd give his other arm for the pair of spiked log-walking boots he'd tossed into one of the wagons along with the oddments of equipment and camp gear the men had cobbled together. All he had to work with now was instinct, a partner who might obey his orders if she was frightened enough, and a large helping of dumb luck.

Maybe it would be enough. "Don't move, Meggy. Just hang on no matter what."

He heard her muffled response, but couldn't tell what she'd said. He tightened his left arm over the log floating alongside them and gritted his teeth.

How far was it to the junction with the south fork of the Tennant, where the river would widen and slow?

How long could he hold on?

He tried to anticipate the motion of the log beneath them, worked to reduce the roll by clinging to the adjacent log with one foot and one hand. He pulled it toward him until his back muscles quivered.

His left leg started to go numb.

He rested, gasping for breath, praying for strength, then pulled again. They had survived so far, hadn't been caught by the fire and hadn't drowned in the river. He'd be damned if he'd let her die now.

Indian Joe ran his hand over the neck of the riderless gray gelding that had barreled down the mountain trail. "Look. Mane singed by fire."

O'Malley grunted. "Why wouldn't Tom ride his own horse down the mountain? Think, man, think!"

The Indian shrugged and pulled up the horse's front leg to peer at the underside of the hoof. "Horse sound. Man has broken arm," he said slowly.

"Leastways, that's what Price says." The sergeant lowered his voice. "Not like Tom to abandon his horse, 'specially if he's injured."

Indian Joe examined the horse's other three legs. When he straightened, his black eyes flicked to where Vergil Price sat in the back of one wagon. "Horse swim." He laid a small brown leaflet in O'Malley's hand. "Tom ride into river."

"What're you sayin'? That he's drowned?"

The Indian shook his head. "Not drown. Swim, maybe."

"Swim! Not bleedin' likely with his arm broke. Didn't Price say Tom cut loose a side-stack of timber?"

"Yeah, that's what he said, but—"

Before he finished the sentence, Indian Joe swung up onto the horse. "I will search."

O'Malley turned to study Vergil Price. The man's eyes met his for an instant, then shifted away. So he'd been watching them, had he? Mick sure would give a leprechaun's purse of gold to know what that son of a gun was thinkin'.

He gazed past the two wagons and the animals

gathered into the makeshift pen to where the water glinted silver in the waning sunlight. Just beyond the stand of cottonwoods on the far side, the river widened.

As he looked, something long and dark floated into view. Looked like a piece of timber. And another!

Logs! Hundreds of them, looking for all the world like they'd been rafted by seasoned river drivers. He squinted into the light. Not a sign of a cable or a length of rope... What was holding them together? Sure and certain they hadn't just floated downstream like that, nice as you please.

He raised his hand to scratch his beard and froze. *Jesus, Mary, and Joseph! The answer was there, right before his eyes.*

He started toward the crew. "Peaveys, lads! Grab yer river spikes, we've got work to do!"

The men raced down the road toward him and sloshed into the river, shouting and brandishing their iron-tipped hooks.

"Lookit that, will ya? There's timber drifting all over the river!"

"Boss musta cut 'em loose upriver."

"Guess we'll get our wages now for sure, eh?"

"Get offa my roller, Eight-Bit!"

"Naw, you get off. This one's too frisky for a big-footed Swede like you."

"Watch behind! One of them suckers is broadsidin' into the center."

"Get out there and give it a poke, ya damn fool! Ride the boom! Unless you fancy spending all day sortin' out a logjam."

O'Malley could kiss every grubby, sweaty river pig on the crew. To men like these, a mass of timber was more than a week's wages, it was a challenge. A matter of honor. Even that troublemaker Vergil Price had pitched in. He'd already log-walked smack out into the middle of the river, and there he was, flailing his peavey like a man possessed of the devil.

The sergeant grabbed the last hook and waded in to join the rest. Seeing the timber comin' down to meet them was a fine thing, all right. But pretty quick now he wished he'd clap eyes on Tom and Miss Meggy.

Tom raised his head. A man was coming toward them, scampering from one spinning log to the next, nimble as an antelope. Thank God.

He couldn't hold on much longer. His thigh muscles jerked with the effort it took to hold their makeshift raft together. His left arm ached all the way down to his fingertips from pulling; his right shoulder screamed whenever he moved. The break was high up, he guessed. No matter how hard he tried, his elbow refused to bend.

"Meggy?"

"Yes, I see him."

"Hang on tight. I want him to bump another log up close to us."

Her clear voice floated back to him without a pause. "No, you don't, Tom. It's Vergil Price."

Price! Tom swore under his breath. Was the man crazy? What was he doing here, when he could be halfway to Washington territory by now?

The truth dawned with terrible clarity. Because we know what he's done, and he wants to make sure we don't tell anyone.

"Meggy, listen. When he gets here, roll off into the water and duck under. Stay down as long as you can."

"Tom, I'm afraid." She called the words over her shoulder.

"I know," he yelled back. "I'm afraid, too. Nothing to do but pray to God and swim toward shore."

"W-what are *you* going to do?"

He groaned, but softly so she wouldn't hear him. "I'm going to try to sit up."

Chapter Twenty-One

I'm gonna kill him. Her, too, if I have to. Guess I do have to, since she heard everything I said about startin' the fire, and she watched me draw my bead on Tom. Things can sure get into a mess with a woman around. He shoulda never let her stay. She never shoulda been so pretty in the first place.

No two ways about it, now I'm gonna have to do it.

Price expertly rolled the log under his feet to within a few yards of the cedar to which Tom and Meggy clung. "Think yer pretty smart, don'tcha?" he yelled.

"Matter of fact," Tom replied, "I'm feeling more disgusted than smart."

"Yeah? How's that?" Price poled the log closer.

"Should have shot you both when I had the chance."

Tom snorted. "I should have run you off this mountain like a wild dog when *I* had the chance. Hindsight's not worth much at this point."

"Wild dog, huh?" Price snickered. "That's real army humor, Colonel. Considerin' that I'm the one that's run *you,* and the lady, off of Devil's Camp. Kinda makes me the one in charge, now, don't it?"

Tom nudged Meggy's booted foot with his chin.

"How do you figure that, Verg? None of these river pigs crawling over this mess of timber seems to be taking orders from you."

"They don't matter," Price scoffed. "It's you that matters. You an' Miss Meggy are gonna do what I say."

"Sure, Verg." The log Price was walking edged alongside. Tom pressed Meggy's foot again. When the two timbers thunked together, Meggy relinquished her hold, slid off her perch and slipped beneath the surface without a sound. It took all Tom's willpower not to reach for her.

Good girl. Now just let us slide past before you come up.

"What the—?" Price jabbed his peavey into the river. "Where the hell is she?" He stabbed downward again, swearing in frustration.

With his last ounce of strength, Tom pushed himself up with his good arm and maneuvered his body until he sat straddling the thick cedar log. It started to roll under him, and he made a grab for Price's cant hook.

"Oh no, you don't," the logger snarled. He danced

backward out of reach. "No reason you shouldn't drown right along with the lady."

He rammed the pointed tip into Tom's log and shoved hard. Tom felt the log beneath his knees start to turn over. He lunged for the birdcage, grabbed it up and tossed it toward Price. The terrified raven flapped and squawked as the cage sailed toward its target. "Broke-broke-more-more-nevermore."

For the first time since he'd adopted the nestling, Tom was glad he'd taught the bird to talk. Price jerked backward in surprise, but managed to keep his balance while the cage splashed into the water and bobbed downriver. Tom watched it float out of reach, then glimpsed a dark head break the surface and a small white hand close around the rope. His heart hammered until he thought his chest would burst. Now all he had to do was deal with Price.

The peavey bit again. This time, Tom leaned toward it, grasped the tip and yanked it forward. The sharp metal sliced into his palm, but he didn't let go. Price, clinging to the other end, shoved back, and the two men began a desperate battle for control.

Tom rammed the tool backward, forcing Price to fight for balance as the slippery log spun under his feet. Price recovered and jabbed the peavey forward, but Tom was ready for him. He let the tip slide so close to his calf he could feel the cold metal through his trouser leg.

Then, instead of thrusting the peavey away in the

same seesaw pattern, he grasped it and yanked it forward, hard. The startled man lost his balance and tumbled into the water. With a cry, he disappeared.

Tom hoisted the hook, waiting for Price to surface. He'd never killed a man in anger. Army fighting had been either a cold, calculated attack or self-defense, never personal hatred. Could he take a man's life in cold blood? Even a man who had twice tried to kill him? Had tried to harm Meggy?

Gripping the log with his thighs, he scanned the water, the peavey growing heavy in his left hand. He wouldn't have to aim it, just push Price's head under and keep him there until…

He dropped his arm and laid the hook along the length of his log. He couldn't do it.

He watched the shiny surface of the river, but there was no sign of Price. Except for the ripples made by floating logs, the smooth water shone like polished satin. Then, from the far corner of his vision, he saw two things happen at almost the same moment.

In the shallows at the river's edge, a horse—his horse, if he wasn't mistaken—dashed forward into the water. The rider reached down to steady a sodden figure in black, swaying in waist-deep water. Against her chest she cradled a birdcage.

He opened his mouth to yell, then caught sight of something else. In the middle of the river, the logs began to jumble up like matchsticks. A center jam. It would take skilled log-walkers hours of wet, dangerous work to sort it out. He strained his eyes, waiting and watching, until finally the truth began to dawn on him.

Price was trapped underneath the pile of logs.

"Tom! *Tom!* Speak to me, boyo."

The Irishman worked his way toward him across the drifting logs. Behind him, Eight-Bit Orrin's powerful arms pushed and shoved with his cant hook to clear a path.

"Tom? I saw Price come after you. What happened?"

Tom pointed at the building logjam.

"Serves him right," Orrin growled. "Smelled something about the man I couldn't stomach."

Tom held O'Malley's gaze. "Meggy?"

The sergeant tipped his head toward the far bank. "Indian Joe's got her. She's safe."

Tom's stomach muscles clenched, then began to uncoil. "Guess I'd better go tell her about Price."

O'Malley snorted. "Guess you'd better go let Fong fix you up, first. Pardon me for puttin' it like this, Colonel, but...that's an order."

Fong lifted Tom's broken arm and bound it between two splint boards. Though he made little noise, every strangled moan that escaped Tom's tightly compressed lips brought tears stinging into Meggy's eyes.

She held his left hand tight in both of hers, but the

sight of his sweat-beaded forehead and the occasional gasps that escaped his whitened lips felt like knives slicing into her belly.

Oh, how wrenching it was to care for someone!

How blithe and foolish she had been only a few short weeks ago when she'd come out to marry Mr. Peabody, a man she had never even been introduced to. She hadn't given a thought to whether she could ever care for him. At the burial, staring down at his stiff body lying in the coffin, she had felt nothing at all. She had not known Mr. Peabody, as she now knew Tom. Had not loved him.

She turned her face away. She couldn't bear to see Tom's face twist with pain.

Lord, what a puzzle life was. Only fools and spinsters like Aunt Hattie escaped the agony of watching someone they loved suffer. Meggy closed her eyes at the thought.

You, Mary Margaret Hampton, were neither raised to be a fool nor destined to be a spinster. And for that awakening, she had Colonel Tom Randall to thank. She blushed at the unbearably sweet memories she had locked away in her heart.

But what now?

Tom lay half-conscious in the back of a wagon, crushing her fingers every time Fong laid his quick, sure hands on him. When the cook was finished with his ministrations, the men would hitch up a team and drive the colonel into Tennant, where there was a doctor.

From the smoke and ash hazing the air, she knew the fire still burned up on the mountain. Mr. O'Malley had told her the wind was now pushing it east, away from the town and the sawmill five miles downriver at Dixon Landing. It would likely burn itself out before morning.

The crew had finally managed to break up the center jam and form the timber into a huge floating log boom. "Held together with manila rope and spit," the Irishman joked.

Price's body had not been found. The only other casualty, besides her realization of a perilously vulnerable heart when it came to the colonel, was the colonel himself.

"Now," Seth Claymore bragged, "both Colonel Tom 'n me are wounded." Young men did grow up with the oddest ideas of what constituted manly honor. If *she* ever had a son…

The thought stopped her heartbeat. "Oh," she murmured aloud. But first they must be wed!

And Tom had not proposed.

Perhaps he wouldn't. Perhaps he had gotten too strong a taste of how stubborn and difficult she could be, and he was thinking better of it.

She glanced down at him. Two blue eyes were fixed on her face. "Meggy," he croaked.

She bit her lip. "Yes, Tom?" She waited an eternity for him to speak. "Yes?"

"Meggy, I'm sorry. That was an awful thing for you to have to undergo."

"It wasn't awful, Tom. It was frightening and unsettling, but it never did get to 'awful' until this very minute."

"Had I known—ouch! Do that again, Fong, and you're fired."

The slim Chinaman rocked back on his heels. "You not fire me, boss. No, never. Too much exciting happen all time, keep you too busy."

"Huh." Tom snorted.

"Besides, you terrible cook. Men not stay one week to cut trees if I not do cooking."

Tom closed his eyes with a groan. "Meg, tell me. What is it that's awful about this very minute?"

She would tell him, right here and now. Just blurt it out. *Mama would pitch a fit at such unladylike behavior!*

Well, she couldn't help that. She had told him she loved him, right before the fire jumped the river, and when they came up for air he'd never mentioned it. *That* was what was awful. He hadn't even acknowledged that he'd heard her!

That was no way to start a proper life together.

O'Malley stepped to her side. "Tom, can you hear me, boyo?"

Tom grunted but didn't open his eyes.

"Whaddya thinkin' to do, Tom? After we get you to the doctor, I mean."

"You mean if the doc doesn't kill me or truss me up like a Christmas goose so I can't move?"

The sergeant grinned at Meggy. "Well…I mean, what were you thinkin' about that fine log boom the crew manhandled together? Just leave it fer the beavers?"

"Tomorrow we'll push it on down to Dixon Landing."

"And then what?"

Meggy stilled. Yes, and then what? *Was he going to propose or not?*

"Then we'll move on to Number Two Camp and cut some more timber."

"All of us?" O'Malley gave her a sidelong glance.

"All of us. We'll keep the two Claymore boys with us. Seth's going to make a fine skid greaser, once his arm heals. Besides, sending them off to another crew might be dangerous for the young one."

Meggy resisted the impulse to drop the man's bandaged hand and stomp away into town on her own. How *could* he forget about her like this? Why, he didn't so much as mention her name! Had a few hours in the river made her invisible?

Meggy closed her mind and tried her best to quiet her plunging heart. She would not let it matter. She would lift her chin and straighten her spine and conduct herself like a well-bred Southern lady, even if it killed her.

But it does *matter. What would an* Oregon *woman do?*

The sergeant turned toward the men beginning to straggle up from the river. "Load up, boys. Let's get the colonel into town."

Chapter Twenty-Two

Tom wanted to say something to Meggy, but he didn't know what. She rode beside him in the wagon, along with the Claymore brothers and Fong, whose black-capped head nodded against a bushel basket of potatoes. Other supplies the men had rescued from the cookhouse pantry filled the wagon—a burlap bag of coffee beans and a hundred-pound sack of flour. But no whiskey.

His arm hurt like hell, a crushing ache that pulsed from his shoulder to his wrist. But if he had to pick a spot where it hurt the most, it would be his chest. Beneath his bruised ribs his heart pumped pure sorrow into his veins.

He'd lost Devil's Camp to the fire, had managed to salvage only a tenth of the timber he needed to fulfill his contract and pay the men their hard-earned jack. Worse, another man had lost his life during the ordeal. Maybe Vergil Price deserved to drown under a logjam for what he had plotted, but that didn't make Tom feel any better about it. Poor dumb son of a—

O'Malley's voice cut his thought short. "When we get to town, I'm thinkin' the colonel's gonna treat us all to some special 'toothache medicine' at the Golden Goose."

A ragged cheer went up from the men following in the other wagon.

O'Malley grinned and sidled his mount close to the turning wheel. "That okay with you, Tom?"

Tom lifted his good arm. "Sure, why not? Keep you busy while the doc fixes me up."

And it would keep the crew's mind off the long trek they'd have to make in the morning to Number Two Camp.

He shot a glance at Meggy. Her face was pale but composed, her gray-green eyes looking into his with an odd expression, as if she wasn't sure who he was. He had to chuckle at the thought. Right now he wasn't so sure who he was, either.

For some reason he thought of Susanna. He saw his sister's small, determined chin, her delicate hand writing away at the cherry-wood desk in her sitting room. Susanna had always felt strongly about things, and she acted on her feelings. Meggy was a lot like her.

Ever since that night in Meggy's cabin, when he had spoken of his sister, he'd begun to realize something. Did it really matter whether Susanna had in fact been a spy for the Union army? Whether she was guilty or not, her death was just as agonizing for him. Since the day he'd watched the dirt clods rain down onto her coffin, he had kept himself from loving anyone, especially a woman. He never wanted to feel such pain again.

His belly clenched. That fear had crippled him. His inability to save his sister had frozen his heart into a chunk of granite.

Until now. Now there was Meggy.

But Lord knew he couldn't ask her to come to Number Two Camp. She deserved a fine house with fancy gingerbread around the front porch, a grand piano in the parlor, a white picket fence to grow roses on.

The more he thought about it, the worse he felt. She'd captured the hearts of his crew; his rough, uncouth loggers treated her like a duchess.

He lay back in the wagon and closed his eyes. And damned if she hadn't captured him, as well. Mind and body and soul. The problem was, he didn't know what to do about it.

Meggy paced the perimeter of the small room Sergeant O'Malley had procured for her at the Mountain View Hotel.

She couldn't possibly!

You could.

Mama would just die! And Papa...

Mama and Papa are gone, Meggy. And the old ways with them. You alone must decide.

She swerved to avoid the chiffonier and the tall bureau jutting out from the wall. And the big, quilt-swathed double bed. She hadn't slept in a double bed since...since— Was it only hours ago that she and Tom had lain in each other's arms? The prospect of stretching out alone on that bed brought her no joy.

What *was* she to do?

She would leave, that's what. She would take the noon stage tomorrow, catch up with her trunk at Eagle Point. And then...

And then what? Go back to Chester County and take up residence with Aunt Hattie? Tend to nieces and nephews for the rest of your life?

It would be safe there. She would belong. She would have family close by—sisters and their husbands and their offspring to fill her days.

Meggy circled the room again, reversed direction and retraced her path. Her wet shoes squeaked at every step. She tried not to look at the bed. It suggested...well, it reminded her...

It's him you want. Not Aunt Hattie and a passel of your sisters' babies. Admit it. You want lean, dark-haired, short-spoken Colonel Tom Randall.

Oh, devil take it, she wanted him in the worst way. She wanted him and only him, and she wanted her own babies. Tom's babies.

But he hadn't spoken for her.

And it doesn't look as if he's planning to.

She twitched her still-damp skirt away from the yellow counterpane. Well then, she could live without him.

He had a broken arm, tons of logs to float downriver and a new camp to set up. Tom's life was already overfull. He had Sergeant O'Malley and Fong and the rest of his crew; why would he need her?

For the same reason you need him, you goose. Because the thought of being without him made her feel cold and dark inside. Because she loved every stubborn, set-in-his-ways, male thing about him.

Because he didn't laugh when she drank too much whiskey and sang "Bonnie Blue Flag" at the top of her voice.

Tom Randall was the only man she'd ever known who saw her as she really was, who saw things in her she didn't even know were there until they were reflected in his eyes.

Such feelings are what life is all about, Meggy. You cannot give that up.

The late-afternoon sunlight slanted across the bed. Meggy studied the way the shaft turned the air to a golden haze, made the yellow counterpane glow. Well, then, like any soldier, she must move forward.

With a stiffened spine, she opened the door, stepped out into the hallway and headed down the stairs toward the Golden Goose.

Singing.

"'We are a band of brothers, and native to the soil....'"

Chapter Twenty-Three

She had never set foot in a saloon before. The swinging doors beckoned, and at the same time they threatened. Papa would never believe she had come to such a pass.

It would be simple, she told herself. Just walk on in and then...

Then what? Somehow she knew this was a momentous step, a true digression from The Path she had been taught to regard as paramount in her very-proper-respectable-lady life. Her life before coming out West.

Up until now.

Correction. Up until Tom. From the moment she had gazed at his tall, loose-jointed form, at his steady eyes, dark as spring violets, her feelings had zigged and zagged away from The Path, and her behavior had followed suit.

Was that wrong?

It depended on how one looked at it.

Why did she not care?

Tom had not ''led her astray,'' as Aunt Hattie would put it. Rather, he had drawn out her real self, which she'd kept hidden inside for the past twenty-five years. The self she had always *thought* she was.

Well, she was almost twenty-six now. Almost too late.

She laid her shaking hand on the scrolled oak panel before her. Did one pull it forward or push on in? If she pushed inward, she could not retreat gracefully, not without someone noticing her.

That settled it.

For courage, she drew in a deep breath just as a burst of male laughter boiled from behind the hinged doors. *Oh Lord, Lord. What will I say?*

Head held high, she walked on in. After all, she was fighting for her life. Her *real* life.

The first thing she laid eyes on was the startled face of the bartender, a tall man with a mere sprinkle of hair rimming his otherwise bald head. He looked like a monk, she thought irrationally.

Whatever must *she* look like?

The man watched her, but at the same time wiped a cloth up and down an expanse of shiny mahogany. She sent him a shaky smile, and his polishing hand came to a stop.

His lips moved, speaking to someone. She caught

only the word *out* before Mr. O'Malley stepped to her side.

"Meggy, lass, this is no place for the likes of you."

"Possibly not, Sergeant, but I have some, um, business to see to."

His rusty eyebrows waggled upward. "Business, is it? What would a well-brought-up colleen such as yourself want in a public house?"

"I came to find you. The crew, I mean. All of you."

"Lass, 'tis a bit early to be lookin' for Tom. He's still at the doctor's, gettin' his arm fixed up. And 'tis a bit late to stop us from celebratin' the fact that he's got an arm at all."

"I do not mean to halt your celebration, Mr. O'Malley. It's just that…well, you see…" She ran out of words.

Brows furrowed, O'Malley peered into her face. "Miss Meggy, it can't be you're wantin' to *join* us?"

"Oh, no. I merely thought…that is…oh, I may as well just say it."

All at once the noise in the room faded away until all she could hear was the tick-tick of the clock on the wall. Even the bartender set the square glass bottle in his hand on top of the bar so quietly it made no sound.

"Just say what, lass?" the Irishman said in a low voice.

"Mr. O'Malley…Michael…I must talk to you. The crew, I mean. All of you."

His voice dropped to an undertone. "What about, Meggy?"

"About, well, about Tom."

"Tom," he echoed.

Meggy sucked in a lungful of the smoky air. "Well, actually, about…me."

"Aha." O'Malley nodded unconvincingly. "I see. About you."

"I mean, about…Tom. And me."

"Aha," he said again. "I see the way of it now. Come with me, lass."

He gestured to the barkeep, then cupped her elbow and guided her to the round table smack in the center of the room. The floor, she noticed, was polished to a shine, even though it was just planking.

"Gather 'round, lads. Miss Meggy has somethin' on her mind."

Voices burst out. "Miss Meggy, you kin tell us!"

"Mebbe she don't want to?"

"Hell, she's here, ain't she?"

"I thought she said somethin' about Tom."

"Tom 'n *her,* you numb-nut. Clean yer ears out."

"And, by golly, act surprised!"

Even the bartender had something to say. "Haven't had this much excitement since some feller hypnotized old man Crockett's prize laying hen and the boys all made bets to see when it'd wake up. Business was real good that night.''

The men shuffled chairs until she was surrounded by a sea of eager faces. Suddenly her tongue seemed to freeze into a lump of ice.

''Go on, Miss Meggy. Say it.''

''Ve are yer friends, by golly.''

She didn't know where to begin.

Then Sergeant O'Malley stepped over to the scarred oak table, swept the glasses off onto the floor with one swipe of his arm, and lifted her off the floor. ''Step up on that bench, lass, then up onto the table. A good speech deserves a platform.''

Aghast, Meggy steadied herself on the tabletop and then looked down into the familiar faces of the crew. *Oh, well, in for a penny, in for a pound, Mama used to say.* At the moment it felt more like in for a bushel. A barrel, even. Maybe a whole wagon load of barrels.

She cleared her throat. ''Gentlemen...'' She cleared her throat again.

''You see, it's like this.'' She swallowed and started over. ''Well, I really do not know *what* it's like, as I have never before found myself in such a position. I...well, Tom...that is, Colonel Randall... Excuse me, Mr. Bar Man, might I have something to drink?''

In complete silence the barkeep uncorked the bottle at his elbow, sloshed a bit into a tumbler and handed it up to her with a little bow.

Meggy took a swallow. Her throat burned. Her eyes watered. But after the initial shock of that dreadful-tasting stuff numbing her mouth, and the rush of heat as it settled below her stays, she gathered her courage, took another gulp and proceeded.

"You see, I have come to have a great deal of regard for Colonel Randall."

Another sip. "And it is very difficult to think about going away, leaving, you see, because...well, it is possible that the colonel returns my regard. But he hasn't *said* so, which suggests that I may be mistaken and... Oh, dear, this is so much harder than chasing a Yankee over the back fence!"

She gripped the glass until her knuckles whitened. "And you understand, of course, that it would not be proper for me to remain under these circumstances."

"Not proper a'tall," someone echoed.

She let another mouthful of whiskey roll around her tongue. "If I leave—that is, take the stagecoach tomorrow to Eagle Point—I will never see Tom, um, Colonel Randall again. And...well, I would *want* to see him. Very much. I mean, I would miss him dreadfully."

She paused for another sip. "In fact, for the rest of my life." Another sip.

"Forever, to be honest." She tried to steady her voice. "But...but Colonel Randall intends to start up another camp. A Number Two Camp, he calls it. He has made plans for himself, and all of you—his crew—are to go with him.''

She blinked away the stinging moisture in her eyes. ''And so, gentlemen, I do not know what to do. I just d-don't know…what to do.''

She closed her eyes and extended the now-empty glass toward the bartender. ''May I have another one of these?''

''This here's a democracy, ain't it?'' a voice shouted. ''Let's vote on it!''

''Yeah,'' someone agreed.

Fong waved from the back of the room. ''That very good idea, missy. American way.''

O'Malley stepped forward. ''Sure and we must do this nice and proper-like. Swede, get some paper.''

The burly man rose and poked his face into the fascinated bartender's field of vision. ''Ve gonna vote, so need some ballots.''

''Don't have no paper. How 'bout a deck of cards?''

''Need someone to tally the votes,'' O'Malley said. ''Who kin add and subtract?''

''I can, Mister O'Malley,'' Seth Claymore shouted. ''I reckon I can do it left-handed, since my right arm's busted up like the colonel's.''

''Seth!'' Meggy saw him for the first time, hidden behind Swede Jensen's bulky frame. Nobby popped up beside his older brother. ''I'm here, too, Miss Meggy.''

My stars and chicken feathers, two young boys in a barroom!

"Seth Claymore, what are you doing in this place?"

She gulped. She might as well ask what a respectable Southern lady was doing there, too!

Seth gave her a wide-eyed look, then his face split into a grin. "Same as you, I reckon. Jawin' with the Devil's Camp crew."

Jawing? She certainly was not. She was…well, she was asking advice. *From a rough, unshaven, uncultured Oregon logging crew!* What *was* her life coming to?

But it felt right. She liked the men, all except for Mr. Price. They might be unschooled, crude in their speech, lacking in polished manners, but they were good men, with kind hearts and an underlying regard for each other despite the ribald joshing they inflicted on one another.

She had observed them, gathered for tea on the front porch of her little cabin, and she knew without a doubt that they respected—even loved—Tom.

And they respected her. Even liked her, out of place as she was. It would be almost as hard to leave them as it would be to leave Tom.

O'Malley shouted for order. "All right, lads. Miss Meggy's laid it before you, the question she's got to resolve before the stage arrives at noon tomorrow. Let's see what we can do to help her out."

He lifted her down from the table to the accompaniment of cheers and stamping boots. "Pass out the cards, Nobby. We'll write on the backs."

"What about Indian Joe?"

"What about him?"

"He cain't write."

The Indian rose from his chair in the far corner of the room. "I make my mark. I can make picture."

Tears pooled under Meggy's lids. She blinked them back, but they kept coming. She bowed her head.

Out of the corner of her blurred vision she watched a thick hand tip the whiskey bottle to fill her glass.

O'Malley's voice boomed behind her. "Nobby, make sure every man gets a ballot, will you now, lad?"

"An' me an' Seth, too?" The boy accepted the deck of playing cards the bartender handed over, but stood resolute before the sergeant. "Colonel Tom'd let us vote, I know he would. He calls us men, just like he does the others, and 'sides, we're part of the crew same as Swede and Indian Joe and Eight-Bit."

The boy's brown eyes challenged every man in the room. "Ain't we?"

"Aren't we," someone corrected.

Seth joined his brother. "If'n I don't get to vote, I ain't gonna tally up."

"Aren't gonna," suggested the same voice.

Meggy wondered if either Seth or Nobby had attended school, or was Seth's arithmetic self-taught?

How can your mind wander so at such a crucial time? Her insides fluttered like shimmies on a clothesline.

"Let the boy—I mean, man—vote," Eight-Bit shouted.

Nobby grinned and began to circle the room, the playing cards in his hand. Seth resettled himself at a battered oak table, and the bartender brought a cigar box to collect the votes, then stuffed a pencil stub into his hand.

Beneath her shirtwaist, Meggy's heart squeezed and began a rhythmic hammering. *Tom…Tom…Tom.* She watched the faces of the men as they solemnly accepted one card apiece from Nobby's hand.

Swede produced a chewed-up lead pencil and hunched his shoulders over his ballot. After what seemed an interminable wait, he grunted with satisfaction, folded the card in half and propped his elbow on top of it. Then he passed his pencil to Eight-Bit.

Meggy almost groaned aloud. Except for the stub of lead Seth clutched in his left hand, the crew was sharing one single pencil! Voting would likely take all night.

The bartender stepped about the quiet room, whiskey bottle in hand, filling glasses.

"How do you spell *summer?*" Orrin whispered.

"*S-U-M-U-R,*" someone intoned. "There's only one *R.*"

"Nah, there's two *R*s," a voice interjected. "Summerrr. Hear it? Two *R*s."

Meggy choked back a giggle. Then she began to wonder what Orrin was writing that had to do with summer. Summer was fast drawing to a close, and the logging season with it. Already the leaves on the willows and maples down by the river were yellowing. Soon they would turn to gold, and then to orange and scarlet as winter closed in.

Where would she be then? Where, oh where, could she go to find even a shred of happiness after this glorious, upside-down season at Devil's Camp?

Certainly not back to Seton Falls and Aunt Hattie!

How her imagination was running on as she sat trying to appear calm and dignified while awaiting the wisdom of the only friends she had at the moment.

This is my doing. Rather than just give up without a fight, I brought matters to a head. Now she suffered the anguish of the congregation when the preacher went on too long.

Had she done the right thing?

She was *not* a Western woman. She was not brave and tough in the face of heartbreak. At this moment, she was perilously close to tears and so frightened she couldn't think sensibly. She cradled the glass of whiskey between her trembling hands.

Then again, Mary Margaret, you have come this far. Survived a forest fire nipping at her skirts, chopped away at a stack of timber higher than her head, avoided drowning in the river, even floated for miles and miles on top of a log no wider than Aunt Hattie's kitchen shelf. Surely, after all she had been through, all she had learned about the world outside of Chester County, about her very self, she was not to be deterred by a little bobble in her life like Colonel Tom Randall?

The pencil passed to Sam Turner, the silver-haired bullwhacker who kept the oxen in line with his deep, rumbly voice and his whip. Sam chewed the pencil end for a long minute, then bent forward to mark his ballot.

Sam had never stopped at her cabin for tea, Meggy recalled. From the look of his flushed face, and judging by the amount of liquid the oversize glass in his fist had once contained, Sam preferred whiskey.

At this moment, so did Meggy.

Lord, what took them so long to scratch a single word—*Go* or *Stay*—on a scrap of paper?

Fong waved the pencil away without even looking up. Instead, he hunched forward with peculiar intensity, shielding whatever he was doing with the long, floppy sleeves of his black cotton jacket.

She couldn't stand it any longer. Any second Tom would walk in the door, broken arm or no broken arm, and demand to know what was going on.

Her head buzzed. Her mouth felt tingly, and her lips kept smiling no matter what. She wanted to sing ''Bonnie Blue Flag'' to strengthen her resolve, but she knew Northerners would probably not appreciate that.

She tried to recite a prayer instead. The one that came to mind began, "Now I lay me down to sleep..." She got no further than "lay me down" when she remembered Tom touching her in intimate ways, his hands gentle and sure. Her face grew hot.

Seth and Nobby conferred over their cards. Seth had finished his and dropped it into the cigar box; now he was helping his younger brother to write something. Seth's left hand traced letters, while Nobby struggled to keep hold of the wobbly pencil stub.

O'Malley strode up and ostentatiously placed his folded card in the box next to Seth. Then he took the box up in his hands and walked about the room, waiting for the votes to be dropped in.

Meggy could not take her eyes off that box. L. L. Tanner, Fine Cigars it said in graceful red lettering. Why two *L*s? she wondered. Lawrence and Leland? Luther and Lavinia? Law and Largesse? She giggled. No, perhaps it was Land and Liberty.

Life and Love?

A sobering thought. She was beginning to suspect God intended to bless her with one or the other, but not both. The thought made her a bit light-headed. Or maybe it was the whiskey.

Charlotte understood about life and love, and Charlotte had never touched a drop of spirits in her entire life. Meggy guessed that she, being the oldest at almost twenty-six, needed a little extra help.

Merciful heaven, what was taking so long? Her heart was so jumpy she could scarcely sit still.

"Now, then." O'Malley's voice rolled over her. "All votes in?"

Meggy stiffened, gulped one last swallow of whiskey and focused on Tom's logging crew, the men whose advice she had sought. One by one, their arms lifted and cards fluttered into the box Sergeant O'Malley proffered.

Fong refused to fold his, and slipped it to the bottom of the pile, a sly smile playing about his lips. Indian Joe refused to add his vote as well, waving O'Malley past with a brusque gesture. Then the darkhaired man stood abruptly and stalked toward Meggy, his card in his hand, his black eyes on hers.

He thrust it toward her. "Read last," he said without a hint of expression. She closed her hand around it, curling her fingers around the edge. It seemed larger than the others.

"Now, then, Seth. Tally up the votes."

"Yessir!"

The Irishman dumped the lot on the table and sat down while Seth went to work. "I trust you can read as well as cipher?"

"Oh, yessir. Cain't spell too good, but I shore can read 'bout anything that's writ down."

O'Malley nodded.

"'Cept this one, Sergeant." Seth lifted an unfolded card from the pile and showed it to O'Malley.

"Aha," the Irishman said. "'Tis a rune, it is. Some kind of magic sign like they used in the old days." He brought the card to Meggy.

It was the ace of diamonds. Carefully inscribed on the face with a complicated Chinese character, meticulously drawn in charcoal.

"It say 'Long life,'" Fong sang from the back of the room. His black eyes danced. "It say 'Many children.'"

"*Skoal,*" Swede added.

"Whazzat mean?" Eight-Bit demanded.

"It means 'Shut yer trap,'" Swede retorted. Everyone guffawed.

"Finish the tally," Sam Turner shouted. "I wrote mine in American."

Seth bent his head over the box, separated the cards into two piles, one considerably taller than the other, and then raised his eyes. In a surprisingly mature voice, he then announced, "The votes are duly recorded." He grinned up at her. "You wanna see 'em, don'tcha, Miss Meggy?"

He delivered the larger pile first, then placed the short pile—one card—across the table just out of her reach.

"Read these ones first, ma'am."

Meggy reached for the top card. Inside was written a single word. "Stay."

Her pulse leaped. The next one read, "Don't never goe."

The third card, folded over twice, was splotched with whiskey and contained a long, printed message. "Stick till next sumurr, sea what coms."

Her hand faltered. Fighting back a sob, she opened the next, a jack of clubs with a mustache and a broad smile drawn on the face. Inside were printed three words. *"MARRY THE COLONEL."*

Oh. *Oh.* Her stomach turned a slow somersault under her rib cage.

The last card from the tall stack read, "Dere miss meggie the kernal he is lik a fater i want yu to bee my mother please nobby."

"Oh, now, Miss Meggy, don't cry, lass." O'Malley pressed a snowy handkerchief into her fingers. "Here, here's the last one." He slid the card she held in her hand, Indian Joe's vote, out of her fingers.

"Read it out loud," the Irishman urged.

It was two cards, really. Joined together at the side by a bit of string threaded through two tiny holes on each edge. Meggy smoothed it open and stared down upon the king and queen of hearts, facing each other. From each figure stretched two skillfully drawn arms, and at the end of each arm, two hands, clasped together.

She burst into tears.

Chapter Twenty-Four

"Colonel, darlin', wake up." A grinning O'Malley bent over Tom, touched one freckled hand to his shoulder. "Colonel?"

"What is it, O'Malley?"

"'Tis past eight, Tom."

Tom groaned and opened one eye. "What difference does that make? We've no timber to cut today."

"'Tis yer weddin' day, boyo. Get up now, or you'll miss all the doin's."

Tom bolted upright. "My *what? What did you say?*"

O'Malley regarded him with patient resignation. "Colonel, you're gettin' married today."

"Are you loco? Whatever gave you that idea?"

"Ten o'clock sharp at the Tennant Methodist Church. And 'twas your skipjack loggers gave me that idea."

"The crew?" Disbelief roughened Tom's voice. "Swede? Orrin? Indian Joe?"

The Irishman nodded. "Even the Claymore boys."

Tom stared at his sergeant. "Where is she?"

"Aye, you'll be wantin' to mention the idea to her directly, I'm thinkin'."

Tom grabbed O'Malley's shirtfront. "Jumping scorpions, I must be dreaming. I remember Doc gave me some laudanum when he set my arm. Next thing I know I'm gettin' married. Mick, tell me, am I dreaming?"

A rumble of laughter rolled out of the sergeant's broad chest. "Well, boyo, it's like this. This dream you're havin', it's one of those that's gonna last awhile. Sure as my name is Michael Brendan O'Malley, you're awake, and I'm awake, and you're gettin' married in two hours. Correction, one hour and forty-five minutes. I'm standin' up with you."

"But—"

"'Tis like this, Colonel. Miss Meggy—now there's a fine, spunky lass—Miss Meggy joined us at the Golden Goose last night, while you was at the doc's. That's where we proposed the idea."

"Proposed," Tom echoed. He might be awake, but his brain felt as if it was rolling around in his skull like a loose marble. "I didn't set foot in the Golden Goose last night. After Doc Brannan finished with me, I couldn't even stand up."

O'Malley gazed out the lace-curtained window, a

faraway look in his eyes. "Aye, 'twas a beautiful thing, so it was. There she stood, brave and bonny as you please, her dress still soppin' wet, her hair stringin' down. Climbed up on a table she did, to make herself heard. And the men listened like polite little lambs—ah, you would have been proud of yer lads, Tom. Not one of 'em even twitched till she finished cryin'."

Tom shook his head. Any minute he'd wake up, and when he did, he'd find that girl and—

"First she kinda choked up some, then she took herself in hand and never flinched, not even when the men started cheerin'."

Tom clamped his teeth together so hard his temples pounded. "O'Malley, get to the point!"

The sergeant snapped to attention. "Yessir. The point is, you've been spoken for, and the wedding's at ten o'clock."

Tom groaned. "What, exactly, did Meggy say last night at the Golden Goose?"

"Well, clear as I can recall, she said her trunk had gone on to Eagle Point, but her heart was here in Tennant. So, we told her what she oughtta do."

"You told her," Tom repeated.

O'Malley's rust-colored eyebrows waggled. "Well, it was Swede who called for the vote. Nobby Claymore passed out playing cards for ballots, and Seth Claymore did the countin'. That lad's got a fine head for arithmetic. Then Miss Meggy cried and said thank-you, and could she have another whiskey. After her third shot, she decided she needed a gown for the weddin', and by the time I escorted her back to her hotel room, she was thinkin' up names for the little ones.''

Tom's head jerked up. ''What?''

''Tom Junior, first. Then Lacey, after her mother, you know. An' after that... Colonel, you'd better hurry.''

The instant Tom put his foot on the carpeted floor, his head spun. *Tom Junior? Lacey?*

''Help me get into my trousers, Mick. I've got to see Meggy.''

Chapter Twenty-Five

"Tom!" Meggy tucked the parcel under her arm, picked up her skirts and raced across the rutted street to where he stood swaying on the plank walkway. His right arm, encased in white plaster, was bent at an angle. He took care not to bump it against her.

"Tom, I've done the most dreadful thing. Something I never dreamed I would do, but I did do it, and now…oh, you will never forgive me, will you?"

"Never," he said in a gentle voice. "Let's take a walk, Meg. Straighten things out." He was moving before he finished speaking.

She fell into step beside him. "Where are we going?"

"Someplace that's private."

He didn't say another word until they reached a stand of drooping cottonwoods at the edge of town. He guided her into a sun-dappled area screened all around by frothy green branches, then turned to face her and touched her hand.

"I like to do my own asking," he said. "Especially in the matter of a wife."

She studied the grass at her feet. "I don't know what came over me, Tom. One minute my heart was cracking in two like a dried-out ginger cookie, and the next minute I was so mad I wanted to strangle you."

"Any particular reason?"

"Well, yes, as a matter of fact. Back on the river, right before the fire jumped over us, I...um, I told you I loved you, remember?"

"I remember. I kept thinking if we were going to drown, I was glad we were doing it together. Then I was breathing again, and I realized I couldn't let you die, no matter what. Thought I told you that."

"No, you did not tell me that. But I guess you did show me what you felt. You worked hard and bravely to get me to safety."

"I would have done the same whether you'd said what you said or not."

Probably shouldn't have admitted that, he acknowledged to himself.

"I know," she said, her voice soft. "Then you talked about floating your log boom down to the sawmill, about Number Two Camp, and...well, I knew right away how things would work out. You've got to turn those logs into lumber, and you've got to establish a new camp and start again. So I…well, I confess I went along with the crew to the Golden Goose, and I, um, well…the men sort of mentioned—''

''Yeah.'' He stepped in close and pressed his cheek against her forehead. She smelled like rose petals.

''I've made such a mess of things,'' she said in a small voice. ''And it's all because of my idiotic notion of what a woman should do when there's someone she wants and she'll die if she lives all the rest of her life without him.''

He blew his breath out in a sigh. ''Have to say it makes sense to me.''

''A lady, especially one raised in the South as I have been, is not supposed to— *It does?*''

''It does,'' Tom murmured. It was getting hard to talk over the ache in his throat. ''I love you,'' he said in a quiet voice.

''But I fear the West has altered my perceptions— *You do?*''

''Oh, God, Meggy, you know I do. I've loved you ever since the day you plunked yourself down on that cabin floor like a damn general and refused to move.''

She tipped her head up and looked into his face. ''Oh, Tom, can you ever forgive me?''

He brushed her mouth with his lips, once, twice, then with a groan pressed her closer with his good arm and kissed her again.

''Nope,'' he said when he could speak. ''I want

you with me from now on, for better or worse. I want you to marry me, Meggy.''

The green eyes that met his shone with tears. ''Yes, Tom. Oh, yes.''

He touched the string-wrapped package under her arm. ''What's in the parcel?''

''I…well, Mr. Johnston, the saloon keeper, introduced me to his wife. She works as a seamstress, and she—''

Tom laughed aloud. ''Anything else you need?''

Meggy looked up at him with brimming eyes. ''Only you.''

He pulled her close. ''That,'' he announced when he had kissed her thoroughly for much longer than he thought prudent, ''can be arranged. In fact, I don't know how much longer I can stand to wait.''

At exactly ten o'clock that sun-splashed morning, Thomas Lawrence Randall, of Zanesville, Ohio, took Mary Margaret Hampton of Seton Falls, South Carolina, to be his lawful wedded wife. Sergeant Michael O'Malley stood up with the groom. Swede Jensen and Indian Joe escorted the bride down the aisle. Nobby Claymore held the bouquet of wild roses she carried when it came time for Tom to slide the gold wedding band onto her finger.

When the minister pronounced them wed in the sight of God and those assembled, the men cheered and O'Malley mopped his eyes with his handkerchief.

Arm in arm, the couple left the church under an archway of metal-tipped peavey hooks.

That night, Number Two Camp welcomed the couple with a flapjack and sausage supper Fong prepared under the stars. Shortly thereafter, the honeymoon commenced in the colonel's tent.

Where, hanging from the center pole, Tom's pet raven swung in its wood-slat house and sang "Meggytom-meggytom-meggytom" until a silent, purposeful figure rose naked from a heated embrace and drew a blanket over the cage.

* * * * *

LYNNA BANNING

has combined a lifelong love of history and literature into a satisfying career as a writer. Born in Oregon, she has lived in Northern California most of her life, graduating from Scripps College and embarking on her career as an editor and technical writer, and later as a high school English teacher.

An amateur pianist and harpsichordist, Lynna performs on psaltery and recorders with two Renaissance ensembles and teaches music in her spare time. Currently she is learning to play the harp.

She enjoys hearing from her readers. You may write to her directly at P.O. Box 324, Felton, CA 95018, or at carolynw@cruzio.com. Visit Lynna's Web site at www2.cruzio.com/~carolynw.

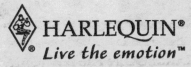

Can't get enough of
our riveting Regencies
and evocative Victorians?
Then check out these enchanting
tales from Harlequin Historicals®

On sale May 2003

BEAUTY AND THE BARON by Deborah Hale

Will a former ugly duckling and an embittered
Waterloo war hero defy the odds in the name of love?

SCOUNDREL'S DAUGHTER by Margo Maguire

A feisty beauty encounters a ruggedly handsome
archaeologist who is intent on whisking her away
on the adventure of a lifetime!

On sale June 2003

THE NOTORIOUS MARRIAGE by Nicola Cornick
(sequel to LADY ALLERTON'S WAGER)

Eleanor Trevithick's hasty marriage to Kit Mostyn
is scandalous in itself. But then her husband
mysteriously disappears the next day....

SAVING SARAH by Gail Ranstrom

Can a jaded hero accused of treason and a
privileged lady hiding a dark secret save
each other—and discover everlasting love?

COMING NEXT MONTH FROM

HARLEQUIN HISTORICALS®

- **LADY ALLERTON'S WAGER**
  by **Nicola Cornick,** author of THE BLANCHLAND SECRET
  Lady Beth Allerton's wager with the Earl of Trevithick was the most
  dangerous thing she'd ever done. If she won, her prize would be an
  estate. If she lost, the penalty was to become his mistress!
  HH #651 ISBN# 29251-1 $5.25 U.S./$6.25 CAN.

- **McKINNON'S BRIDE**
  by **Sharon Harlow,** author of FOR LOVE OF ANNA
  When Jessie Monroe's husband was killed in the arms of another
  woman, she vowed never to experience that kind of pain again and
  set off for her brother's ranch. There she met Cade McKinnon, who
  fell in love with her at first sight, determined to win her hand and
  her heart. But when Jessie learned he'd been lying to her, would she
  ever be able to forgive him?
  HH #652 ISBN# 29252-X $5.25 U.S./$6.25 CAN.

- **ADAM'S PROMISE**
  by **Julianne MacLean,** author of
  THE MARSHAL AND MRS. O'MALLEY
  Madeline Oxley eagerly traveled to Canada to marry
  Adam Coates, the man she'd adored since childhood. Upon her
  arrival, however, she discovered that he really wanted to marry her
  older sister. Unable to return to England, Madeline hoped Adam
  would learn to love her. But when her sister arrived, which one of
  them would Adam choose?
  HH #653 ISBN# 29253-8 $5.25 U.S./$6.25 CAN.

- **HIGHLAND SWORD**
  by **Ruth Langan,** book one in the *Mystical Highlands* series
  A fierce warrior traveled to the Mystical Kingdom, a hidden land in
  the Highlands where ancient magic has not been forgotten, to find a
  woman to heal his dying son. But little did he expect this woman
  would heal his broken heart, as well!
  HH #654 ISBN# 29254-6 $5.25 U.S./$6.25 CAN.

KEEP AN EYE OUT FOR ALL FOUR
OF THESE TERRIFIC NEW TITLES

HHCNM0303